POCKET-47

POCKET-47

A Novel

JUDE HARDIN

Oceanview Publishing
Longboat Key, Florida

ISBN: 978-1-60809-011-2

Published in the United States by Oceanview Publishing
Longboat Key, Florida
www.oceanviewpub.com

2 4 6 8 10 9 7 5 3 1

PRINTED IN THE UNITED STATES OF AMERICA

For Corey. A fine lad.

Acknowledgments

The publication of a novel is always a collaborative effort. *Pocket-47* has gone through several incarnations over several years, and many people have helped make its publication a reality. Please forgive me if I have forgotten any names.

I would like to thank my editor, Pat Gussin, for her meticulous and tireless work on the manuscript, and for seeing its potential on first reading.

Thanks to all the wonderful folks at Oceanview Publishing: Bob Gussin, Frank Troncale, Susan Greger (enjoy your retirement!), Mary Adele Bogdon, John Cheesman, George Foster, Kylie Fritz, Sandy Greger, Joe Hall, Susan Hayes, Maryglenn McCombs, and Cheryl Melnick. An author only gets one debut, and I would like to express my deepest gratitude to all of you for making mine an occasion I will never forget.

In no particular order, I would like to thank all my friends, family members, and colleagues, for their help on my journey toward publication: Pat Boling, Kathy Ledford, Amy Marin, Alicia Dixon, Jay Poynor, Lainey Bancroft, Kathy Calarco, Eric Christopherson, Bob Florence, Kris Montee, Kelly Nichols, Aaron Lazar, Stephen Parrish, Marcus Sakey, Susan Grace, Mark Terry, Leighton Gage, Dusty Rhoades, Jon VanZile, and a couple of blogging editors called The Crabby Cows (you know who you are, even if nobody else does!).

And a special thanks to authors Erica Orloff, Tess Gerritsen, and J. A. Konrath for their guidance and encouragement. I promise to do my best to pay it forward.

POCKET-47

CHAPTER ONE

My stepfather taught me three important survival skills: how to use a baitcaster reel, how to filet a bass, and how to adjust for the kick of a .44 magnum. I had gotten up at six a.m. and exercised the first. By nine, I stood under the shade of a loblolly pine, busy with the second.

I never quite mastered the third. That's why I carry a .38.

I wore khaki shorts, no shirt, a pair of Top-Siders, and a ball cap that said Guinness. Typical north Florida fishing attire.

I scraped the scales off my third and final fish, looked up and saw a little red car turning from Lake Barkley Road onto my gravel driveway. It was one of those cars I call a Bic. Like the lighters, they're cheap and disposable. You buy one fresh off the lot, and by the time it needs new tires it's ready for the junkyard. An internal timing device insures that all working parts take a dive at the precise moment the warranty expires.

It struggled up the hill and parked beside my GMC Jimmy. The driver's side door opened and a young woman got out, wearing what at first appeared to be a hearing aid. It was one of those cell phone gizmos you hang on your ear so everyone thinks you're loony tunes walking around talking to yourself. In the future, they'll implant a computer chip directly into your brain and you'll be perpetually connected, via satellite, to people you don't want to talk to anyway.

I was hoping I'd die before anything like that ever happened when the woman said, "I'm looking for Nicholas Colt. The private eye. Is that you?"

She surveyed my home sweet home—a 1964 Airstream Safari travel trailer—my ten-year-old SUV, my bloodstained picnic table littered with catch-of-the-day carcasses. She had an expensive-looking hairstyle, clipped shoulder-length, dark brown with bourbon highlights, and a *what-is-that-smell?* expression. She wore a navy blue skirt and jacket, silky white blouse, some sort of shoes that didn't tread well on my sandy yard. White leather purse. I doubted she was old enough to drink.

"If you're selling something, I'm broke, so don't bother. If you're from the loan company, I'm really broke, so really don't bother." I was six weeks behind on my car payment. I expected to wake up any day now and find my Jimmy not there. A tow truck hadn't followed her in, so I figured I was safe for the moment.

She stepped forward and extended her hand, briefly breaking eye contact to glance at the scar on my belly. Her perfume was light and spicy, very nice. I put the filet knife down and opened my palms to show the fish grime. She frowned and laced her fingers together against the front of her skirt, quickly giving up on the idea of a handshake. Tiny beads of sweat studded her forehead.

"My name is Leitha Ryan. I need help finding someone, Mr. Colt. Is that something you might be interested in?"

She raked her hair back with her fingers and chewed on her upper lip as if she were hoping I'd say no.

"My clients usually call first," I said. "Kind of caught me at a bad time."

"I apologize. I did try to call, but—"

The sandy-haired dog we call Bud crept up from behind and pushed his muzzle under her skirt. Bud has some Great Dane in him. He looks like a Labrador on steroids. Leitha screamed.

"Don't worry," I said. "He doesn't bite." Dylan Crawford, my friend Joe's son, likes to think Bud is his dog, but Bud belongs to nobody. I like that about him. He showed up at the lake one day a couple of years ago, mangy and half-starved. Joe took him to the vet and got him straightened out, and he's been with us ever since. Sometimes he sleeps at my place, sometimes on Joe's porch.

Bud trotted toward the lake wagging his tail, apparently satisfied with the smell of Leitha's crotch.

"Was my phone disconnected?" I said.

Leitha nodded.

"Sorry. Been a little slow lately. How did you find my place?" I don't tell many people where I live, and I don't advertise the address.

She hesitated, took a step back toward the Bic. There was a St. Christopher statue on the dashboard, similar to the one my mother had when her '65 Fairlane met with a tree. The statue survived. Mom didn't. Mom was a Baptist.

"Can I get you a cup of coffee or a glass of iced tea?" I said. "I'm having fish for breakfast. You like fish?"

She looked at the mess on the picnic table and her face went pale. "No, thank you. I already had breakfast. Maybe I should come back some other time. Sorry I interrupted what you were doing there."

She turned to leave.

"Wait," I said. I needed the work. My bank account had bled to death waiting on a couple of previous clients to pay up, and I wasn't in the mood to shoot the repo man when he came for my Jimmy. "If you can hang around for a few minutes while I get cleaned up, I'll be happy to discuss your problem."

She halfheartedly followed me inside, visibly relieved that my air conditioner was functioning. I washed my hands, put some ice cubes in a glass, filled the glass with sweet tea, and handed it to her. I switched on the television so she'd have something to do while I took a shower. I put my bass filets in the refrigerator and closed the partition on my way to the bedroom and bath.

The shower in an Airstream is slightly larger than a coffin. I scrubbed my body and toweled off and gave my beard a quick trim. I pulled my hair back in a ponytail and returned to the living room wearing fresh khaki shorts and a Hawaiian shirt. They were talking about the local weather on television. No surprise there. High in the mid-nineties, 100 percent humidity, chance of afternoon thundershowers.

Leitha had helped herself to one of my Marlboros from a pack on the coffee table. Beside the cigarettes were a box of toothpicks, a stack of nicotine patches, and a package of peppermint chewing gum. I'd been trying to quit. Rule #6 from Nicholas Colt's *Philosophy of Life*: Shit happens, especially when you give up smoking. I was seventeen the first time. My stepfather blew his brains out that week, with the same .44 he'd used to teach me how to shoot. Years later, I had the gun melted down to a blob. It's on my desk now, next to Mom's St. Christopher.

At first I thought Leitha was talking to herself, but she was connected to someone on that goofy ear thing. She said goodbye when she saw me coming. I poured myself a glass of tea, sat on the sofa beside her, and picked up the cigarette pack.

"Mind if I have one of these?" I said.

She smiled. "I should have asked."

"No problem. *Mi casa es su casa.*" I lit my cigarette.

Leitha crossed her legs, which I noticed were first-rate. Rule #3 from Nicholas Colt's *Philosophy of Life*: Love will break your heart, and lust will break your bank account. Rule #3 has been proven many times, and is universally accepted as being true.

She stood and examined the gold record hanging on my wall, the only one I hadn't pawned for blow in the '80s. An awkward moment of silence inevitably follows when someone realizes I'm *that* Nicholas Colt, the one who crawled from the wreckage of a chartered jet seconds before a massive fireball consumed his wife and baby daughter and everyone in his band. I let it tick off and then said, "You're trying to locate someone?"

"Is this your wife and little girl?" She pointed at the framed photograph hanging near the gold record.

"Yes," I said.

"They're beautiful."

Twenty-some years had passed, but it was still difficult for me to talk about the tragedy. Especially with a stranger.

"You're trying to locate someone?" I repeated.

Leitha blew smoke at the ceiling. "My sister. She ran away from home."

"Sister. How old?"

"Fifteen." Her voice broke slightly when she said it.

"I figured you to be about that age."

"I'm twenty-three, Mr. Colt." She sounded offended.

"Where's home?" I asked.

She sat back down on the couch. "We live in Jacksonville, downtown in Springfield. I work at the hospital there. We're orphans, Mr. Colt. Grew up in foster homes. When I graduated from nursing school, the state allowed me to take custody of Brittney. So, basically, I'm raising her."

"My girlfriend's a nurse," I said. "I should have done something like that. Good money, never any shortage of work."

Leitha laughed. "You should have been a surgeon. Seem to be pretty good with a knife."

I cleared my throat. "How long your sister been gone?"

"Almost two weeks. She did it once before, ran away, but she came back after two days. I kept thinking she would come back again this time, you know?" Leitha stubbed out her cigarette. Her eyes were red now, on the verge of tears.

"You've contacted the police?"

"That's the thing. I'm afraid to. I'm afraid they'll take her away from me and put her back in foster care. Please don't tell the police, Mr. Colt."

"Call me Nicholas. You sure she ran away? Sure she wasn't kidnapped or something?"

"We had a fight. It was a week ago Saturday, August fifth, right before she left for her tennis lesson. She'd started hanging out with a guy named Mark Toohey. He was way older than her, like nineteen, I think. Seemed like an all right guy, just too old for Brittney. I told her Mark could come to the house when I was home, but that she wasn't allowed to go off with him in his car. She freaked. She called me a bitch and said I wasn't her mom and all that. You know, the usual bullshit. I told her that as soon as she got home from her lesson, she was grounded for a week. Next morning I found this note under my windshield wiper."

Leitha reached into her purse, pulled out a crumpled paper that had been torn from a spiral notebook. It seemed the note had gone to battle with a half-eaten red Twizzler stick. She peeled the sticky candy away, handed the note to me. I found my glasses and read it.

Leitha,
You are so fucking mean. I can't live with you anymore.
B

"Well," I said, "she certainly knows how to get to the point. Sounds like you got yourself a runaway all right. Can you afford to hire a private investigator?"

"You look different with the glasses on. More intelligent or something," Leitha said.

I took them off. "What do I look like now? A moron?"

"Come on, Mr. Colt. I mean Nicholas. You're good looking and you know it."

I kept chanting rule #3, the lust part. "You trying to butter me up?" I said.

"Is it working?"

"Maybe. The thing is, I can't work for free. I wish I could, but I can't. You didn't answer my question. Can you afford a PI?"

"I talked to an agency in Jacksonville. They were going to charge me a hundred an hour. I can't afford that. Plus, they said they could try to locate her, but that the police would have to actually pick her up. As I told you before, I don't want that if there's any way to avoid it. They gave me your name, said you could probably do it for less. They said you specialize in runaways."

"What agency?"

"Brett Hershey and Associates."

"Ah. Brett. All the beat cops call him 'Candy Ass.' Did you visit his fancy office downtown? That's why Brett charges a hundred an hour. He's right about the cops being the pickup guys, though. Most PIs won't pick up a runaway."

"Why not?"

"We really don't have any authority to use force. Say I pick her up and she alleges abuse or something. Runaways don't want to be caught. They'll lie through their teeth to get revenge. You could sue me."

"I wouldn't do that."

"If you want me to pick her up, I'll need you to sign a contract giving me twenty-four hour custody rights."

"Okay. How much are you going to charge?"

"So, Brett sent you down here to Hallows Cove, to me, the remainder bin, the clearance rack. You drove forty miles down here thinking you'd get a bargain, right? I like you, so I'm going to do something I never do. I'm going to give you a flat rate. Thousand bucks, win, lose, or draw. If it takes me two hours to find her and bring her home, I make five hundred an hour. If it takes me two weeks, I make twelve fifty an hour. If I haven't found her after two weeks, we'll renegotiate. Can you live with that?"

"What's your hourly rate?"

"Hundred dollars."

"But you don't have a fancy downtown office."

"Yeah, but I'm good. I have the right connections when I need them. Plus, I dedicate myself to one case at a time. Like Brett told you, I specialize in runaways."

"I'll take the flat rate, I guess."

"Fine. Do you know where Mark Toohey lives?"

"Yes. It's only a few blocks from our house. I went over there and talked to him, but he says he hasn't seen Brittney."

"Does he have a job?"

"He delivers pizza for the Domino's in Springfield."

"I'll talk to him. What about school?"

"She was supposed to start tenth grade last week. Didn't show up for any of her classes."

"Friends? Anybody she might have gone to stay with?"

"She spends a lot of time on the computer. Facebook and all that. I really don't know of any friends."

Leitha dug in her purse and produced a plastic ID card. I looked it over. Stanton College Preparatory School. Blue eyes, sandy blond hair, 5'3", 105 lbs. I knew a little bit about Stanton. It's a public school, but you have to apply to get in.

"She must be smart," I said.

"She's very bright. She struggled for years with dyslexia, but seems to have it under control now. We were so excited last year when she got accepted to Stanton. I can't believe she's throwing it all away like this."

"She drink or do drugs?"

"I'd kill her."

"Medical problems? Any psych history?"

"She's healthy. We've both been to counseling but, you know, she's not crazy if that's what you mean."

"What about hobbies?"

"She reads a lot, and plays on the Internet. She swims. Oh, and there's tennis. Her last foster parents were big into tennis. They gave Brittney lessons. She played on the JV team at Stanton last year."

"How long did she live with the tennis people?"

"Almost two years."

"Did she like them?"

"It's a doctor and his wife. They were planning to adopt Brittney. They still pay for her tennis lessons. Every Saturday morning Doctor Spivey picks her up and takes her for her lesson. They usually have lunch, and then he brings her home."

"But you said she didn't come home after her lesson a week ago Saturday. I assume you've talked with the Spiveys."

"Yes. Doctor Spivey said he dropped her at the house and waited to make sure she got inside. I was at work at the time. The

Spiveys are very worried about Brittney. They wanted to call the police, but I talked them out of it."

Ordinarily, that would have raised a red flag. But I understood why Leitha didn't want the police involved. She didn't want Brittney forced back into foster care.

"Can you give me the Spiveys' address and phone number?"

Leitha wrote it on the back of the paper Brittney had used for her note. The address was in Ponte Vedre. Rich people.

"I'll talk to the Spiveys," I said. "Who was giving her lessons?"

"A pro in Ponte Vedre named Kent Clark."

"Kent Clark?" I laughed. "Like Superman, only backward. Any reason to believe she might have been involved with him? Other than the lessons, I mean."

"I don't think so. He's old, like forty or something."

I raised an eyebrow at that. "Does Brittney have any scars or tattoos? Piercings?"

"She wears earrings. That's all."

"She got a cell phone?"

"She's on my plan. Here's the bill from last month."

I took the phone statement and put it with the note. "I want to get started right away," I said. "I'll need the money up front."

Leitha wrote me a check. I wrote my cell phone number on the back of a business card and handed it to her. "As of today, my cell still works. I leave it turned off most of the time, so leave voice mail and I'll get back to you. Call me right away if you hear from Brittney or if she comes home."

Leitha nodded. She rose and offered her hand again, then moved toward the door.

"Will you be home later?" I said.

"I have to work tonight. Why?"

"I'd like to take a look at Brittney's room."

"I'll be home from work around eight tomorrow morning, if you want to come then."

"I'll be there," I said. "Any questions?"

"Just one. How—"

She hesitated, but her eyes and facial expression spoke volumes. I finished the thought for her. "How does a world-renowned blues guitarist with homes on both coasts end up as a PI working out of a camper? I ask myself the same question every day."

She stepped out into the August heat, avoiding further eye contact. I stood in the doorway and watched her drive off in the Bic.

Bud barked and chased her a quarter mile down Lake Barkley Road. He finally stopped and sneezed a couple of times, from all the dust she had stirred.

CHAPTER TWO

After Leitha drove away, I shuffled through the pile of bills on my desk, putting them in severity-of-delinquency order.

My answering machine had one message on it, from yesterday before Ma Bell shut down my landline. It said, "Hey sweetie. Don't forget to meet me for lunch at Lyon's Den tomorrow. Love you." It was from Juliet Dakila, my girlfriend. I'd saved the message so I wouldn't forget our date.

I have an amazing memory, but I'm absentminded as hell. Juliet knows this about me, so I'm sure that's why my cell phone rang shortly after I played the message.

"What's wrong with your home phone?" Juliet asked.

"I was a little late paying the bill. I'll get it turned back on today or tomorrow."

"You need money?"

I skip-traced a guy one time who made his living sponging off girlfriends. Loser. I'd borrowed from Juliet before, always paid back every penny. Didn't like to make a habit of it.

"I'm all right," I said. "We still doing lunch today?"

"Of course. Among other things."

"Other things like what?" I asked. I had a feeling I might be in for one of her famous shopping trips. Juliet would live at the mall if they let her. She has to stop at every store, look around, try ten things on, and finally remember what she really wants is on sale at Penney's. Here's my idea of shopping: You know you need something, some paint for example. You know the type, color, and quantity before you ever leave the house. You walk into the paint store, tell them what you want, pay for it, leave. Shopping done. Juliet, on the other hand, will spend two hours picking out a pair of shoes. It's not one of the things I love about her, and I don't know why she ever asks me to tag along. I get grouchy after about ten minutes.

I was trying to think of excuses not to go shopping with her when she said, "You're going to meet my mother today."

"Sure," I said. "We'll just hop on a plane to the Philippines and—"

"No, silly. She's here. I told you she was coming to stay with my sister for a while, remember? To help with the kids."

"Oh, yeah. How could I forget that?" Joy. I suddenly wished for that shopping trip I'd been dreading only seconds earlier. Misery is always relative, and relatives are always misery.

"She flew in late last night," Juliet said. "I haven't even seen her myself yet. We'll go over to Abby's place right after lunch. Unless you have other plans."

Juliet's sister Abby didn't have any kids until she turned thirty, and then started cranking them out once a year, sure as the first pitch in the World Series. She had three boys and one girl, and was pregnant with the fifth—another girl, according to the sonogram. I loved hanging around Abby's house and playing with the kids sometimes, but the thought of meeting Juliet's mom gave me an acid burn just below my heart. I've never been very good at meeting mothers.

"Actually," I said, "I need to work on some research for—"

"This is my *mother* we're talking about, Nicholas. No excuses, dude. You're coming. Don't worry, she's very nice. She doesn't know much English yet, so you won't even have to talk to her a lot. Please say you'll come. For me?"

"All right. I'll come." The things we do for love. Maybe Freud had it right. Perhaps all motivation stems from the desire to get laid.

"Awesome," Juliet said. "See you at Lyon's Den in a little while."

It was just past ten, and we weren't supposed to meet until noon, so I had time to do a couple of background checks on the computer. I transferred my bass filets from the refrigerator to the freezer, crammed my bills into a drawer, sat down, and started with Mark Toohey.

Leitha was right about his age. Some things she probably didn't know: Mark Toohey was born in Waterloo, Iowa, where he dropped out of school the day he turned sixteen. He'd had a variety of addresses since then, one being the state penitentiary in Starke, Florida. He served six months on a burglary charge, and still had four years of probation time left. His proud parents still lived in Iowa. I printed the data on him, including his current address and phone number, and that of his employer.

Nine times out of ten, when a young girl like Brittney Ryan has an older boyfriend, she is easy to find. Find the boyfriend, find the girl. I didn't bother to call Toohey because, also nine times out of ten, the boyfriend will lie to protect the runaway. I planned to make a surprise visit to Mark Toohey's place the next day, put this little job in the scrapbook.

I heard Bud barking, so I opened the hatch and let him inside. He danced around on my vinyl tile floor for a minute, gave my leg a hug, climbed on the couch and settled there with a smile on his face and his tongue out.

I ran Kent Clark, the tennis pro, next. He graduated from the University of Miami in 1986 with degrees in communications and physical education. He taught high school in Boca Raton until 1998, but his employment history was sketchy after that. He didn't file a tax return in 2001, but did file for bankruptcy and a divorce.

I looked up the number and called Seminole High School in Boca Raton on my cell phone. After several rings, a lady with a nasally grandmother voice answered.

I introduced myself as principal Steven Gill from Hallows Cove Junior High. Gill was the principal when I went to school there thirty years ago, but I was counting on her not knowing that.

"I'm checking references on a Mr. Kent Clark," I said. "His résumé says he taught down there from nineteen eighty-six to nineteen ninety-eight. Is that correct?"

"I'll have to pull his file," she said. "Can you hold?"

"Of course. Thank you." I waited, started wondering how much collective time, the world over, is wasted on *hold* every day. Probably thousands of hours. Why couldn't all that time be put to use somehow? What do most people do while they're on hold? I guessed most people just sat there with the phone pressed against their heads, like I do. How many man-hours, man-*years*, are sucked into the abyss while waiting for people to come back to the phone? Someday I'm going to find out, and give everyone on hold something to do. Clip their toenails or something. I'll probably win the Nobel Prize.

When she clicked back on, I detected some nervousness in her voice, a slight raise in pitch.

"Yes. He was employed here during those years. Anything else I can help you with today?"

"Can you tell me why he left?"

"By law, I really can't give you any details, Mr. Gill. I'm sure you know that."

"Right. May I speak with the principal?"

"You can, but it's a different principal than when Mr. Clark was employed here. Do you want to speak with her?"

"No, that's okay. Could you give me the name of the principal who was there the same years as Mr. Clark?"

"That would have been Mr. Tsirulnopolis."

"Could you spell that for me?"

She spelled it. "Everyone called him Mr. T, because his name was so hard to pronounce."

"Yeah. It's all Greek to me. What was his first name?"

"You know, I don't even remember. Everyone just called him T. We do miss our Mr. T."

She started sounding all gushy and nostalgic, so I figured it was time to hang up. Rule #216 in Nicolas Colt's *Philosophy of Life:* Things twenty years ago weren't all that goddamn great either. "Did he wear a lot of heavy gold chains around his neck?" I said.

"Pardon?"

"Never mind. Thank you very much."

I clicked a few keys and found Tsirulnopolis' phone number and address. My lucky day. He was the only person named Tsiulnopolis in the entire state of Florida. I called, and he picked up on the first ring. I heard a television blaring in the background.

"This is T," he said.

I decided to be myself this time. "My name is Nicholas Colt. I'm a private investigator, and I'm trying to get some information on a man I think you worked with previously. His name is Kent Clark."

"Is he in trouble again?" Mr. T said.

"Not that I know of. I was hired to find a fifteen-year-old runaway, and he's her tennis coach. I was just trying to get some information before going to talk with him."

"Can't help you. He was never convicted. Anything I say would, in essence, be slander."

"Never convicted of what? You can tell me the arrest charges. That's not slander. It's a matter of public record."

"Actually, he had it all expunged. You won't find it in any public records, Mr. Colt."

"A fifteen-year-old girl is missing," I said. "With all due respect, that's serious shit. My client wants to avoid getting the police and the court system involved, but if I need to get a subpoena—"

"I'd like to help you, but—" He sighed. "I'm retired from the school system, Mr. Colt. The only repercussions I fear are from Kent Clark himself. He could sue me if he found out."

"He won't find out," I said. "My word."

He hesitated. "All right. Mr. Clark was terminated for inappropriate behavior with one of his female students. Criminal charges were filed, but he beat them in court. I'm sure he'll never teach school again. He got off light if you ask me."

Bud put his head on my lap, started nudging my elbow with his muzzle. He was telling me to get my ass off the phone and get him something to eat. I ignored him, and he finally went back to the couch.

"What was the 'inappropriate behavior'?" I said. "Could you

turn your television down a notch?" The Beverly Hillbillies theme song was playing, and I wasn't in the mood for a story about a man named Jed.

He ignored my request. "One of the girls claimed that he fondled her. Sexually. He denied it, but the girl had a witness so we had to believe her. It's never easy firing a teacher, Mr. Colt, but I think we did the right thing where Kent Clark was concerned."

"Sounds like it. Thanks for the info, Mr. T. Hope you're enjoying retirement."

Mr. T chuckled. "Well, my golf swing has never been better. I'll say that."

Too bad the same can't be said for your hearing.

We said goodbye and hung up.

I put Kent Clark on my list of probable causes for Brittney's running away. It was possible he had tried something with her, maybe even succeeded. I've seen it happen more than once. A trusted uncle, teacher, priest, whatever, molests a minor and then threatens to do them and their family harm if a word is ever said. It's a compelling reason for a fifteen-year-old to bolt.

I opened the pantry door and got Bud a Milk-Bone. He crunched it into small pieces on the floor and gobbled the small pieces, hyperfocused on doing everything as quickly as possible. I gave him an old pair of deck shoes a while back. He knows which pair is his. He took one of them to the couch and gnawed on the heel.

I ran a quick check on Dr. Michael Spivey, Brittney's former foster father. He graduated from the University of Florida in 1982 with a double major, music and biology, and then from the university's school of medicine in 1985. He was active in the National Foster Parent Association and Big Brothers Big Sisters of America. He'd done a three-year tour in the military after med school. No police record, and no bankruptcies or anything.

I'm always a little suspicious of anyone who's that clean.

CHAPTER THREE

A sign near the parking lot entrance, one of those yellow portable jobs on wheels, said TONIGHT KING WATERS AND ONE GIA T LEAP. The N in GIANT had apparently taken a leap of its own. Lyon's Den's board-and-batten exterior had always reminded me of *Little House on the Prairie*.

I made it there a few minutes before noon. The nightclub is located just north of the Hallows Cove pier, and many of the tables in the restaurant upstairs have a spectacular view of the St. John's River. Every December, Juliet and I make it a point to go up there and watch the Christmas parade of boats. Hundreds of mariners deck their vessels with yuletide decorations and twinkling lights, and sail down to St. Augustine. Jules and I talk about getting our own boat someday. Guess I could always weld some pontoons onto the Airstream.

Inside, Neil Young moaned "Harvest Moon" from invisible speakers. An L-shaped mahogany bar stood in front of a large mirrored wall, and beyond a row of bistro tables were the dance floor and a raised stage. The entire area was about the size of a basketball court. Antique signs, rusted farm tools, and other pieces of old junk were tacked to the walls and ceiling Cracker Barrel style.

I sat on a stool. Sonya Shafer slid the wine glass she had been polishing into an overhead rack and slapped a cocktail napkin on the bar in front of me. I've known Sonya since she was a little girl. Her daddy and I fish together sometimes. She wore tight black pants and a white tuxedo shirt, and her blonde hair was long and frizzed out like a rock star's.

"Old Fitz on the rocks?" she said.

"Make it a Carta Blanca this time. And, what the hell, a shot of Quervo Gold. Can you cash this?" I showed her the check from Leitha.

"Not this early," she said.

"Put it on my tab, then. Lunch too."

"You meeting Juliet?"

"Yeah."

"You got it, babe." She brought my drinks, then walked off to serve another customer. I sipped on the beer and read a greasy menu I knew by heart.

Juliet came in a few minutes later wearing jeans and a T-shirt one of her friends from the bank had given her. It said *Severe Penalty for Early Withdrawal.* I loved it when she wore that. My lucky shirt. She sat beside me, picked up my shot of tequila, and sucked it dry.

"Hey. That was mine," I said.

"No liquor for you today. It deadens the senses."

"My senses just might need some deadening," I said. I was about to go crazy just looking at her. Juliet had gotten all the right genes from her American father and Filipino mother. She was 5'3", long black hair, olive complexion, smile like a search light, brown eyes warm as apple pie. She leaned over and kissed me.

"You taste like tequila," I said.

"After lunch, you will come to my house and give me great pleasure."

"Well, okay. If I have to," I said. "I have to get up early in the morning, though, so I'll need to be asleep by midnight."

"You have a job?" she said.

"I do." I told her about the runaway named Brittney Ryan and about the research I had done earlier.

"That gives us less than twelve hours then."

"We could always skip lunch," I said.

She kissed me again. "We will starve. But we will die happy."

"I thought we were going to Abby's. For me to meet your mom."

"They went out shopping. Probably be gone all day. We'll have to make it another time."

"Shucks," I said. I couldn't believe my good fortune. I had a thousand dollar check in my pocket, I was going to get laid, and I didn't have to meet any mothers. The day kept getting better and better.

I followed Juliet to her house. Three hours later, I went out and brought back some Chinese take-out. Fried rice, chicken and broccoli, egg rolls. We ate the food and drank a bottle of cheap champagne and went back to bed.

Someone outside was riding around on a dirt bike. The noise from the whiney little engine gave me a headache.

"Mind if I shoot your neighbor?"

"Do you love me?" Juliet said.

"Very much," I said. "I'll love you even more if you give me permission to kill that inconsiderate—"

"Will you marry me?" She was lying on her stomach, her hands laced together supporting her head. She looked me directly in the eyes.

"You sure know how to kill a beautiful moment," I joked. "Sure. I'll marry you. Someday."

"Why not today? Tomorrow? I want to have a baby with you. Take me out right now and buy me a diamond ring. You should at least come and live with me here. There's no reason for you to stay in that crummy old camper."

"I like having my own space. It's not *that* crummy. As for the baby thing, I think you know where I stand on that."

"You were a daddy before. Why not again?"

"Let's not get into it, Jules."

"Never say never," she said.

"I am saying never. Trust me, I'm never going to be a father again. Never in a million years."

She left it alone. "Well, I still think you should move out of that camper. Couldn't you at least rent a decent apartment somewhere?"

"Are you ashamed of where I live?" I said.

Juliet frowned. "Sometimes people at work ask me, 'What part of town does your boyfriend stay at?' I don't know what to tell—"

"Tell them I'm on waterfront property in Clay County. That should shut their nosy asses up. Listen, if you're ashamed of me—"

"I'm not. That's not what I'm saying. I just wish you had a better house."

"I'll get something better when I can afford it. In the meantime, it's not all that bad. I have enough room to eat and sleep and run my business, and I can go fishing anytime I feel like it. I stopped worrying about keeping up with the Joneses a long time ago. I'd rather live life on my own terms. Make sense?"

"I guess. When you *do* meet my mother—"

"Is that what this is all about? Shit. I should have known. You're going to be embarrassed for your mom to find out how I live. Is that it? You're afraid your mother will think you're dating a loser? I think I need to go now." I got up and put my shirt on, started buttoning it.

"Please don't go, Nicholas. I'm sorry. It's just that my mother, well, she's very conservative and—you know how mothers are. They want the best for their little girls. I think you *are* the best, but I just don't want to hear a bunch of crap from her."

"Maybe it's best that I never meet her. What do you want me to do, lie to her about where I live?"

"Would that be so bad? She's only going to be here for a few weeks, until Abby gets settled in with her new baby. Then she'll be going back to the Philippines."

I looked out the window. A gray rabbit, looking very content, was munching on one of Juliet's tomato plants. The dirt bike was still doing donuts in my skull.

"Sorry, Jules. I'm not going to lie to anybody about where I live, what I think, or anything else. If you can't accept me as I am—"

"Please come back to bed. I love you today."

It was something we said to each other often, *I love you today*, knowing that relationships have to be taken one day at a time. We both knew that *forever* was a myth. As long as we loved each other today, tomorrow would take care of itself.

I took my shirt off and climbed back in bed with her. I stared at the ceiling for a few minutes, absently fingering the smooth and hairless scar tissue on my lower right abdomen, debating whether or not to make the compromise, to let Juliet's mother think I had more than I really did.

"Jules," I said.

"Yes?"

"I would do anything for you. I'd die for you. But like the sailor said, 'I yam what I yam.' I'm not going to pretend to be anything else."

"I can respect that," she said.

She kissed my chest, made a trail with her tongue down to my belly and rested her head there. What she did next made me think hard about going out and buying that ring she wanted.

CHAPTER FOUR

Leitha Ryan lived in a Craftsman-style bungalow painted yellow with white trim. The yard had recently been mowed, and the St. Augustine grass was thick, lush, and deep green. Baptized in the morning dew, it *smelled* green. I'm always impressed with anyone who can make grass grow in this part of the country. I was never very good at it myself.

She had wicker furniture on the porch and some hanging plants and a copper mailbox. I rang the bell and she let me in.

"Nice," I said. "How many bedrooms?"

"Just two." Leitha's hospital scrubs swallowed her tiny frame, and the circles under her eyes announced the hangdog look of someone who'd either missed way too much sleep or had a serious illness. I remembered working the night shift at a warehouse before I got my PI license. Your body never gets used to that schedule.

The house reminded me of a place I lived when I was a kid. Hardwood floors, built-in bookcases, wainscoting you won't find at Home Depot. It was the kind of house you used to be able to buy cheap, but since Springfield had been designated a historic district a few years ago prices had swollen. I figured it set her back two-fifty, maybe more. A mortgage is something I'll never have again. Been there, done that, bought the whole rack of chips. They tell you it's a good investment, but when you're in your forties and take on a big heavy debt like that your options are suddenly limited. You have to keep working at a job you hate until you're practically dead, and then you get to sit around and watch TV with an oxygen canister beside you in the house you worked half your life to pay for until you're really dead. Then the lawyers and the government take their fat share and your family is left to fight over the rest and take all your measly shit to Goodwill. Some investment. Errol Flynn got it right. Any man who dies with more than ten thousand dollars in the bank is a failure.

The living room was furnished with modern junk, buy-now-pay-later garbage that ends up costing ten times more than what it's worth. A red denim sofa and matching love seat with chrome legs invaded the bulk of the space, along with some chrome and glass tables, and a pair of stainless steel lamps. The only thing halfway genuine was a stained-glass window in an oak frame serving as a mantle decoration. A big yellow rose bloomed from its center, each petal a separate cut.

Leitha led me into a short hallway. "This is Brittney's room," she said. "Sorry about the mess."

I looked in the closet first. The hundred-year-old cedar still smelled like cedar. You couldn't have slid a piece of paper between the clothes on hangers. A red Wilson tennis bag, a backpack, and a set of leather-bound Harvard Classics were arranged neatly on the overhead shelf. One of the books had been pulled out, and lay separate from the others. It was something called *Two Years Before The Mast* by Richard Henry Dana, Jr. A playing card—the seven of clubs—had been used as a bookmark, and "the latitude of Point Conception" was highlighted in yellow at the bottom of page 54. The paragraphs were dense and unbroken by dialogue.

"She reads this stuff?" I said.

"We found those at a thrift store. Got the whole set for thirty dollars. I was going to sell them on eBay, but then Brittney said she wanted them. Yes, she's read them all. Like I said, she's very bright."

"I'll say." I saw titles from Cervantes, Dante, Darwin, Shakespeare, Locke, and some I'd never heard of. Give me James Patterson and a six-pack and I'm set for the evening.

"Is this her school backpack?" I said

"That's her old one. I bought her a new one and filled it with supplies from a list Stanton gave us. She must have taken it when she left."

"What color was it? The backpack."

"Red."

"I'll need a recent photograph of Brittney," I said. "One with a good shot of her face."

"I'll see what I can find."

Leitha left the room. A few seconds later, I heard some drawers being yanked open across the hall.

A couple dozen pairs of shoes, looking as though they'd been thrown off in a hurry, littered the closet floor. A dusty bowling ball bag and a set of blue and white cheerleader pompoms had been abandoned in one corner. I saw no remnants of kiddy toys like you see in some teenagers' closets. Barbie dolls, Hot Wheels, board games, and whatnot. No boxes of family photos. No evidence of a childhood, happy or otherwise.

Leitha came back and handed me a nice five-by-seven of Brittney in her tennis outfit.

"You didn't tell me she was a cheerleader," I said, pointing toward the pompoms.

"She tried it for a while in eighth grade, but didn't like it very much," Leitha said. "She's athletic, just not very outgoing. You know?"

I nodded. "You mind if I look around by myself in here for a few minutes?" People always get nervous when you go through underwear drawers and everything, but I needed to find out if Brittney had any secrets or bad habits she'd been keeping from her sister.

"I'll be in the kitchen if you need me," she said. Her nurse shoes squeaked on the wood floor as she walked away.

In one corner of Brittney's room stood a wooden desk painted blue. In the drawers I found the usual assortment of office supplies, along with a stack of index cards she had used for a research paper on autism. The cards were secured with a rubber band. I picked them up and flipped through them. I liked the feel and smell. I wondered if a teacher had mandated the cards, or if Brittney had been kicking it old-school on her own.

A newer-model HP Pavilion computer and monitor, and a ceramic frog with pens and pencils sticking out of its mouth, graced the desktop. Brittney's bed was next to the desk and had been left unmade. It had pink sheets with tiny white polka dots and a poster of the rock group KISS on the wall behind the headboard. I had to respect someone who reads Shakespeare and listens to KISS at the same time. I got on my knees, lifted the mattress and felt under it. Nothing.

I went through her dresser drawers. Everything had been folded and put away neatly, which somewhat astounded me. The socks had been arranged in rows by color. I was impressed. Most teenagers have trouble even keeping the dirty separated from the clean. I went back to the closet and opened the bowling ball satchel and the tennis bag and the backpack, and found a bowling ball and two tennis racquets and some eraser dust respectively. Next I started feeling through the tightly packed clothes on hangers. There was a Stanton letterman jacket sandwiched a foot or so left of center, with something hard and rectangular near the snaps on front. I pulled the jacket off the hanger, unzipped the lining, and found half a pack of menthol cigarettes, two condoms in a box made for three, and an unmarked VHS-C videotape. I slid the tape and the condoms into one of the side flap pockets of my shorts and left the cigarettes where they were. I went through the rest of the clothes, but didn't find any other secret hiding places.

I walked out and took a quick look in the bedroom across the hall, Leitha's room. She had an Arts and Crafts oak bed, very sturdy looking, and a matching dresser and mirror. An old steamer trunk, padlocked, with an embroidered pillow and floppy straw hat on top, anchored the foot of the bed. Everything waxed and shiny. No dust bunnies under the bed. On top of the dresser was a bill from the electric company and a pay stub from the hospital where Leitha worked. I assumed she got paid every other week, and some quick math put her at about sixty grand a year. Better than average—

especially for a young single person—and enough to afford the house she was in and the new Bic in her driveway. A framed photograph of a school-aged girl sitting next to a toddler hung on the wall beside the dresser. It was a little crooked, so I straightened it.

I walked to the kitchen. Leitha was busy unloading the dishwasher.

"Did you know she's sexually active?" I said. I tossed the condom box onto the countertop.

Leitha dropped a glass, a stemmed red goblet textured with grape bunches that everyone's grandmother had a set of at one time. It didn't break. She picked it up and set it in the sink. She opened the refrigerator and pulled out a plastic bottle containing some kind of sports drink the exact same color as Windex.

"Can I get you something?" she said.

"I'm good."

"I have beer."

Breakfast of champions. "Okay, I'll take a beer."

She handed me a bottle of one of those ultralight brews that are supposed to make you young and slim and sexy. I twisted off the cap, watched the vapors rise, and swallowed about half of it. It didn't taste very good, but at least I was watching my carb count.

I reached into my pocket and pulled out the VHS-C tape. "Any idea what's on this?"

"No."

"Can we watch it?"

"I don't even have a VCR. Everything's on DVD or the computer now."

"Mind if I take it with me?"

"Of course. Take anything you need." She paused, glancing back at the condoms. "I hope she's not pregnant. Hope that's not the real reason she ran away."

"Did she give you any reason to think she might be?"

"No. I work nights—" Leitha capped her drink and pressed the bottle against her chin. She couldn't finish what she was about to say.

"It'll be all right," I said. I always say something stupid when a woman cries. Odds were that it wouldn't be all right. I had a hunch something had set Brittney off, something other than the threat of being grounded for a week. Maybe she was pregnant; maybe it was something else.

I drained the last of the watered-down beer. I wanted a cigarette, but Leitha's house smelled like you weren't supposed to smoke there.

"Since I'm already here in Springfield, I'm going to talk with Mark Toohey first," I said. "If I don't have any luck, I'll drive up to Ponte Vedre and check out the Spiveys and Kent Clark."

Leitha nodded, and I left her house while she was still crying.

CHAPTER FIVE

I call my GMC Jimmy *Jimmy*. He's like a trusted old friend, a partner. We've been through a lot together—167,000 miles worth. I take care of him, and he takes care of me. That's the way it always works with partners. On the way to Toohey's, I cashed Leitha's check, secured the bills in my gold fishhook money clip, and put the wad in my pocket. I stopped at the Shell station on the corner of 8th and Boulevard, examined the oil level and tire pressure, and topped off the gas tank. I bought a fried cherry turnover and a cup of Bean Street for myself, and a pint of STP for Jimmy. Later I planned to go by the title loan place and pay what I owed.

Mark Toohey lived on the third floor of a Victorian converted to rentals. The Painted Lady, glorious I'm sure in her prime, was now plagued with peeling paint, curling shingles, rotting wood. I climbed the stairway, its varnish black with age, the smell of incense hovering like a sickly sweet ghost. I knocked on Toohey's door. Waited. Knocked again.

I called Domino's Pizza, but the manager said Toohey had the day off. So much for wrapping this up in two hours.

I moved Jimmy to a shady spot across from the house and waited.

I carry a Smith and Wesson model 640 .38-caliber revolver. Stainless finish, hardwood grips, two-inch barrel. It's a lovely gun. I own several handguns, none of them automatics. A very expensive nine jammed on me at the firing range one time. If the target had been shooting back, I'd be dead right now. Revolvers don't hold as many rounds, but as long as there's a bullet in the chamber, every time you pull the trigger it will come out. Rule #7 from Nicholas Colt's *Philosophy of Life*: if you pull a trigger, it's always best if a bullet comes out. I call my .38 Little Bill, for no good reason. Little Bill lives in a little holster that slides onto my belt. The tails of my Hawaiian shirts keep Bill out of sight. I also keep a sawed-off double-barrel shotgun strapped to the back of Jimmy's passenger seat. The shotgun has no name.

I sat there for a long time. Waiting, sweating, chewing toothpicks, and trying not to smoke. The exciting, pushing-the-envelope, living-on-the-edge life of a private investigator.

At 7:30, I drove three blocks down 8th Street to McDonald's, got two Big Macs, a large order of fries, and a large black coffee. Every time I go to McDonald's I want a McDLT, which they haven't made in about twenty years. It came in a Styrofoam container that kept the cheeseburger part warm and the lettuce and tomato part cool. Brilliant design for a burger to go. The reason they stopped selling it had something to do with Styrofoam vs. The Environment. I drove back to Toohey's, parked in the same spot, thought about how biodegradable the Big Mac boxes and I were.

At 8:37 the streetlights came on. At 8:38 a black Mustang pulled to the curb. A man I figured was Mark Toohey got out the driver's side. He had a high-and-tight Marine haircut, silver hoops dangling from both ears, ballooned biceps from six months of nothing to do but pump iron. He walked around and opened the passenger's door and a girl got out who wasn't Brittney. She was tall and blonde with cleavage like a cartoon. Toohey gave her a slap on the butt as they approached the threshold. I gave them enough time to get upstairs and into the apartment and then waited ten more minutes so it wouldn't appear as though I'd been waiting for them.

The stairwell still smelled like incense, this time mixed with the distinctive aroma of cannabis. A rap song blared from the second floor apartment, the bass so loud it made my teeth hurt.

I knocked. Toohey's girl, who looked to be in her mid-twenties and stoned, answered. She had on a white terrycloth bathrobe monogrammed *MT*, long blonde hair, heavy makeup, black bag-gage under her eyes. Perfume that screamed, "Smell *me*, every-body. Smell *me*."

"Can I help you?" she said.

"I doubt it. But maybe your boyfriend can." I flashed a counterfeit smile, showed her my ID.

"Mark. There's a private dick at the door." She emphasized *dick*, and giggled. Charming as bubble wrap, Toohey's girl.

Toohey came to the door in Tommy Hilfiger boxers, the leafy stench of marijuana oozing from every pore. He had prison ink on his right arm, an immature goatee on his chin, a torso sculpted from marble.

I showed him my ID. "I need to talk with you for a few minutes," I said. "I'm looking for a girl named Brittney Ryan."

"Can't you see I'm busy? Can't you see I got a date, man?"

"It'll only take a few minutes. Can we talk in private?"

The blonde wasn't giggling anymore. She stood by the fireplace, arms folded over her chest, glaring at me.

"Fuck," Toohey said. "Hold on."

He closed the door. A few minutes later, he came out wearing baggy shorts, a wife-beater T, and sandals.

"Let's walk outside," I said. The rap music and the smell of the place gave me a headache. I let Toohey take the lead down the stairs.

I threw my toothpick on the sidewalk and lit a cigarette. I offered Toohey one.

"That shit's bad for your health," he said.

"Lots of things are. Where's Brittney?"

"How the fuck should I know? I look like her daddy or something?" He stood with his arms slack, head cocked, lips pursed. The bravado too many hits on a pipe can give you.

"You look like you might have been in some trouble, Mark. You look like you might be on probation. You look like a pizza delivery guy who drives a brand-new car and wears ten-dollar underwear and a Rolex."

"I don't have time for this shit, man. You ain't no cop. I told you, I don't know where the bitch is. Fuck off." He shot the bird, about eight inches from my face. He didn't know how close he was to an emergency room visit. I let it go.

"You're right," I said. "I'm not a cop. But I have friends who are. I have friends who could cramp your lifestyle like you wouldn't believe."

"I ain't seen her," he said.

"When was the last time you did see her?"

"Couple weeks ago."

"Did you know she ran away from home?"

"Not my business."

"Well, it *is* my business, and I have a hunch you might know where she is. Were you having sex with her?"

Toohey's cheeks were shiny with sweat. He looked at the sky. "That shit's personal, man."

"I'll find her, Mark. With or without your help. You help me out, I might not have you arrested for statutory rape. Not to mention the drug charges."

He sighed. "She's hookin'. You didn't hear it from me."

I hadn't expected that. Brittney had been gone for two weeks and, a hungry kid—even a smart one—is an easy mark, easy prey for street vultures. But I couldn't understand why she would choose prostitution over going back to Leitha's. It didn't add up.

"Who's the pimp?" I said.

"Fat guy they call Duck. Black dude. Lives on the west side. He's a bouncer at The Tumble Inn. You didn't hear any of this shit from me." Toohey glanced up at his apartment. The blonde was standing there by the open window with her breasts flattened against the panes, trying to eavesdrop.

"Close the fucking window," Toohey shouted.

She closed the fucking window and backed away. A purple Caprice with huge tires and shiny rims inched along the hot pavement in front of Toohey's house. It clipped by at about twenty-five miles per hour, probably looking to score some dope. Or sell some. I watched Toohey's expression, which didn't change.

"What's your girlfriend's name?" I said.

"Why you need to know that?"

"Forget it. She turning tricks too?"

"Fuck you. She's legit, man. Got a bookkeeping job at a car lot."

"Classy." I handed him a business card. "Thanks for your help. Call me if you hear from Brittney or see her."

Toohey turned his head and spit in the grass. I walked across the street, started Jimmy, headed for the west side.

A man I assumed was Duck sat on a stool outside the front entrance, his shaved head shining blue under The Tumble Inn's neon sign. He wore black jeans, a black T-shirt, black leather sneakers, everything triple extra-large.

It was nine thirty on a Wednesday night, and the line to get into the club stretched half a block down the sidewalk. Everyone in the crowd was white. Most of them wore black clothes and had shiny sharp things stuck in their faces. Vampire complexions, bootblack hair. I watched from Jimmy with a pair of binoculars.

Duck checked the customers' IDs one by one. Some were admitted, some sent to the back of the queue. Nobody was arguing about it. They were having their own little party on the sidewalk, a cemetery residents' circle-jerk.

After an hour or so, the ones who'd been turned away started giving up and the line disappeared. I walked to the door and handed the big man Brittney's student ID.

"This some kind of joke?" he said.

The band inside played a weak rendition of Steppenwolf's *Born to be Wild*. The singer's voice was too smooth, as if Frank Sinatra had put together a heavy metal group.

"My name is Nicholas Colt," I said. "I'm a private investigator. The girl's a runaway. I got a tip she's working for you."

"Ain't nobody working for me, bro. I'm just security, you know what I'm saying?" He handed Brittney's ID back to me. His fingers reminded me of those hotdogs that "plump when you cook 'em."

"You're Duck, right?" I said.

"He off tonight."

"Hell, everybody's off tonight. You know where I might find him?"

"He probably at the crib, man. You know what I'm saying? I don't keep up with the motherfucker, but he probably at the crib."

"You wouldn't happen to know his address, would you?"

"I don't know shit, bro. You know what I'm saying?"

"Yeah. I know exactly what you're saying. If I bring some cops over, and we go inside and card everybody, we won't find anyone under twenty-one, will we? We won't have to shut the club down and take all the employees to jail, will we?"

"Fuck off, bro. Everybody inside got valid ID." His Oakley shades leaned half a bubble off level, as if his ears were not quite symmetrical.

"I need to speak with the manager," I said.

"He busy."

"I'm busy too."

I walked around him and opened the door to the club. Next thing I knew, I was flat on the sidewalk with a size fourteen Nike on my chest. I pulled Little Bill from his holster and wedged the barrel into Fatboy's crotch.

"Get off me," I shouted.

He didn't say anything. He had the dark glasses on, so I couldn't see what his eyes were doing. The little revolver glistened under the neon light. I clenched my teeth and hissed in a few short breaths, trying not to pass out. I couldn't really shoot him. He would collapse and mash me like a potato. Legal aspects aside, it just wouldn't have been practical. He was smiling, knew he had the advantage even though I had the gun.

A white guy wearing a suit came out of the club with a lit cigar in one hand. The top three buttons on his shirt were open, exposing the black fur on his chest. "What's the problem here, Shep?" he said.

"Motherfucker trying to get by me, Mr. Clemons."

"What do you want?" Mr. Clemons said to me.

"First of all, I want Magilla Gorilla here to get his goddamn three-hundred-pound foot off me."

"Let him up, Shep."

Shep twisted his foot enough to give me a burn, and then backed away. He took the Oakleys off for a second and pulled his shirt up to wipe his eyes. Bin Laden and a few close friends could have hidden out in his belly button.

I stood up and holstered the pistol.

"Are you the manager?" I said.

"I'm the chief cook and bottle washer," Mr. Clemons said. "I own the joint. What's this all about?"

I took a deep breath, lit a cigarette, showed Clemons my PI license. "I just need to talk with you for a few minutes. There was no cause for any of this bullshit."

"Talk to me about what?" He puffed on the cigar, which smelled expensive. I got a whiff of his cologne, which didn't. His face was shiny and red, his nose bulbous and broken at least once.

"I'm looking for a runaway girl," I said. "Fifteen."

"Can't help you. You know how much a liquor license is worth in this town? I don't cater to minors."

"That's not what I'm saying. I have reason to believe one of your employees—"

"Which one?" An ash fell from the cigar and landed on his shoe. Turquoise Capezios. He pulled a handkerchief from his pocket, bent down, and wiped away the grime.

"Can we talk in private?" I said. Big Shep stood a few feet behind Clemons, trying his best to look menacing.

"Come on in," Clemons said.

I followed him through the hazy crowd of zombies. Sinatra was singing *Bad to the Bone* now. Not really fair to Frank. The singer sounded more like Bing Crosby with a cold.

The office had a full-length mirror on one wall, a desk with a phone and computer and a loose pile of receipts. Clemons offered me a cigar. I took it, put it in my shirt pocket.

"Can I buy you a drink?" he said.

"Thanks, but I'll be leaving shortly. I'm trying to find one of your employees, guy they call Duck."

"Is he in some sort of trouble?" His cigar was getting short. He took a painful hot puff, exhaled jets of blue smoke through his nose.

"Not from me," I said. "I was hired to find a runaway, and rumor has it Duck's been pimping her. I got no beef with Duck himself. I just want the girl."

"I have no control over what my employees do in their spare time." Clemons looked exasperated, as though he were talking about a child who'd chosen a risky hobby. Skateboarding or something.

"I understand that," I said.

"What makes you think she's with Donald?"

"That his real name?"

Clemons nodded. He extinguished the cigar in a congested ashtray that stood sentry beside his desk, an amber glass disk supported by a metal stand. Probably from the same era as his shirt. "Again, why do you think that girl's with my man Duck?"

"Let's just say I heard it through the whisper stream," I said.

"Yeah. I really can't give you any personal information on one of my staff members. Not without a warrant or something. You understand that, don't you?"

"You like cops, Mr. Clemons?"

He laughed. "They tend to make me nervous."

"Me too. We can do this the easy way, or I can send a couple uniforms in with paper. That would be a pain in the ass for all involved. You know how cops are. They make one call, they start hanging around, looking for other things. Maybe everyone here is twenty-one, maybe not. The kids are pretty sophisticated with fake IDs these days. It's amazing what you can do with a two hundred dollar printer. Maybe none of these darling customers of yours are trading Ecstasy in the heads. Maybe nobody's—"

"Fair enough," Clemons said. "I've worked too hard building what I have here to let a two-bit punk like Donald Knight bitch it up. Anyway, I'm pretty sure he's been skimming on the cover charge. I'm going to give you what you need, long as you swear to keep quiet about where it came from."

"Pinky promise," I said.

He punched some keys on the computer, ripped the bottom off one of the cash register receipts, wrote down an address.

"Appreciate it," I said. I turned to leave the office.

"Mr. Colt."

"Yes?"

"Try not to come back here again. Shep usually isn't as gentle as he was tonight."

"Yeah. I'll try. Thanks for the stogie."

I walked toward the club's exit. One of the ghouls—a female, I think—asked me if I'd like to dance. I kept walking.

CHAPTER SIX

It was almost midnight when I found Duck's house. If Leitha had hired Brett Hershey to find her sister, or if she'd been paying me by the hour, her thousand dollars would be gone now.

I switched on my cell phone. No messages. I made a mental note to go by the Bellsouth office tomorrow and have my home phone turned back on. No telling how much business I was losing. Then again, it hadn't been ringing much lately.

Duck lived on the second floor of a two-story brick apartment building, a cube with a roof. I tooled around the block a couple of times, checking out the neighborhood and searching for a place to park. Most of the homes had been built back in the fifties, before every family had two or three cars, so the shallow and narrow driveways naturally spilled out to the street. Parking places were scarce. I drove in circles until someone finally pulled out, half a block away. I hadn't parallel parked in years, and it took me three tries to finally wedge into the space. I couldn't see Duck's building from there so I got out and took a casual midnight stroll.

The neighborhood was quiet, very few lights still on. An ambulance siren wailed in the distance. I walked the perimeter of the apartment building, looking for obstacles that might hang me up if I found Brittney and got her away from there.

A wooden privacy fence surrounded the back lot. I opened the gate enough to slide through. A jaundiced naked bulb cast a gloomy haze over a swing set with no swings and a jungle gym and a basketball goal with BITCH spraypainted on the backboard. Playland at the McDonald's in hell.

Two metal ladders, bolted to the brick siding on back of the building, led up to two different second-floor windows. I figured the apartment had four units, two on bottom, two on top. A light was on in one of the downstairs flats, filtered through a bed sheet with pictures of *Sesame Street* characters on it.

I walked back to the front of the complex. There was a bus stop across the street, with a steel bench and plywood shelter, and I went over there and had a seat, waited and watched with Little Bill at my side. At 12:37 my cell phone rang.

"Hi, sweetie," Juliet said.

"Hi yourself. What are you doing? Thought you had to work tonight."

"I'm on my lunch break. What are you doing?"

It always struck me as funny for someone to be eating lunch in the middle of the night.

"I'm working, too," I said.

"That runaway you told me about?"

"Yeah. I'm hoping to wrap it up tonight. Right now I'm sitting at a bus stop watching the apartment building where I think she'll show up."

"Sounds boring."

"It is. How's it going at the hospital tonight?"

"Lots of sick people. If it wasn't for the patients, we might be able to get some work done."

She tells me that every time I ask her about work. "Yeah," I said. "I can see how all those pesky sick folks might hold up production. What are you having for lunch?"

She started talking, but my attention turned to the Cadillac Escalade pulling into the apartment building's driveway.

"I need to go," I said.

"I'll see you tomorrow?"

"For sure."

I'd thought Shep was big, but Duck was a monster. I guessed him to be six four, three hundred fifty pounds. He wore a dark running suit with white stripes on the sides and a white ball cap turned backward. He was fat, but solid. His arms and shoulders looked as though they might have been carved from railroad ties. Three girls filed out from the back of the Escalade and followed him to the front door. I couldn't tell for sure, but I thought one of them was Brittney Ryan.

I walked back to Jimmy, entered Brittney's cell number as a speed dial on my phone, reached into the glove box and pulled out a package of nylon cable ties. I drove to the building, parked perpendicular behind the Escalade, walked inside and up the stairs to Duck's door, phone in my left hand and shotgun with no name in my right. The apartment was quiet. I knocked. Duck answered, smiling as though he'd been expecting someone. I pressed the barrel of the shotgun against his double chin.

"On the floor," I said. "Hands behind your head."

"Whoa. Go easy now, bro." He looked annoyed. The three girls were sitting on the floor with a Monopoly board and a bong. I'd interrupted their playtime. I pressed the shotgun closer against his neck. He got down on his knees and then went facedown with his hands laced behind his head. He knew the drill.

"What you want, motherfucker? Money? You a cop?"

I looked at the girl I'd thought was Brittney. I hit the speed dial on my phone and immediately heard the theme song from *Sanford and Son*. She got up and ran toward the back of the apartment.

"Call her back," I said to Duck.

"You think you can just waltz in here and take one of my girls? I run a legitimate escort service, motherfucker. Got a business license and everything."

"You got a license to sell fifteen-year-old girls?"

"Bitch got ID say she eighteen."

"She's not. Call her, or the next number I dial is the cops."

"Trixie," Duck shouted. "Get your ass back in here."

A door slammed. I took two cable ties from my pocket, secured them around Duck's wrists and ankles. The two other girls hadn't moved or said anything. One of them was crying. I tied them up anyway. I ran through the living room, into the kitchen, climbed through the window to the fire escape. At the bottom of the steel ladder, I set the shotgun down, ran and caught up with Brittney. She had one leg over the wooden privacy fence. I grabbed her foot, and she screamed.

My lungs were burning. "My name is Nicholas Colt. Your sister hired me to find you and bring you home. You can come on down on this side of the fence and come with me. Or, you can jump to the other side, and I'll call the police and you'll spend the night in juvie and probably go back to being a ward of the state. It's up to you."

"You're not going to kill me?" she said.

"I only kill people I don't like. I like you. Now come on down."

"I can't go back to Leitha's. They'll find me and kill me."

"Who? Fat boy piece of shit pimp in there? Believe me, he won't do anything."

"Not him. He's real nice."

"Who then?"

"I can't tell you."

"Come with me and we'll talk about it. I won't make you go back to Leitha's tonight. Promise."

She swung her leg back to my side of the fence and jumped to the ground. She had on jeans and sneakers and a shirt that didn't cover her belly button. She had remembered to take her backpack. She was about five two, hundred pounds max. She was young and sweet and innocent, and it made me sick to think about her giving blow jobs in the backs of cars.

I picked up the shotgun as we walked around to the front of the apartment building. I opened my car door, and Brittney climbed into the passenger's seat.

"Wait here," I said. "I'll be right back." I figured the threat of juvenile detention would keep her still for at least a few minutes.

I walked back up to the apartment, cut Duck and the girls loose. I still had the shotgun.

"False fucking imprisonment," Duck said. "I'm going to find out who you are, then I'm going to sue your goddamn ass."

I threw a business card on the floor. "There you go. You can sue me, but all my shit together doesn't add up to that Escalade in your driveway. Remember, I know where you live and what you do."

Our eyes locked. He sneered and showed his gold front teeth but he didn't say anything so I left.

Rule # 17 in Nicholas Colt's *Philosophy of Life:* it is easier for a camel to go through the eye of a needle than to get any meaningful conversation from a teenager. It's hard enough with the suburban types, the ones worried about pimples and shoe brands and who did who after the football game. With someone like Brittney, orphaned and exposed to the potential cruelties and uncertainties of foster care from an early age—coupled with time on the streets—it was next to impossible.

Brittney sank against the passenger's side door and sat there stiffly with her arms across her chest. I reminded her to buckle her seatbelt. She did her fencepost impersonation for another minute or so, strapped on the shoulder harness and said, "Just drop me at Leitha's."

"Why?" I said. "So you can run away again?"

"It's not your problem, mister. You did what you were hired to do. Just take me home."

"What did you hope to accomplish by selling your body?"

She straightened up in her seat. "I am not a whore."

"So what were you doing with Duck?"

"Modeling lingerie. That's all."

"Modeling. Let's see, you prance around in some fancy underwear while a guy watches? Is that it? You wag your ass while some drunk bastard plays with himself? I got news for you, little girl. That's a form of prostitution, too. You can go to jail for that. Is that where you want to be? Jail? You'll learn some lessons in jail, all right. You'll learn how to be a thief and a con artist, a druggie and a whore. Maybe even a killer. I don't have any kids, but, if I had one, I'd do whatever it took to keep them out of jail and the court system. That shit's strictly for losers. You're a smart girl. What the hell were you thinking?"

She was silent for a beat. "I need money. Enough to get to California."

"Why California?" I said.

"Have you ever heard of Point Conception?"

"Sure. It's from a book called *Two Years Before the Mast*." I was proud of myself for remembering that.

"It's a real place. The most beautiful place on the planet. I have a friend there, and a job on a ranch whenever I want it. I want to study drama in California. I'm going to be a movie star some day. Plus, like I said, somebody here is going to kill me. I can't stay in Florida."

"Who's going to kill you? Why do you even think that?"

"I saw something—I can't tell you."

"How am I supposed to help if you won't tell me anything?"

"Don't you get it? I don't want your help. If I tell you, you'll tell the police and somebody will be arrested and tried and sent to prison, but they'll still get to me. I know they will. The only way for me to survive is to be far, far away from here. Somewhere they won't find me."

We rode in silence for a few minutes. I turned on the police scanner. A man in Orange Park was holding his wife hostage in their home with a gun. The SWAT team had been called in. I turned it off. Jimmy's tires hummed a monotonous tune on the blacktop.

"I did a little acting one time," I said, trying to find some common ground.

"Let me guess. *Arsenic and Old Lace* in the high school drama club? You were the stiff, right?"

"Nope. I had a bit part in *G.I. Jane*, movie back in the nineties with Demi Moore. They filmed part of it down at Camp Blanding."

"You got to meet Demi Moore?"

"Bruce Willis too. He was hanging around with her during part of the filming."

"Oh my God, you are *lucky*. What part did you play?"

"Have you seen the movie?"

"Only about a gazillion times. I love Demi Moore."

"Remember the restaurant scene? I was the guy two tables over eating spaghetti."

"That's not a bit part. You were just an extra."

"I was still in the movie."

"You were scenery. That's not acting."

"Hey, I'm a method actor. I *lived* the part, ate spaghetti for years preparing for my role."

Brittney giggled. "Well, I'm impressed that you met Demi and Bruce."

"How about you?" I said. "Done anything yet? You know, any acting?"

"No. But I know I'll be good at it. I do scenes by myself sometimes, from Shakespeare. You ever read any Shakespeare, Mr. Colt?"

"I usually wait for the movie," I said. Got another laugh.

I slid a CD into the player. The first track was a song I cowrote called *On the Verge*. It still got decent airplay on classic rock stations.

"Don't you have anything from this century?" Brittney said.

"You don't like these guys?"

"They're all right."

"I was the guitar player," I said.

"Now I know you're lying. They all died in a plane crash, like, before I was born."

"All but one."

"Are you serious? You played guitar for Colt Forty-Five?"

I nodded.

She looked out the window into the darkness and listened to the song.

It was two in morning and traffic was light. I took the interstate and got off at the Green Cove Springs and Hallows Cove exit. I almost creamed Juliet's mailbox when I turned from State Road 17 onto her driveway.

"Is this your house?" Brittney said.

"My girlfriend's. You'll be more comfortable here."

"Won't we wake her up?"

"She's at work. Graveyard shift, Hallows Cove Memorial."

"She's a doctor?"

"Nurse."

"My sister's a nurse. I couldn't do it, give people shots and all that crap."

We got out and I unlocked Juliet's front door. I switched on the light in the foyer, disabled the alarm, smelled the vanilla-scented candles Juliet keeps on a stand in the entranceway.

"This is a pretty house," Brittney said.

We walked into the living room and I turned more lights on. Jules had forgotten her stethoscope on the coffee table.

"I'll give you the grand tour tomorrow," I said. "Right now, I want you to go to bed. First door down the hall, on the right. The bathroom's right across the hall."

She didn't argue. Her eyelids looked as though someone had tied boat anchors to them.

"You have a toothbrush?" I said.

"In my backpack."

"Anything to wear?"

"No."

She brushed her teeth, went into the spare bedroom, and shut the door. A few minutes later, I knocked and handed her a set of Juliet's pajamas. Brittney's eyes were red and swollen, from fatigue and maybe from crying again. I told her goodnight.

I went to the kitchen, plunked some ice cubes in a glass, filled the glass with bourbon. I grabbed a pack of crackers from a tin on top of the refrigerator, opened the sliding glass door to the back porch, and stepped outside. The deck chairs, beaded with dew, glistened silver in the moonlight. I got a towel and wiped one off and sat down with my drink and looked at the stars. I ate a few crackers, and then lit the cigar Mr. Clemons had given me.

The cigar was first-rate, a product of the Dominican Republic. The bourbon was first-rate, a product of Bardstown, Kentucky. I sat there enjoying them, pondering how two very different things from two very different parts of the world went so well together. Like Juliet and me.

I sat there in the dark, thinking about Brittney's claim that someone was trying to kill her. It was possible she fabricated the story to delay returning to Leitha's care. From a teenager's perspective, there's no way Big Sister is going to be "the boss of me." I've heard plenty of bogus stories from plenty of runaways who didn't want to go back home for one reason or another. Leitha's threat to ground Brittney might have been all there was to it. It was also possible Brittney was telling the truth, and her life really was in danger. If that was the case, I needed to find out who, what, when, where, and why, and make sure whoever had threatened her got a solid message to leave her alone.

I reactivated Juliet's alarm system. If Brittney tried to sneak out, a siren would go off. I took a hot shower, climbed into Juliet's bed, and fell asleep within minutes.

CHAPTER SEVEN

I was dreaming about black-eyed peas with Tabasco sauce and cornbread when I felt Juliet snuggle in behind me.

"Who's been sleeping in *my* bed?" she said. I was naked except for my underwear, and she was naked except for the silver crucifix she always wears.

"The big bad wolf?" I said.

"Wrong fairy tale."

Juliet's hair was damp and she smelled like cocoa butter. She wedged her hand between my thighs, tickled me with a fingernail.

"What can I say?" I said. "Nobody ever read to me when I was a kid."

"Want me to tell you a bedtime story?" She kissed the back of my neck.

I turned over and faced her. "Do they live happily ever after?"

"Always."

"I need to pee first."

"How romantic. Go on, you."

When I raised my head, someone with tympani mallets started pounding in my brain. It was my inner troll. He attacks various parts of my body at various times. Today it happened to be the area behind my eyeballs. "You got any Tylenol?" I said.

"There's two full bottles in the cabinet over the sink."

"Thanks. I think one full bottle will be enough."

I got up and used the bathroom, then quietly opened Brittney's bedroom door and peeked in. She'd kicked the covers away and curled into a fetal position in the pajamas I'd given her. Her hair was braided into one long pigtail, and a darkened area the size of a quarter stood out against the otherwise pale skin on the back of her neck. Someone had either been kissing or hitting her, I thought, until it occurred to me she might have bumped her neck climbing out that second-story window last night. I'd probably gotten a few bruises myself. I gently shut Brittney's door. I went back to the bathroom and looked my body over. I didn't find any bruises. I splashed some water on my face and ran Juliet's brush through my hair and beard. I squeezed out a thread of paste and brushed my teeth.

I noticed Juliet had disabled the alarm. I punched in the code for reset, swallowed two headache tablets with some cold water, and went back to bed.

"I heard you open the refrigerator," Juliet said. "You didn't drink out of the jug again, did you?"

"Of course not."

"Yes you did. I would have heard if you'd gotten a glass out."

"What are you?" I said. "The bionic woman or something? You got super hearing? So what if I drank out of the jug?"

"I have super everything." She kissed me on the mouth.

"I was trying to be quiet."

"What's up? You hiding another woman here somewhere?" She smiled, unaware she'd rolled a seven.

"The runaway I told you about. I picked her up last night."

Juliet sat straight up, switched on the bedside lamp. "Here? In my house? Have you lost your fucking mind?"

"Shh. She might hear you. I can explain."

"Don't shh me. This is my home, Nicholas. It's not a flophouse for your juvenile delinquents."

"I think you'll like her."

"I can't believe you brought her here. Why didn't you take her home?"

I told her why.

"Someone's trying to kill her?" she said.

"That's what she told me."

"So now I have to worry about murderers coming here?"

"Nobody knows she's here. I haven't even told her sister yet. That reminds me, I need to call her."

"Why didn't you take her to your place?"

"I figured she needed more privacy than she could get at my place. And there's always the possibility she might fabricate abuse charges or something. I need your help on this one, Jules."

"You could have at least called before you brought her here."

"Didn't want to bother you at work. Sorry. I'm hoping it'll only be for a couple days. If I can get her to trust me, maybe she'll tell me who threatened her."

"Two days, Nicholas. You'll have to think of something else if it takes longer than that."

"All right."

"I have to go to sleep now. Goodnight." She blew me a sarcastic kiss, turned over, and buried her head under the pillow. I told her goodnight, even though it was nine o'clock in the morning.

I couldn't go back to sleep, so I got up and started a pot of coffee. Juliet says I make the world's worst. I use about twice the recommended measurement of grounds, and it comes out looking similar to oil drained from an engine with too many miles on it. At least you can taste my coffee. Juliet's reminds me of weak tea. We always have to make two pots.

When I opened the front door to get the newspaper, the alarm started wailing. I quickly punched in the code to silence it, heard scuffling noises coming from Brittney's room. I walked in there and found her sleepy and confused, trying to escape through the closet. She was wading through a rack of clothes, desperately trying to find her way.

"Brittney. It's okay. It was just the burglar alarm."

She came out of the closet and looked around, her bottom lip trembling. She sat on the bed, folded her arms across her chest.

"I forgot where I was," she said. She untied the pigtail and ruffled her hair into frizzy strands with her fingers, then pulled out a brush from her backpack and vigorously stroked it into shape. "Usually nothing wakes me up. Leitha always says I'd sleep through a hurricane."

"It's all right. You can go back to sleep if you want."

"I don't think I can."

"You drink coffee?"

She nodded. We walked to the kitchen, and I poured us each a cup. Brittney sat on a barstool, her bare feet dangling. I stood beside her.

"This coffee sucks," she said. "When did you make it, last week?"

"It's fresh. I like it strong."

"I'll say. You got something I can dilute it with, like a gallon of paint thinner maybe?"

"How about some milk? They say turpentine is bad for your health."

"Milk would be nice. You got a cigarette?"

"Those things are *definitely* bad for your health."

"Lots of things are."

I couldn't argue with that. We walked out to the back porch, and I gave her a little stainless steel pitcher of half-and-half for her coffee and a Marlboro. My fine Dominican Republic butt from last night was squashed and wet in the ashtray. I took the ashtray inside and wiped it clean, walked back out and sat beside Brittney in one of the deck chairs, lit a cigarette for myself.

The sky was aspirin white, a thin layer of benign clouds blocking the morning sun. The guy with the drum mallets had stopped beating so hard.

"Did you sleep okay?" I said.

"Like a fucking rock."

I coughed out about three lungs worth of smoke. "Okay. Rule number one. Nice girls don't say fuck."

"Your girlfriend said it." Brittney dribbled half her coffee onto the deck and replaced it with some of the cream.

"Yeah, well, who said she's a nice girl? You heard that?"

"Uh-huh. Then I fell back to sleep."

"Okay. Nice fifteen-year-old girls don't say fuck."

"She sounds mean. She doesn't want me here."

"Juliet's not mean. She was surprised, that's all. She was tired from working all night. You'll see. She's really a nice person. How's your coffee now?"

"Why can't I stay at your house?"

"My house is a seventeen-foot camper on a rental lot on the lake."

"Sounds cool."

"There's only one bed, and it hurts my back to sleep on the couch."

"I'll take the couch," Brittney said.

"I don't think it's a good idea. Come on in and we'll get some breakfast."

"I'm not hungry."

"Then come on in and watch me eat some breakfast."

I cracked a half-dozen eggs into a clear glass Pyrex mixing bowl, handed the bowl and a whisk to Brittney, told her to scramble the eggs for me.

"I don't know how," she said.

"You've never made scrambled eggs?"

"So? Have you ever read Dante's *Inferno*? Can't we just go to Burger King or something? This is stupid."

I took the bowl and demonstrated. "Now you try," I said. "It's not stupid to learn how to take care of yourself."

"Maybe, but Burger King has better coffee."

After a while she got into a rhythm and mixed the eggs while I turned on the electric griddle and started laying out strips of bacon. Pretty soon the room smelled good and I was starving.

"You're going to cook the eggs," I said.

"I don't know how to cook. Nobody ever showed me."

"That's what I'm here for."

I showed her how to set the stove and melt butter in a skillet. Once the butter started bubbling, I told her to gently pour in the egg mixture. The eggs landed with a satisfying sizzle, and I showed her how to keep stirring and turning them with a spatula so they wouldn't burn. I put four slices of whole wheat bread in the toaster.

"I don't like brown bread," she said.

"This is for me. You're not hungry, remember?"

"Maybe I'm a little hungry."

We sat at the table and ate bacon and scrambled eggs and toast.

"Wicked delicious," Brittney said.

"*Wicked* delicious?"

She smiled. "I knew a girl in school from Cape Cod. She was always saying wicked this and wicked that."

"Oh. What was your friend's name?"

Her smile disappeared. She shook her head slightly and didn't say anything.

I filled our mugs, mine with coffee and hers with coffee-flavored milk. Brittney drank it and ate the wheat toast without further complaint.

It was strange having a teenager around. Strange in a good way. I've often wondered what my life would have been like if my baby had survived. Sitting at the table with Brittney made me think about what Harmony might have been like at fifteen. It made me sad.

After breakfast, we went outside and had another cigarette and some more coffee.

"Can't I at least *see* your house?" she said.

"You like to fish?"

"Sure. Love to. Marlin is my fave."

"You've never been, have you? Maybe you've read *Old Man and the Sea*, but I bet you've never been fishing." I winked at her.

"It doesn't mean I'm stupid. I live in a different world than you do, Mr. Colt."

"Call me Nicholas. Since I taught you how to cook eggs, maybe I could teach you how to catch a bass."

"You're afraid of me, aren't you? You're afraid if I stay at your place, I'll say you tried to rape me or something, huh?"

That caught me off guard. "I'm going to be straight-up with you. I'm afraid of a lot of things. I'm afraid the human race is going to fall flat on its ass any day now. I've dealt with a lot of teenage runaways, most with lives harder than yours. I've seen twelve-year-old mothers with crack babies. I've seen girls your age with two kids already and trying to have a third so they can get more money from the government. I've seen boys lying in the gutter with white shit coming out their mouths, so strung out they can't remember their last meal. That's where you're headed, Brittney. Don't think California is the land of milk and honey, either. I went all the way to Hollywood one time chasing a sixteen-year-old boy who thought he was going to be the next Tom Cruise. I found him in a motel room—"

"All right," she said. "Jesus."

I took a sip of coffee. It was lukewarm and bitter now, and I thought about going inside and topping it off with some of the Kentucky whiskey. "You hear what I'm saying, though? Running away from home is not the answer."

"It is if someone's trying to kill you."

"Ah. Now there's a good subject. Why don't you tell me all about that."

"Maybe. If you take me fishing."

"Tell me first."

"Take me fishing first."

"Do you know the meaning of the word extortion?" I said.

She nodded.

"Figures," I said.

CHAPTER EIGHT

I tiptoed into Juliet's bedroom and got a pair of shorts and a T-shirt with Jacksonville Jaguars pictures on it for Brittney. I had nearly completed Operation Clandestine when the cell phone in my pocket trilled. Before I had a chance to answer the call, Juliet squinted my way and said, "Where the hell you going with my clothes?"

"Brittney needed something," I said. "I think you guys are about the same size."

"You could have asked first."

"Didn't want to wake you."

"Well, guess what? I'm awake now."

"Okay. May I please borrow this shirt and this pair of shorts for my poor runaway who doesn't have anything to wear?"

"Of course. But put that shirt back. It's a sleep shirt, three sizes too big. She'll look like a bag lady. Get that cute peach-colored top. It will match the white shorts."

I did as instructed, then walked to the bed and gave Juliet a kiss. "Thanks, sweetheart."

There was a message on my phone from Leitha. I called her from the kitchen.

"Is she okay?"

"She's fine," I said. "The thing is, she doesn't want to come back to your house. She thinks someone is trying to kill her."

"That's crazy. Let me talk to her."

"She's in the shower right now."

"So who does she think is trying to kill her?"

"She won't tell. Maybe if I can spend some time with her, I can get to the bottom of it."

"I want her home with me." Leitha said.

"I understand that. And I'll bring her right now if you insist. But she'll probably just run away again. I'd like to get to the root cause of why she ran away in the first place."

Leitha's voice quivered. "When do you think you'll bring her home?"

"As soon as I can. I'm going to take her fishing in a little while. Maybe she'll open up."

"Will you have her call me as soon as she gets out of the shower?"

"Sure."

We said goodbye. Juliet came into the kitchen wrapped in a fuzzy pink bathrobe and matching slippers. She didn't say anything and poured herself a cup of coffee. Her hair was a mess from sleeping on it wet.

"Good morning," I said.

She ignored me, took her coffee out to the back porch. I poured myself a cup. The bourbon was getting low, so I added half a shot of tequila and followed Juliet outside.

"Sorry if we woke you," I said.

"Oh, no problem. I can make it on one fucking hour of sleep. I'm goddamn bionic, remember?"

"I just love it when your Irish half shines through," I said. "We'll be leaving soon, so you can go back to bed. You have to work tonight?"

"Think, Nicholas. Have you ever tried that? Just thinking for once? I took off tonight because you invited me to come along with you and Joe to your Thursday night pool game at Kelly's. He's bringing his wife, and we're going to make a night of it. Any of that ring a bell?"

"Crap. I did forget this is Thursday." I lit a cigarette.

"Yeah. So now you have that girl to worry about. I suppose that means the date is off?"

"This is my work, Jules. If it interferes with my social calendar—"

"This coffee is horrible." She got up and walked to the railing, dumped the contents of her cup into the sand below. "You were hired to find her, not babysit or try to straighten out her life. How much are you charging for all that?"

"Doing it because I want to. If I have an opportunity to actually help a kid in trouble—"

"Just leave, okay? I'm really not very happy at the moment. I'm starting to think that I need more than you're capable of giving, Nicholas."

"What are you saying?"

She leaned, elbows on knees, hands over face, voice an octave higher. "I'm saying maybe we need a break."

"You're dumping me?"

"Don't say it like that."

"How else am I supposed to say it?" I drained the last of my tequila-spiked coffee. "Consider me gone, babe."

I wasn't too worried. Jules and I break up every couple months. We always end up back together.

My place on Lake Barkley is only seven miles from Juliet's house. When we crossed the Shands Bridge, Brittney said, "Did you know the St. John's is one of the only rivers in the United States that flows north?"

"Geography was never my best subject," I said.

"What was your best subject?"

"Music. And nap time."

We pulled into my drive around eleven. The cloud cover had dissipated, the sun high and hot now. I unlocked the door to my camper and we climbed inside. I switched on the air conditioner.

"This place is cool," Brittney said. "It's like living in a spaceship or a submarine or something."

"Never thought about it that way," I said. "Serves the purpose for now, I guess."

"Will you play for me?" She pointed toward the guitar case propped against a bulkhead.

"I don't play anymore."

"Why not?"

"Because I don't."

She scrunched her lips. "Okay. Can I get on your computer?"

She goofed around on the web while I rigged a couple of fishing rods. It wasn't the best time of day for catching fish, but I figured I could teach her some things and then go out again in the evening when it got cooler. After I had everything ready, I dragged her away from the computer and we went outside.

"I'm going to teach you to cast from the bank first," I said. "Then we'll go out in the boat."

"You have a boat?"

"It's one of my landlord's rentals. He lets me borrow it. In exchange, I provide some security around the campsites here. And I get a reduced rate on my lot. My landlord happens to be my best friend."

"I think he should give you the lot for free."

"I think you're right. Maybe I'll bring that up."

We walked down the hill to the lake. I carried the rods, and Brittney toted my tackle box. I'd given her a cap to wear so her face wouldn't get sunburned. She had her hair in a ponytail and looked cute as a girl going fishing for the first time possibly could.

"I don't have to touch a worm or anything, do I?"

"Just a plastic one," I said. "We'll save the live bait lessons for another day."

I took the rod with the spincast reel and demonstrated how to use it. Brittney tried, fumbled a few times, finally got the hang of it.

"Your thingy's different than mine," she said.

"This is called a baitcaster reel. It's a little tricky. Once you get good enough with that one, I'll teach you. Deal?"

"Okay."

We'd been fishing for about an hour, with no luck, when Brittney said, "This is quite conducive to somnolence."

"What?"

"It means I'm getting sleepy."

"You always go around talking like the Professor on *Gilligan's Island*?" I said.

"Who?"

"Never mind. Tell me something. Did your tennis coach ever make a pass at you?"

"Kent?"

"Yeah. Kent Clark."

"Oh! I think I got one." Her rod bent, and she started reeling feverishly.

"Wait a minute," I said.

She didn't have a fish. She had snagged onto a log or something. I took her rod and gave the line some slack, hoping to free the hook. No dice. I had to break the line.

"Now what?" Brittney said.

"Now I teach you how to tie a new hook on the end of the line."

"This is hard."

"No it's not. It's fun. See that tackle box? That's called being prepared. If we came out here with just one hook, we'd be screwed now, huh? What about Kent Clark? He ever try anything?"

"Oh, hell no. He's old. Like forty-something, I think. Plus, he's married."

"That doesn't stop some people."

"He was always a perfect gentleman."

"All right. Ready to go out on the boat?" I said.

We walked to the dock and shoved off. Brittney insisted she was a good swimmer, but I made her wear a life jacket anyway. I started the engine and motored toward the east side of the lake, to some breaklines where I'd had some luck previously. The water was calm and glassy.

Thursday, or any weekday, was a good day to fish. On weekends, the ski boats and Jet Skis and party barges pretty much ruined any angling action. If I were King of the World, I would do away with all gasoline- and diesel-powered vehicles, anything that ran on fossil fuels. We would have sailboats, rowboats, and bicycles.

Anything that made more noise than an acoustic guitar would be outlawed. Rule #12 from Nicholas Colt's *Philosophy of Life*: you're never going to be King of the World, so just deal with the bullshit best you can.

Brittney faced the bow, her long blonde ponytail blowing in the wind. I slowed down, cut the engine, dropped a concrete anchor from the stern, and instructed Brittney to do the same on her end. The boat didn't have a live well, but I had a good-sized basket on board in case we caught a few.

"Cast toward the shore," I said. "Then reel it in slowly."

Brittney got a hit on her second cast. She shrieked. A good-sized largemouth surfaced and jumped about ten feet from the boat.

"Let him run with it a little," I said. "Use your drag like I showed you."

A few minutes later she had him reeled in close to the boat and I reached out and snagged him with a long-handled net.

"Wow. That's a beautiful fish," I said. I hung him on a scale from my tackle box. He weighed nearly five pounds.

"You're right," Brittney said. "This is fun."

"You want to take him off the hook?"

"Maybe you better."

"You need to learn how."

"I'll watch. Next time, I'll do it myself."

I gently brushed back the dorsal fin, wrestled the hook from his bottom lip.

"Should we keep him, or throw him back?" I said.

"Why would we want to keep him?"

"To eat, silly."

"Oh, no. I don't want to kill him. He's so powerful. And beautiful."

I lowered him back to the water. He flopped, swam away.

We fished for about two more hours, until it started to get dark. Brittney caught one more, and I didn't catch any. Beginner's luck. She released the second fish all by herself.

✿   ✿   ✿

When we got back to my camper, Brittney asked me what was for supper.

"We could have had those two big fish you caught," I said.

"Is that what you do? Eat the ones you catch?"

"Sometimes."

"Don't you think that's cruel?"

I thought about that for a minute. "I would never kill anything just for the sake of killing it," I said. "But survival depends on death. Where do you think those strips of bacon you ate this morning came from?"

"I'm thinking seriously about becoming a vegetarian. How do you feel about stem cell research?" Brittney said.

"What?" I couldn't figure how her mind worked sometimes.

"You said survival depends on death. Isn't that the same thing? They use tissue from potentially viable embryos and fetuses, thinking they might be able to cure certain diseases someday."

"I don't know much about it," I said. "I guess I would say the life of a human is inherently more valuable than the life of an animal."

"That's egotistical. Let's forget about animals for a minute. Do you believe in the concept of sacrificing one for the good of many?"

"Depends on if I'm the one being sacrificed, I guess. There you go talking like The Professor again. What are you, a budding young philosopher or something? I'm going to grill some hot dogs for dinner. I guess you can just have a bun."

Brittney bit her lip. "Hot dogs sound good."

We ate outside on the picnic table with a citronella candle a few feet away to ward off mosquitoes. I had a Dos Equis and Brittney had a Coke. We smoked cigarettes afterward and I had another beer.

"Why is there a picture of your wife hanging on the wall?" Brittney asked.

"Obviously because I loved her and I miss her," I said.

"But doesn't it make your girlfriend sad when she sees it?"

"I don't know. I never thought about it like that."

"Sometimes you have to let go of the past and cling to the love you have now."

"And sometimes, young lady, you have to mind your own business."

We sat in silence for a few minutes.

"Make you a deal," I said. "I'll quit smoking if you quit."

"I can quit any time I want to. I go days at a time without smoking sometimes. It's no big deal for me."

"That means you're not hooked yet. You should quit now, before it becomes an addiction."

"Okay. So I'll quit now." She dropped her cigarette and smashed it into the sand with her sneaker. She grabbed the Marlboro pack from the picnic table, twisted it, rolled it into a ball, threw it over her shoulder. "There. Now we quit."

"I didn't mean right this second," I said. "Damn, girl. You do have a flare for the dramatic. I'm sure you'll be a great actress some day."

"I have a present for you," she said.

She climbed inside the camper, came back out with her backpack. She unzipped it, reached in, and pulled out a paperback book. I lit my Zippo and read the cover. It was a pocket-sized dictionary and thesaurus.

"So you can improve your vocabulary," Brittney said.

"Gee, thanks. You think I'm a dummy or something?"

"You didn't know what 'conducive to somnolence' meant."

"I knew what it meant. It just sounded strange coming from a fifteen-year-old. I have a damn good vocabulary. But thanks anyway for the book. What else do you have in that backpack?"

"Just some things for school. Check this out." She opened the front pocket and pulled out a silver cylinder about the size of a firecracker. She aimed it, and a tiny red dot appeared on Joe Crawford's house half a mile across the lagoon. "It's a laser pointer. Cool, huh?"

"Awesome. Why do you need that for school?"

"It was on the list of supplies for my speech class." She put the pointer in her pants pocket, reached in the backpack, and pulled out a calculator. She handed it to me. "I have a super power."

"Oh yeah? What's that?"

"I can tell you the square root of any number. You know, as long as it's a number *with* a true square root."

"Sure you can."

"Try me."

I multiplied forty-three times forty-three on the calculator. "Okay," I said, "what's the square root of one thousand forty-nine?"

"Forty-three," Brittney said.

"How did you do that?"

"I don't know. I've been able to do it since third grade. It's like a talent some autistic savants have. It can't be explained. I'm not autistic. I guess my brain's just wired funny."

"Amazing. Okay, now that I taught you how to fish, you have to tell me why you think someone is trying to kill you."

"First, you have to tell me why you don't play the guitar anymore," she said.

"Nope. A deal's a deal. I taught you how to fish, so—"

"I said *maybe* I would tell you. I've decided against it. In fact, it was a lie. I made it up. Just take me back home, to Leitha's."

"If it was a lie, why did you run away?"

"Leitha was going to ground me for a whole week. Just because I called her a bitch."

"And why did you call her that? Because of Mark Toohey, right?"

"I love him. Leitha just doesn't understand."

"Toohey's a scumbag," I said. "If I take you home, I want you to promise to do what Leitha says. And, I want you to promise to stay away from Mark Toohey."

"I promise."

She was full of shit. I didn't know what to believe, but if she wanted to go home I had no choice other than to take her there. My twenty-four-hour guardianship paper would expire in a few hours. I called Leitha's home number, no answer. I tried her cell and she picked up on the third ring.

"Now she says she wants to come home," I said. "Says she lied about someone trying to kill her."

"I'm at work right now," Leitha said. Her voice sounded happy. "I have a short shift tonight. You could—"

"How about I just drop her off in the morning? Eight or nine?" It was a long drive to Leitha's house, and the beers had made me sleepy. It would be safer to wait until morning, and there was always a chance she might open up with some more information between now and then.

"Great. I'll fix you guys breakfast. Can I talk to Brittney?"

I handed Brittney the phone.

"I want to come home *tonight*," Brittney said. She was quiet for a minute while Leitha responded, then hung up without saying goodbye. She tossed my phone on the table. "You can't hold me prisoner. I'll hitchhike home if I have to."

"There's the road," I said. She got up and walked away, calling my bluff. I caught up with her and grabbed her arm.

"Let me go, you son of a bitch."

"What the hell's your problem?" I said. "I'm responsible for you until I deliver you to Leitha. You understand that?"

"I don't want to sleep at your girlfriend's house."

I hadn't told her about the little fight Juliet and I had while she was in the shower. I gave her the illusion of victory. "All right," I said. "We'll stay here. You can take the bed, I'll take the couch. Just don't try to sneak out, okay?"

She calmed down some. "Can we go fishing again in the morning?"

"We'll see."

We watched television for a while, and then I made Brittney go to bed. I put on a nicotine patch, sat up and drank a few beers until I fell asleep on the couch, knowing my back would pay the price.

CHAPTER NINE

The living room window exploded.

I heard another shot, followed by glass raining on the galley table.

I reached into the storage compartment under the couch, pulled out my .357, and belly-crawled through the curtain partition to the bedroom.

I tapped Brittney on the shoulder.

"Hey. You okay?" I said.

She didn't answer. I nudged her again.

"Just five more minutes, Leitha," she said.

She was okay.

I didn't turn the lights on, in case the shooters were still out there. All I needed was to be a nice silhouette target, a sitting duck for maybe some drunken kids who'd been shooting frogs down by the lake. Did they know they could have killed us?

I padded to the kitchen, peeked through the blinds, saw taillights winding up Lake Barkley Road. The car was an old Chevy station wagon, white, a '63 or '64. I grabbed my binoculars, but fog had settled in and I couldn't make out the numbers on the plates.

I found my car keys and wallet, opened the camper's hatch and stepped out barefoot onto my yard of damp and uncomfortable pine needles. I took a quick glance at the windows. Totaled.

The old Chevy was out of sight now, probably a mile away. I had to at least get the plate numbers.

I fired up Jimmy, slung a ton of gravel on my way out to Lake Barkley Road.

I switched on the fog lights, not much help. Visibility was about ten feet. I accelerated to sixty, downshifted into the curves, hoped I wouldn't meet a brick wall in the form of a logging truck or something.

I made it to the blinking red light at the intersection of Lake Barkley Road and State Road 13. I looked both ways, saw nothing but a smoky white veil.

Left or right? State road 13 snakes east and west along the St. John's River. A left turn would take me through Orangedale, populated only by a few tobacco and soybean farms, strictly rural. A right would take me through Hallows Cove, what we call "town," and then on up to Jacksonville.

I took a right. I didn't think I'd seen the old Chevy before, and I had a hunch it probably came down from Jacksonville.

I motored into town, ignoring the 35-mph speed limit, second-gearing it through the red lights. I caught up with the white Chevy Impala station wagon at the intersection of 13 and Cypress, where it had stopped for the red light.

The car was a mammoth relic, an antique from the days when gas was thirty-five cents a gallon. It would have been a nice thing for me to own, to pull my house around with if I ever had the occasion. From the same era and all.

I shook all those irrelevant thoughts and looked down at the license plate: W-H-A-L-E. The A was hidden by a mud splatter, but the tag made sense. The Great White Whale.

The light turned green and The Whale heaved forward, greasy puffs of black smoke from its exhaust mingling with the fog. I tailgated it through Remington Park, switching my brights on and off in an effort to get it to pull over.

It sped up, and I followed suit.

Then, in my rearview mirror, I saw a sight any sane driver wearing nothing but Sponge Bob boxers and a shoulder holster would naturally dread: the flashing blue strobes of a Florida state trooper.

I pulled into the lot of The Parkside Motel, known affectionately among locals as the "Come and Go." I gripped the steering wheel as the trooper ambled my way, didn't want him to get edgy when he saw my unconcealed weapon.

The cop was short and thin and walked with the authority only a badge and a gun can give you.

"Step out of the vehicle," he said. His right hand rested on the butt of his 9-mm Glock.

I did as instructed. I heard a few cars passing on 13 and was happy now that the fog was so thick.

"Hands on the car."

Again I complied, felt my holster go light when he lifted my piece. He cuffed me. Didn't say good morning or read me my rights or anything.

"Am I being arrested?"

"I'll ask the questions, sir." At least he was being polite now. I guess he could afford to be, now that my wrists were chained together and pinched like sausage links.

"Have you been drinking tonight?"

"No sir." It was a lie. But it had been a couple hours since I'd had anything, and I certainly wasn't drunk. Adrenaline from chasing The Whale had burned off any residual alcohol in my system.

"Driver's license, registration, proof of insurance," he demanded.

"In the glove box," I said, giving consent for search and seizure.

He reached in, opened the glove compartment, pulled out my wallet and a couple of envelopes. He shuffled through my IDs and credit cards.

"Why didn't you tell me you're a private detective?"

"You didn't ask. Sir."

"Not a wiseass are you?"

"No sir." Another lie.

"The address on your driver's license and your PI license is a post office box. Where do you live?"

"Lot twenty-seven, over at Joe's."

"Joe's?"

I was starting not to like this guy more and more. What kind of cop didn't know about Joe's? I reminded myself that the State boys moved around a lot, and he was probably new to the area.

"Joe's Fish Camp," I said. "Over on Lake Barkley. I have an old Airstream parked over there."

"You pull a camper with the Jimmy?"

"The camper's not going anywhere. The bearings are shot. No exterior lights. If I ever decide to move, I'll just sell it. Or keep it for a weekend place."

The trooper relaxed a little, and I even saw his thin lips creak toward a smile. "So what brings you out this morning, so early, with the nice undies?"

"The bad guy got away," I said. I told him about my camper being shot at, gave him The Whale's description and plates.

"For some reason, I believe you," he said. "Have you called in a police report yet?"

"It just now happened."

"When you get home, call the Clay County Sheriff's Department. They'll send someone out."

No shit, Sherlock.

He uncuffed me and I shook some circulation back into my hands. He gave me back my wallet and the envelopes and my gun. Told me to drive safely.

When I got back to my camper, I walked to the bedroom and switched on the reading lamp to check on Brittney.

She was gone.

CHAPTER TEN

I picked up my shorts and checked the pockets. The fishhook money clip was there, but the cash was gone. Nine hundred dollars. My life's savings. "Fuck," I said, and threw the shorts across the room. After I stomped around shouting expletives for a few more minutes, I put my clothes on and walked outside.

"Brittney," I shouted. No answer. I figured she had hitched a ride, maybe to Leitha's house, maybe to the Greyhound station for a ticket to the West Coast. With nine hundred dollars, she could have gone anywhere.

I tried to reach Leitha on the phone. No luck. I figured she was still asleep. She'd gotten off work at one and it was a little past seven now. I decided to drive on up there. Springfield was as good a place as any to start looking for Brittney again. If she didn't go to Leitha's, maybe she went to Mark Toohey's place.

On the way I remembered the VHS-C tape I'd stolen from Brittney's room. I'd put it in one of my pockets, and left those shorts at Juliet's house in the dirty clothes hamper. I stopped by Juliet's to get the tape.

A newer model Mercedes, white, with vanity plates that said GAS MAN was parked in her driveway. Juliet's car wasn't there, or maybe she had put it in the garage for once.

Everything that had happened earlier had me on edge. I pulled Little Bill from his holster, walked around the perimeter of the house. Everything seemed to be in order. I used my key to open the front door. The house was quiet. I made sure the alarm wasn't on, walked to Juliet's bedroom and into a nightmare.

Juliet sat up in bed, clutching the top sheet to cover herself. "Nicholas. What are you doing here?"

"Question is, what is *he* doing here?" I pointed Little Bill toward the guy lying beside Juliet. He was snoring. I felt like giving him an extra asshole, size .38.

Juliet got up, grabbed her bathrobe from the floor, quickly put it on and tied the belt. She stalked out of the bedroom. I followed her to the kitchen.

"Don't you think it's just a little rude to barge into my house like this?" she said.

"You gave me a key, remember? Last week you were practically begging me to move in with you. Don't you think it's a little rude to be fucking Mr. Anesthesiologist in the bed I helped you pay for?"

"How did you know—"

"I saw the plates on his goddamn Mercedes. Gas man. What else could it be? You fucking somebody from the utility company?"

She looked up at me with teary eyes. "Okay. Last week I wanted you to move in. And for the umpteenth time, you said no. I need some kind of commitment, Nicholas. Can't you see that? On again, off again. That's us. I just can't take it—"

"You don't have to take it anymore. We're off again. Forever this time. You in love with that guy?"

She started crying. "I was drunk. I was mad at you. He... I'm in love with *you*, you jerk. I'm almost forty years old, Nicholas. I need—"

"You need a goddamn spanking," I said. I put Little Bill in his holster, slammed the front door on my way out.

Now that my personal life was good and fucked up, I was determined to make sure my professional life wasn't. I felt responsible for Brittney getting away from me. I should have taken her to Leitha's last night. Soon as she said she wanted to go home, I should have taken her there.

I drove to Springfield, pulled into Leitha's driveway. Her car was there. I tried her landline and cell, no answer at either. I mounted the porch, rang the doorbell, and then knocked hard. She should have been awake by now. She was expecting me to bring Brittney, and had even planned to cook breakfast for us. I found it odd that she didn't answer the door. I needed to tell her Brittney was on the loose again.

I walked around back, opened a chain-link gate, followed some concrete stepping stones to the patio and a set of French doors. One of the panes near the lock had been broken, and the door was ajar.

I ran back to Jimmy and got the shotgun. I pushed Leitha's back door open with my foot, stood back, and waited for a few seconds. Nothing happened. I walked through the door and into the master bedroom, the shotgun's barrel leading the way.

The stench of human waste was so thick I could taste it. Leitha lay faceup on the bed, her arms and legs spread and tied to the frame with electrical cords. There was a pillowcase knotted tightly around her throat.

My face went numb. I leaned against the wall, shotgun in hand, my heart thumping and fluttering like a bird in a box.

Leitha's nipples had been burned off, probably with a cigar or cigarette, and a tilted cross had been carved into her forehead. Her eyes were open, glazed, and fixed. Her jaw was slack, the tip of her tongue sticking out. She'd lost control of her bowels and bladder.

I walked outside and vomited, my chest heaving and burning. I couldn't get enough air. There just wasn't enough.

I managed to calm down enough to phone the police. I sat in the cool grass under a sycamore tree until they arrived.

CHAPTER ELEVEN

By two that afternoon, Leitha was in the morgue and I was homeless.

I sat in the interrogation room, Sheriff's Department Substation 4, wearing a nice set of orange coveralls too tight in the shoulders and too short in the legs. The clothes I'd been wearing were taken for evidence, my hands checked for gunshot residue and blood. Negative for both. I wasn't under arrest, but they'd sealed off the Airstream and the perimeter of my lot pending arrival of an FBI forensics team. Somebody had tortured and killed Leitha. The cops figured the same someone had kidnapped Brittney. Since Brittney had last been seen at my place, the Clay County guys were in on the investigation.

"How you doing?" A homicide detective named Barry Fleming walked in and shut the door behind him. Fleming and I had history. He turned his back to me, straightened his tie in a mirror I knew was two-way.

"You got a video cam behind the mirror?" I said.

"Protocol. It's nothing personal."

I resented being treated like a suspect.

"Let's walk outside," I said. "Then we can talk. No tape recorders, no video."

Fleming cut me in half with his eyes.

He made a signal to the mirror and we left the room. We walked down a long hallway to the emergency exit and I followed him into the sunlight. The deputies had a nice little patio setup out there. Barbecue grill, table with an umbrella, hot tub.

Fleming fished a pair of Ray Bans from a pocket. We stepped into the shade of the umbrella and sat at the table.

Fleming started: "What was your relationship with the victim?"

"The victim has a name. Her name is Leitha Ryan, in case you forgot. She hired me to find her runaway sister."

"Why weren't the police notified?"

I cocked my head to one side and squinted, trying to see Fleming's eyes through the dark glasses. "Leitha was afraid Brittney would be put back into foster care," I said.

Fleming chuckled. "That would have been better for both of them. We've already gotten a prelim back from the M.E.'s office. Her nipples weren't the only thing burned off."

I rose, grabbed Homicide Detective Barry Fleming by his fat tie, lifted him like a marionette. His mouth opened in silent protest. His eyes bulged.

"You little fuckwad," I said. "You think that shit's funny? I should break your fucking neck right now. But I have work to do."

I shoved him away. He tripped over a chair and landed on his ass in the hot tub.

I walked out and started my car, burned rubber leaving Substation 4's parking lot.

All the tools I use to make a living were sealed up in the Airstream. Computer, cameras, binoculars, micro-cassettes, everything. And the cops had confiscated Little Bill and the rest of my handguns, as well as the shotgun with no name.

I needed cash, clothes. Some sort of weapon, at least one. And I needed a place to stay.

I drove to The Parkside Motel.

The day clerk looked up from the magazine he was reading when I stepped inside. His cheeks were red, hair bleached from the sun. He took one look at me and laughed.

"Nice suit, Mr. Colt."

"I'm not in the mood, Patrick. I need a room."

"By the hour, or—"

"Very funny," I said. "I need a place to stay. Maybe for a week."

"Cash or credit?"

"Neither. I'm broke."

"I'll have to clear it with Mrs. Mason, of course."

"Do it."

Julie Mason owned The Parkside. We weren't exactly friends, but she owed me a favor.

Patrick walked to the back office. I heard him punching numbers into a phone before he shut the door. I picked up the book he had been reading, let it fall open to the marked page. It was a poem by M. W. Jones. I don't know much about poetry, but this one didn't seem to be very good. Patrick came back to the front desk.

"How can you read this crap?" I said.

He ignored my question. "Mrs. Mason said you can have room two-oh-eight for as long as you need it. She'll put it on your tab."

Patrick handed over the key, and I left the office.

I ordered a pizza from the room, paid for it with a bad check. I choked down three slices and washed it down with a cup of chlorinated water from the bathroom faucet. Now that I had satisfied two of my basic needs—food and shelter—I needed to work on getting some clothes. Jailhouse orange just wasn't my color.

I called Joe Crawford, my landlord and best friend.

"Where are you?" he asked.

"Over at The Parkside. Two-oh-eight. They got everything sealed off over at my place, and I was wondering if you could run through Alvy's Discount and grab me a few things."

"Check out of that dump," Joe said. "You can stay at my place."

"I appreciate it, Joe. Thing is, a young woman was murdered this morning, and I'm going to find out who did it. I don't want that kind of trouble following me to your front door."

"Is that why you're not staying at Juliet's?"

"Juliet and I are through. I caught her in bed with another man this morning."

"Shit. Sorry, man. What do you need from Alvy's?"

"Just some shorts and a couple shirts. Get Wranglers, thirty-three waist. You know the kind of shirts I like. Get large."

"Shoes?"

"I have my Top-Siders with me. I'm all right on shoes. Get me a couple pairs of boxers. Oh, and grab me a can of deodorant, would you?"

"No problem. I'll get over there as soon as I can."

"Thanks, Joe. You're a saint, man."

I hung up, opened the drawer on the bedside table and lifted out the phone directory. I was back in the stone ages, using a pencil and paper and a phone book heavy as a TV preacher's heart.

A couple of clients owed me money.

I dialed a lawyer named Dana Glass first. He owed me two grand for nailing a guy in a bogus workman's comp case. Dana's secretary answered.

"This is Nicholas Colt. May I speak to Mr. Glass, please?"

"Mr. Glass is in court this afternoon. May I take a message?"

I knew Dana wasn't in court. He goes to court about as often as Dracula eats garlic bread.

"I did some work for him a few weeks ago," I said. "I've billed him twice, still haven't gotten paid."

"What was your name, sir?"

I told her my name again and she put me on hold. I was treated to an orchestral arrangement of *Eleanor Rigby* followed by *Just the Way You Are*. Three or four minutes later, she mercifully clicked back on.

"That check was sent yesterday, Mr. Colt."

"Listen," I said, "I need that money today. I'll just drive up there now and you can cut me a check. Then I'll burn the one you already sent."

"Mr. Glass would have to authorize that."

"So what time is he—"

"He'll be in court the rest of the afternoon. You might try back in the morning."

"Sure. Don't go changin'."

"Excuse me?"

I hung up on her. You can't win with lawyers. Lawyers and

insurance companies are the worst about paying on time, and unfortunately 90 percent of my clientele fall into one of those two categories.

I picked up the phone book again, flipped to the Gs in the residential section. Then I remembered I'd written Alecia Gibson's cell number on the back of a business card. I found it in my wallet.

"Hello," she said.

"Is this Alecia."

"Yes?"

"Nicholas Colt. I—"

"Oh, Mr. Colt. I know you're not going to believe this, but I'm in line at the post office right now to buy stamps. I'm sending the money I owe you. I have it right here in my hand."

I had a hard time buying that. "Are you serious? And you haven't mailed it yet?"

"No kidding. I have it right here."

Miracle. "Don't mail it," I said. "I'll come by in a couple of hours to pick it up."

She told me where to meet her.

It was only five hundred bucks, but it would keep me in gas and food for a few days. I ate the other half of my pizza and waited for Joe to bring my clothes. The cold Italian sausage tasted exactly like Play-Doh.

CHAPTER TWELVE

I crossed the Shands Bridge. A tangy odor from the paper mill in Palatka rode in on a breeze from the south, permeating my interior even with the windows up. I drove through Green Cove Springs to the Eagle Harbor community. Alecia had told me to meet her at Wal-Mart, in the electronics department.

I browsed the CDs, found a Coltrane boxed set I knew I'd have to have. Maybe when that tightwad Dana Glass finally coughed up my dough.

"Mr. Colt." Alecia marched my way, handed me a sealed envelope.

"Thank you," I said. "You don't even know what a lifesaver this is."

Alecia was in her mid-thirties, dark brown hair to her shoulders, blue eyes that sparkled aqua under the store's fluorescent ceiling lights.

"Sorry it took so long to pay you," she said. "Things have been a little crazy."

"I understand."

She had hired me several months ago to run surveillance on her husband, suspected of cheating. I caught him checking in at The Ritz up on Amelia Island with a blonde in her early twenties. Got some good photos, felt bad for Alecia.

I glanced over at the wall of new TVs, all tuned to the same channel. My Airstream was on the six o'clock news.

"Excuse me for a minute," I said.

I trotted over and turned the volume up on one of the sets. A reporter named Jenny Wells was live at the scene:

"A fifteen-year-old girl was kidnapped early this morning from this modest trailer home at Joe's Fish Camp near Hallows Cove. Barry Fleming, a homicide detective for the Clay County Sheriff's Department, states that the kidnapping appears to be linked to the murder of Leitha Ryan in Jacksonville's Springfield area, also early today. I talked with Detective Fleming this afternoon."

They cut to a taped interview with Fleming.

"Detective Fleming, I know that local agencies are working closely with the FBI in an effort to solve these cases. Do you have any suspects yet?"

Barry said they had a couple of leads. I doubted it.

Alecia walked up beside me. "I heard about that missing girl," she said.

"That's my camper there in the background."

"It happened where you live? You knew her?"

"She was a runaway I was hired to find. She stayed at my place last night. Now I'm kind of homeless for the next few days while the feds pick apart my camper for evidence. It's been one hell of a day, Alecia."

"You do have a place to stay, don't you?"

"Oh. Yeah. I have a motel room. Nothing fancy, but it beats a park bench."

"If there's anything I can do to help—"

"I'm okay. Really. I just need a good night's sleep and—" I hesitated. *And to track down the son of a bitch who killed Leitha and kidnapped Brittney.*

"And?" Alecia said.

"And just relax for a few days until I can get back to my computer and finish some cases I've been working on." Alecia seemed really nice, but one lesson I've learned through the years is to keep my mouth shut. I didn't want any chance of Barry Fleming finding out I was planning to investigate the crimes myself.

"Well," Alecia said, "you have my number if there's anything I can do."

"Thanks," I said. "And thanks again for the check."

I stood in line at customer service, cashed the check, walked back to electronics, and bought the Coltrane CDs. What the hell. You only live once.

I made it back to Hallows Cove early enough to stop in Kelly's Pool Hall for the tail end of happy hour. Some of the deputies from the sheriff's department hang out there, and I wanted to catch any scuttlebutt that might be flying around. I didn't need a drink, but I wanted one.

A few years ago, Kelly O'Conner, the typical cardboard-cutout Irish bar owner any stranger walking into a place named Kelly's would expect to see, dropped dead one night carrying a pitcher of beer to a table. A guy from India named Anil Sircar bought the place after that, but kept the establishment's Irish name. The TV tuned to a baseball game, the clicking of billiard balls in the adjacent room, the cloud of cigarette smoke hovering overhead, and the sounds of Johnny Cash on the jukebox, felt like home. Anil slapped a cocktail napkin on the bar in front of me.

"The usual," I said.

He brought a double Old Fitz on the rocks, and for a minute I thought he was going to say something to me. He didn't. I lit a cigarette and sipped my drink.

Anil's son flipped hamburger patties on the grill, a steamy broadcast of sizzling meat and onions saturating the air.

"Philip," Anil said, "cheese two of those burgers."

Philip obeyed. I think it was the first time I'd ever heard the word cheese used as a verb.

"Hey, Colt. Why can't you just drink Jack Daniel's like the rest of the rednecks in town?"

I looked in the mirror behind the bar, saw Roy Massengill standing behind me wearing black shorts and a faded football jersey. I'd known Massengill for a long time. He once drove an equipment bus for Colt .45. After the crash, he joined the Navy and eventually became a SEAL. Now he worked as a sniper for the Sheriff's Department's SWAT team. He was damn good at what he did. He had burn scars on his neck from a helicopter accident in the first gulf war, the one they called Desert Storm.

I swiveled my stool around, stood up, and shook his hand. "You know as well as I do the only good whiskey comes from Kentucky," I said.

"And Scotland," Massengill said in a convincing brogue.

"Okay. I'll give you Scotland. Too bad the poor sons of bitches have to beg barrels from the bourbon distilleries, though."

Massengill laughed. "Too bad the Kentucky hillbillies are stupid enough to give them away." He sat on the stool next to mine, made a motion to Anil. "Chivas for me, and another cup of swill for my friend here."

Anil brought the drinks, and Massengill threw a twenty on the bar.

"Been working out at Gold's?" I said.

"Going later."

"Thanks for the drink," I drained my first one, shoved the glass aside to make room for the second. "I heard about that hostage situation in Orange Park the other night. Were you in on that?"

"They called me in at one o'clock in the goddamn morning. It was pure bullshit. Some stupid fucker caught his old lady screwing around, figured he'd take her out in style. He slit her throat and then blew his own brains out while Crotchet was on the phone trying to negotiate. I was never able to get a bead on the guy."

"I never understand that shit," I said. "Guy should have killed himself and left the chick alone."

Massengill looked up, glided two fingers down his scarred neck. "So tell me what happened this morning. I've heard the news accounts and the rumors, but I'd like to hear it from you."

"What rumors?"

Without asking, Massengill reached over and took one of my

Marlboros and used my Zippo to light it. "That's good, Nicholas. Answer a question with a question. I'm not at liberty to say what rumors."

Two stiff drinks and two hours of drunken sleep last night surged through my veins like broken glass. I stood, grabbed Massengill's shoulders, got fierce in his face. "Tell me," I shouted.

Massengill did some quick maneuvering, and before I knew it my left cheek was smashed against a soggy napkin on the bar. My right arm was twisted behind my back, my thumb bent at a painful angle toward my wrist.

Massengill whispered in my ear. "Don't fuck with me, Colt. I told you I'm not at liberty to say."

"Let me up," I said.

Massengill loosened his grip. I sat down and wiped my face with a bar towel.

The right sleeve on his jersey had gotten torn in the scuffle, and I got my first glimpse of the finest tattoo I'd ever seen. It was an angel, wings spread, drawn with such detail it looked as though a photograph had been burned onto Massengill's arm.

"Come over to the gym some day," Massengill said. "I'll show you how to break that hold."

I turned up my glass, felt the whiskey burn a trail to my gut. "I know how to break it. Thirty-eight slug to the face. Just didn't feel like killing you right now, that's all. Anil gets pissed when he has to wipe up blood and chunks of skull."

He nodded. "Heard about you dumping old Fleming in the hot tub this afternoon. You know that was a mistake, right?"

"Felt like the thing to do at the time. He was talking about my client like cold meat on a table. She was a human being, you know? Beautiful girl."

"You know how it is with cops," Massengill said. "You have to detach yourself from the vic. Sometimes you even have to joke about it. Take it home with you, and it'll eat you alive. You know you're on Fleming's shit list, right?"

Big revelation there.

CHAPTER THIRTEEN

The next morning I left the motel at nine thirty. Someone had salted my tongue and set it out to dry in the sun. Beef jerky tongue. I had a nasty-tasting film in my mouth, like when you spray for bugs and accidentally inhale some of the poison. My brains were a little on the scrambled side.

After Roy Massengill had asserted his superiority in hand-to-hand combat, he bought me another drink. And another. We talked about old times till wee hours, and I ended up staggering six blocks back to The Parkside.

Now I was standing outside the Clay County Public Library, Hallows Cove Branch, waiting for ten o'clock when someone would open the door.

I had work to do.

Ms. Marcia Gardner, one of the assistant librarians, finally unlatched the deadbolt and let me in. I hit the water fountain first, then walked to the reference room and sat down at one of the on-line computer terminals.

I wanted to find out who had been driving that old Chevy, The Whale. I logged on to one of the background check services I subscribe to and ran the tags. W-H-A-L-E. To my surprise, I got over one hundred hits. WHALE-1 through WHALE-99, and some things like MYWHALE and SVWHALE. No plain WHALES in Florida. There must have been other letters or numbers I hadn't noticed in my adrenaline-buzzed rush. The cops were probably having the same problem tracking the old car.

It took me two hours to go through the entire list, and none of the cars registered was a '63 or '64 Impala station wagon. How could that be? I knew I hadn't hallucinated the whole thing. Maybe Barry Fleming and company were thinking I had fabricated the WHALE story. Maybe that was the rumor Roy Massengill had been talking about.

My hangover was getting a little better, and suddenly a light-bulb switched on over my head.

I typed in W-H-I-L-E, remembering the mud splatter and my bleary eyes and the fog. No luck.

I entered W-H-O-L-E and, bingo, there it was.

The car was registered to a company called Rent-A-Gem, located in the Mandarin area of Jacksonville. I jotted down the address, exited the program, and hurried toward the door.

Marcia Gardner reminded me I had some books overdue.

On my way to Mandarin, I saw a sign advertising free cell phones so I swung in and within twenty minutes had a fully activated phone and a one-year service contract. The phone itself was a fancy flip-top gadget that also took digital photographs. I played with it for a few minutes and then drove to a nearby strip mall and parked in front of Shaky Jake's Gun and Pawn.

I walked inside, browsed the glass counter and found a good weapon at a good price. A Dwight Yokum song blared from one of the old stereos for sale.

The sales clerk probably weighed in at three fifty. Fat oozed over his belt like too much jelly on a sandwich.

"My name's Fred. Can I help you with something?"

"I'd like to see that revolver, please. Would you mind turning the music down?"

Fred pushed his black-framed glasses up to the bridge of his nose. The lenses made his eyes look like bowling balls. His front teeth were about the same size and shade as Scrabble tiles.

He switched off the stereo, produced an oil-stained rag from under the counter, used the rag to pick up the gun. He cupped it in his chubby hand like it was the Hope Diamond and handed it over to me.

"The Smith and Wesson Model Ten, thirty-eight caliber military and police DA. A fine and dependable weapon. Been in production since nineteen-oh-two. Also called the Hand Ejector Model of—"

"I know what it is," I said. "Thanks. Can you tell me what year this one was made?"

Fred frowned.

I examined the gun while Fred researched the serial number on the computer.

"That particular gun was manufactured in nineteen eighty-five," he said. "We got a boxed lot at a police auction last year. That gun's history is well documented."

That's what I wanted to hear. I didn't want to buy a piece that could be traced to a liquor store hold-up or something.

"I'll take it," I said. "Can you print out that history for me?"

"Certainly, sir."

Fred gave me a long form to fill out and wrote down the numbers from my IDs. I guessed Fred had eaten salami for lunch. Or maybe he smelled that way all the time.

"We'll run all your info and, you know, if everything clears you can pick the gun up early next week."

"I was hoping to take it today."

"Not possible. You ever bought a gun in Florida before?"

"Yeah. As a matter of fact I've bought a couple from this store. Is Jake around?"

Fred waddled to the back room and came back, followed by Shaky Jake. Side by side they reminded me of Laurel and Hardy.

"Nicholas." The hot smell of bourbon whooshed out when he said my name. "Good to see you. I heard about what happened on the news."

"Yeah. They confiscated all my guns, and I feel sort of naked going out without one. All my current paperwork is right here on the counter. PI license, concealed weapon permit, everything."

"Of course," Jake said. "Freddie here was just doing his job."

"I understand."

Jake gave Fred instructions on how to document the purchase, and five minutes later I was out the door. Jake let me take the revolver for a hundred twenty-five, and he threw in a belt holster and a box of .38 shells to boot. I loaded the gun, dropped a few extra shells into my pocket, and slid the holster onto my belt.

CHAPTER FOURTEEN

Dozens of vintage automobiles crowded Rent-A-Gem's gravel lot. Gremlins, Vegas, Pintos, Fieros, LeCars. They should have named the place Rent-A-Lemon. They even had a Yugo, a red one with a dented fender.

I parked, got out, and took a stroll.

In the corner, backed up against a six-foot chain-link fence topped with razor ribbon, were four identical Chevy Impala station wagons. I walked around and checked the plates: LTCREAM, SKIM, 2PRCENT, WHOLE.

I looked up and saw a black man coming my way, wearing what looked to be a very expensive tailored suit. Armani or a knockoff. He spoke in a deep baritone.

"You like the Chevy wagons?"

"Tell me about 'em. They for sale?"

Somehow the big man's voice got even deeper and more resonant than before. "Everything's for sale," he said, "at the right price. I picked these up at an estate auction down in Green Cove Springs. You remember Berryman's Dairy?"

"Sure."

"Well, a couple years ago John Berryman died, just dropped dead of a heart attack one day. He'd run that dairy since the fifties, and when he died, it died with him. His widow and children couldn't wait to get rid of the whole shebang. I think someone's raising thoroughbreds on the property now." He pulled out a handkerchief, wiped the sweat from his forehead, and then continued talking. "Anyway, he had this fleet of sixty-three Chevrolet Impala station wagons that I knew were going on the block, and I knew something none of the other bidders knew."

"Yeah?"

"Yeah. These cars were used mostly as advertisements for the dairy." He pointed to the logo on one of the driver's side doors. "They were hardly ever driven. Old man Berryman would park them at the edge of his farm, where they could be seen by the traffic on State Road Seventeen. These cars have very low actual mileage. And I was able to keep the original plates. Check it out."

He guided me to view the license tags I'd already seen.

"Mind if I look at this one?" I said.

"Go right ahead. Keys are in the ignition. I'll be up at the office if you want to deal. Name's Marcus Sharp."

I handed him a business card. "Nicholas Colt."

Sharp walked toward the single-wide trailer that served as an office. I took a few minutes to look the car over, the one with tags that read WHOLE.

I got on my hands and knees and checked underneath. The chassis was well greased, no signs of major corrosion. I rose and inspected the body, found some surface rust along the fender lines. Nothing a good sanding and some primer wouldn't fix.

I opened the driver's side door and climbed in. The interior had a baked and dusty smell, understandable for a car that had lived in the Florida sun for forty years. It had been thoroughly wiped down and vacuumed, so I doubted any fingerprints or other evidence remained. The odometer read 24,827. The gas, brake, and clutch pedals didn't show much wear, so I believed that was the actual mileage.

I put the car in neutral and started it. The gearshift was on the steering column, what they used to call a "three on the tree." The engine sounded strong. I shut it off, got out, and popped the hood. The fluid levels looked all right, oil on the dipstick honey gold. I wanted to find out who had rented the car last night.

I walked to the trailer, opened the door, and stepped into Marcus Sharp's office.

Sharp sat behind a large oak desk, flanked by two guys who were both pointing guns at me.

"Hands behind your head," Sharp said.

Both gunmen were white. The guy on my left held a Sphinx 9-mm. He wasn't as big as Marcus Sharp, but big enough. He looked like the kind of guy that might flip hot hamburger patties with his bare hands.

The other guy was short and fat and bald, but he had an Uzi.

"What's this all about?" I said.

"This is all about you, Nicholas Colt," Sharp said. He rose, walked around the short guy with the Uzi, took a couple of steps toward me. He patted me down, found the .38 on my hip.

"This'll come in handy," he said.

"You didn't answer my question," I said. "Why me?"

Sharp hit me squarely on the jaw with a left hook. My knees buckled. Multicolored dots danced in front of my eyes.

I saw the bottom of Marcus Sharp's shoe as an extreme close-up and, boom boom, out went the lights.

CHAPTER FIFTEEN

I was five years old. I wore a cowboy hat on my head and a six-shooter on my hip. I wandered the interior of a Learjet and saw myself grown and drinking a glass of Champagne and talking to a drummer named Bill Wilder. I saw my wife Susan nursing our baby daughter, Harmony. Sam the bass player and some other guys were playing cards. Through a curtain separating the cabin and the cockpit I heard a deep voice: *Negative. Requesting clearance to land now.*

A monster emerged from behind the curtain. I drew my six-shooter and squeezed off three rounds, but the monster kept coming.

I woke in a cold sweat. My hands and feet were tied, and a rag or something had been stuffed into my mouth and sealed with tape. The rag tasted terrible, like Armor All or something. The purple light of dusk filtered through a shaded window, and for a moment I wondered if I was awake or still dreaming. My head felt like a basketball inflated with too much air. It throbbed with every pulse.

I heard voices in another room. The plan was to make it look like suicide. That's why they hadn't killed me already.

I overheard some other things, making it clear why all this was happening.

Tony, how many times I got to tell you, if the fucking VIN numbers don't match, we don't ship the fucking car. I got a buyer in France about to have a goddamn heart attack, and whose ass you think gonna to get burnt if he can't fix that shit...

It seemed Marcus Sharp and crew were car thieves, and the rental business was just a front.

I tried to wriggle free, but it was useless. They had me wrapped good and tight.

After a while, when the window went completely black, Sharp's thugs came in and carried me outside and folded me into the trunk of a Cadillac.

I wasn't ready to die. I had too much work to do, too many wrongs to try and make right.

Now it was over for me.

The trunk was hot, the air greasy. I was probably near dehydration. They really didn't need to shoot me. They could just park the car somewhere and I'd be dead soon enough. But they wanted it to look like a suicide. I wondered if there would be a note.

The car turned onto a bumpy road and soon came to a stop.

The trunk opened, and I sucked a deep breath of late summer air. A mosquito bit me on the neck.

I saw Marcus Sharp's huge hand coming toward my face. He gently pulled the tape from my mouth and yanked out the rag.

Sharp and his two cronies lifted me out of the trunk. They were handling me carefully, so there wouldn't be any bruises. Maybe they didn't know that residue from the duct tape would be found during an autopsy. My death wouldn't be classified as a suicide, but that fact gave me little consolation at the moment.

Sharp laughed. "You look pretty good, 'cept for that knot on your forehead where I kicked you. That's okay, that'll be a good spot to put the bullet."

I didn't want to die, but I wasn't about to give these punks the satisfaction of seeing me show any fear. I wasn't going to beg these scumbags for my life.

"Fuck you," I said.

Sharp and the boys chuckled.

My Jimmy was parked next to the Cadillac. They carried me and stuffed me into the driver's seat. Sharp had on leather gloves, and he held the little .38 I had bought at the pawn shop earlier. He wrapped my fingers around the grip, making sure my prints were all over it and that some gunshot residue would end up on my hand.

He pressed the barrel against the sore spot on my forehead. There was no hope for me, but I wasn't about to go down without a fight. I ducked and swiveled and managed a kick to the groin with both feet. The .38 discharged, the bullet taking a small chunk of my right bicep on its way out the passenger-side door. The tall punk with the Sphinx had been standing there, and I saw him frantically trying to stop the blood squirting from his leg. Mr. Sphinx's face turned the color of raw biscuit dough and he fell to the ground, shouting for help from Jesus.

I heard a distant report, and saw the left side of Marcus Sharp's skull peel away in slow motion. His ruined head fell in my lap. The short chubby guy with the Uzi ran to the Cadillac and sped off.

I saw a silhouette coming toward me, heard the sound of boots crunching on the gravel lot. When he got close enough I recognized the scars on Roy Massengill's neck. Massengill had a rifle with a night-vision scope. He looked puzzled. His eyes darted back and forth from me to Mr. Sphinx, as though he were trying to figure out exactly what had happened. He turned and watched the Cadillac's taillights fade into the distance.

My crotch was wet and warm. I wasn't sure if it was from Sharp's blood, or if I'd pissed myself. "Goddamn! Get this fucker's head off my lap."

Massengill dragged Sharp's body off of me and then untied my hands and legs. A million fire ants marched through my nervous system. I looked for a cigarette in the glove compartment but couldn't find one and had to settle for a toothpick.

Massengill led me to the tennis courts across the street where his truck was parked. He wrapped a pressure dressing on my gunshot wound. He radioed dispatch and gave them a description of the Cadillac and its driver, and he requested an ambulance for Marcus Sharp and Mr. Sphinx. Not that it would do them any good. They were both dead as conch fritters.

"I take it you've been following me," I said.

"Aren't you glad?"

"What can I say? Thanks for saving my life. Cut it kind of close there, though, didn't you? I mean, the guy was this close to blow-ing my brains out."

"Had to wait for a clear shot. You want to go to the hospital?"

"I'll be all right. I have some Percocets at home. Fleming's idea for you to follow me?"

"Yeah. Like I said, you're on his shit list."

"I know who shot at my camper Friday morning. Guy who bled to death by my Jimmy over there."

"Motive?"

"Marcus Sharp, the big black guy whose head you blew to smithereens, said someone hired them to shoot my place up. Who-ever hired them must have been waiting around. When I chased the shooters, they came in and got Brittney."

"Why was Marcus Sharp going to kill you just now?"

"He knew I was investigating the Chevy station wagon, and he figured I'd eventually find out that Rent-A-Gem was a front for a car theft ring."

"No shit? A car theft ring?"

"Yep."

"We need to talk to Roly-Poly who took off in the Caddy," Roy said.

"Yep."

"No," Roy said. "I meant *we* as in we the cops. You're gonna have to leave this one alone, my friend."

"If it was you, would you leave it alone?"

"Beside the point. You know your Jimmy's going to be im-pounded as evidence, right?"

"Shit."

Fifteen minutes later, three cruisers and two meat wagons showed up, along with Barry Fleming's unmarked Lumina. I stayed in the truck while Massengill walked across the street and took care of business.

Now I was homeless and carless. No girlfriend. No gun. I reached into my pockets. No cell phone, no money. Luckily, I had stashed two hundred dollars back at The Parkside.

When Massengill got back to the truck, I asked him for a ride to the motel.

"You have to talk with Fleming first," he said. "You can do it here, or we can meet him in Green Cove. Your choice. I'm going to be up all night anyway, filing reports and getting grilled by Internal Affairs."

"I'll talk to him here," I said.

I got out and walked back to the scene. I told Fleming everything I knew, and he reminded me that I was a witness and subject to subpoena. He tried to make me go to the hospital, but I refused.

Massengill and I headed north on SR 21. He questioned me for his report to Fleming, and then we didn't say anything for a while.

I finally spoke up. "You all right?"

"You ever kill anyone, Nicholas?" His voice was steady and his eyes stared straight ahead, but I figured he felt it somewhere deep. I figured Massengill would need a few drinks before the night was over.

"I've carried a weapon every day since I got my PI license," I said. "Never had to use it. Lucky, I guess."

"Think you could do it if you had to?"

"If it was me or him, sure. I don't think I'd have a problem with it."

"That's the thing. I'm a sniper. It's never a matter of me or him. My life is never the one in immediate danger. I'm far away, looking through a scope, and it's almost like I become the hand of God. I get to decide if this person lives or dies."

"Marcus Sharp was a bad man," I said. "My brain would be all over the Jimmy's header right now if you hadn't taken him out. You did what you had to do."

"Yeah. But it's never easy. The after part is never easy. You think you could kill somebody like I killed Sharp? You know, with no immediate threat to yourself?"

"I don't know."

"You know what a kill switch is?"

"Sure," I said. "Like on a train or a speed boat. It shuts everything down in case of emergency."

"That's what I have to do when I have someone in my sights. I have to hit the kill switch on my own humanity. Shut everything down. No feeling, no emotion. I become a machine. A life-taking fucking machine. There's no way to explain that moment unless you've been there."

We were quiet for a while. I thought about how much Massengill had changed since the days he drove an equipment bus for my band. He'd been as much of a wildass as the rest of us back then, smoking weed and snorting powder and bedding a different groupie every night. Things had changed for me when I married Susan, and I noticed a change in Massengill during that time as well. Maybe we just grew up.

A trooper car with its lights flashing raced by in the opposite direction.

"Tell me something," I said, "when you saw us leaving Rent-A-Gem, why didn't you call for backup?"

"All I saw was your Jimmy and a Cadillac leaving the lot. I didn't know you were in the Caddy's trunk."

"So you thought I was doing business with those scumbags?"

"What can I say? You went inside, and you were in there for a long time, and then I saw your Jimmy leaving the lot with the Cadillac. I was just doing my job. Count your blessings."

Over the radio we heard that a Sheriff's deputy, unit twenty-seven, was in pursuit of the fugitive Cadillac. A call went out to all units in the area. Massengill put the light on the roof and floored the gas pedal.

We saw the Caddy in Winn-Dixie's parking lot, surrounded by three cruisers with lights flashing. The short, fat guy had his hands against his car and was being frisked. An ambulance and a fire truck had shown up, and a crowd of onlookers with grocery carts formed a semicircle near the front of the store.

We got out and walked toward the scene, Massengill with his badge raised high. He talked to one of the deputies. The short, fat guy's name was Tony Beeler. Massengill climbed into the back of the cruiser, sat beside Beeler, and closed the door. I couldn't hear what they were saying. I stood there holding my sore arm. I was learning what it felt like to be a victim of a violent crime. Nobody was paying any attention to me.

A few minutes later, another deputy knocked on the window and motioned for Massengill to come out. Together they walked to the ambulance where a cluster of officers stood talking. I quietly opened the door and slid in beside the suspect.

"Who hired you guys to shoot at my camper?"

"Fuck you," Beeler said.

"I'm trying to be civil here. I'm going to ask you nicely one more time. Who hired you guys to shoot at my place?"

"Allow me to rephrase," Beeler said. "*Fuck you.*"

I unwrapped the bloody bandage on my arm and tried to stuff it into Beeler's mouth. He clenched his teeth, so I reached down and squeezed his balls until he didn't resist anymore. I broke the toothpick I'd been chewing on, peeled off a splinter and jammed it under his left thumbnail. The bandage muted his scream.

"You talk, I pull it out. Your call."

Beeler's eyes rolled back in his head, and he nodded frantically. I pulled the bandage out of his mouth.

"You motherfucker," Beeler said. "I have rights. I'm going to sue your goddamn—"

The gauze went back in the mouth. I shoved a splinter under the fingernail of his pinky this time. Beeler's ears turned red and then purple. He started nodding again. I pulled the gauze.

"Listen," I said. "I'm not a cop, so don't try any of that 'my rights are being violated' shit with me. I don't give a rat's ass about any of my lousy personal possessions, so go ahead and sue me if you want to. I'm going to ask you nicely once again. Who hired you guys?"

He spat in my face. "You should have died a long time ago, bitch. You should have died with the rest of those motherfuckers on that airplane."

"What the fuck you talking about?"

His eyes bulged and his lips snarled and he whispered hoarsely. "Pocket forty-seven."

I grabbed him by the throat. "What the fuck are you talking about, you slimeball piece of shit?"

Massengill yanked the door open. He and two uniformed officers pulled me away from Beeler.

Massengill got in my face. "You trying to fuck up my collar, or what?"

He was furious, but so was I.

I was about to punch someone and probably get arrested myself when Fleming screeched up in his Lumina. He got out and walked straight to where we were standing.

"Massengill, what are you doing here?"

"Responding to a call for all units, sir."

"What did I tell you back at the scene in Keystone? You're on administrative leave pending an Internal Affairs investigation into the shooting. Now get the fuck out of here before I write your ass up."

"It was a clean shoot, Barry."

"Just finish your report, and then you're done till I.A.'s done. *Comprende?*"

Massengill nodded and walked away. Fleming never even looked at me.

We walked back to Massengill's truck and drove toward The Parkside motel.

"Have you lost your fucking mind, Colt? What were you thinking, climbing into that car with that guy?"

"You ever heard of pocket forty-seven?" I said.

Massengill missed third gear. "Where did you hear that?"

"Beeler. He said I should have died in the plane crash. Then he said something about pocket forty-seven."

"It's nothing. It's a myth."

"What myth? My wife and baby daughter died in that crash. My band died. The pilot and copilot died. Is any of that a myth? I was the sole survivor. That's not a goddamn myth. It's fucking reality. Tell me what pocket forty-seven means."

"Jesus, Colt. Take a Valium. It's nothing. It's a term flyboys use for an unexplained glitch. A mechanical or electrical gremlin. It's like an invisible hand comes along and fucks everything up."

"I don't get it."

"It's slang. It's a myth. It originated in World War Two, I think. Supposedly, the flight suits they issued back then had forty-six pockets. The pilots carried all kinds of shit around with them, but all they really wanted was a little luck. Some of them started sewing an extra pocket into their suits. Pocket forty-seven. It was a place to stow a talisman or a picture of a girl or whatever. Some good luck for the mission. If a guy got shot down, everyone would say he didn't pack pocket forty-seven. Over the years it evolved to mean, like I said, an invisible hand that comes along and fucks things up."

"So how does Beeler know anything about anything?" I said.

"I don't know."

He dropped me at the motel, and I borrowed another roll of gauze for my shot-up arm.

After Massengill drove away, I went to the lobby and logged onto the Internet. I Googled pocket forty-seven. The Wikipedia article echoed what Massengill had told me, along with one startling addition: pocket forty-seven had become common among certain street gangs, used as a verb meaning "to take by surprise in an ambush, or to sabotage." As in: *We fixin' ta pocket forty-seven dey ass.*

Sabotage.

I didn't know what Beeler meant by what he said, and I didn't know how or why anyone could have intentionally caused my band's plane to crash. I clicked off the Internet and walked upstairs, thinking hard about how to find the answers to those questions.

The red light on my room phone was blinking. I called the desk, got the message that my Airstream had been cleared by the FBI. I was free to go home.

I called Joe.

"Think you could give me a ride home?" I said.

I gathered the few things I had in the motel room and put them in a plastic bag.

When we got to the fish camp, around midnight, Joe told me I could borrow his pickup truck until I got my car back.

"Got a gun I can borrow?"

"Never satisfied, are you. What do you want, a pistol?"

"What you got?"

"I have that Remington twelve-gauge."

"Give me that and a pistol."

"Isn't greed one of the seven deadly sins?"

Joe drove the '76 F100 around. The truck, once red, was now a faded and dusty rose color. It was scarred and dented from years of use, and the edges of the rear fenders had rusted through. The windows were tinted black. Joe handed me the key.

"Please, double oh seven, try to give it back in the same condition as you received it."

"Thanks, Q. I'll try."

The feds didn't trash my house too bad. They even left my jug of Old Fitzgerald alone. I poured a drink, found a roll of duct tape, and fixed the broken windows with plastic trash bags. I was lucky it hadn't rained in the past few days.

My head ached and my arm was sore, and I probably shouldn't have been drinking. I felt as though I'd just stepped off a Tilt-A-Whirl. I was shaken, rattled, and rolled, and happy as hell Massengill had come along and saved my ass.

I woke up the next morning in severe pain, my arm red and hot around the bullet wound. I took two Percocets, put some ice on it. An hour later when it hadn't gotten any better I drove myself to the emergency room at Hallows Cove Memorial.

The triage nurse looked at my arm and then put me on the back burner behind some more serious cases. I waited two hours before they called me back to one of the curtained rooms, then another hour before the doctor came in to see me.

The doctor was young, late twenties or early thirties. He had shoulder-length black hair tied in a ponytail, a piercing in each ear and a nice fisherman's—or maybe surfer's—tan. His nametag said J. A. Billingsly, MD, DEPARTMENT OF INTERNAL MEDICINE. He held a metal clipboard with my vitals and medical history and personal information one of the nursing assistants had taken.

"Hi, Mister Colt. I'm Doctor Billingsly." He spoke with a heavy southern accent, from one of the Carolinas I guessed. "Are you allergic to any medications?"

"They already asked me that."

"Just want to make sure."

"None that I know of."

"Okay. Let's have a look at that arm. It's a gunshot wound?"

"Right."

The doctor unwrapped the bandage the triage nurse had put on. "Was it an accident?"

"You could say that."

"The reason I asked, we have to report any criminal activity to the police."

"It's already been reported."

Dr. Billingsly looked at the wound, touched the edges with a gloved hand, frowned. "I'm going to order some blood work, just a CBC and a chemistry, and then admit you so we can give you some IV antibiotics for a few days."

"A few days? Can't do it, doc. I have too much work to do."

"If the infection spreads, you could lose the arm. Or, you could die."

"I can't stay in the hospital."

He reached into the pocket of his lab coat, pulled out a pad, and wrote two prescriptions. He handed them to me. "Levaquin for the infection, Dilaudid for pain. If it doesn't clear up in a few days, you need to get back here right away."

"I understand."

"I'll send in a tech to draw your blood. You can go home after that."

Dr. Billingsly snapped the curtain open and walked away.

Joe's truck was low on fuel and I hadn't checked my mail in a few days so I stopped at the Amoco near the post office and killed two birds. Along with some credit card offers and a couple of bills was, lo and behold, a two-thousand-dollar check from Dana Glass Attorney at Law. Check was in the mail after all. I guess it's not a lie every time. Now I felt bad for hanging up on Dana's receptionist. I felt bad all the way to the bank, where I deposited the check in my anemic account.

There was a Walgreens across the street from the bank, so I went in and filled my prescriptions. I browsed the Foster Grant rack while I waited. A little girl, three or four, came bouncing up to the rack. It took her about five seconds to say, "I want these when I get bigger, Mommy, and I want these when I get bigger." She pranced on, her curly brown hair bouncing in sync with her stride. Her mother stood a few feet away, trying to read the small print on a bottle of medicine. I got a little teary thinking about my baby Harmony, all the years and milestones and joyous occasions that had been robbed from her. From us.

It also occurred to me that I didn't know much about Leitha and Brittney's history. How had they lost their parents? What had life been like for them growing up? Did they have any family besides each other, anyone to take care of Leitha's funeral arrangements? I wondered if Brittney was still alive and if she knew about Leitha's murder.

I found a pair of black wraparounds and paid for them and a bottle of Zephyrhills and my medicine at the pharmacy's register. On my way out I saw the little girl standing near a cluster of gumball machines, crying because she hadn't gotten the flavor she wanted. I asked her mom if it was okay, and then gave the girl all the change in my pocket. She smiled and said thank you.

I took one of the painkillers and one of the antibiotic tablets. My arm felt like a snapping turtle had latched on and refused to let go. Joe's old Ford had a manual transmission, and every time I shifted gears the turtle bit down a little harder.

If Brittney was still in town, and still alive, I figured she was being held against her will. Leitha's murder was all over the news and, if Brittney was able, I knew she'd come forward. I thought the car theft ring probably had something to do with the recent horrors, and the only person I could think of who might have connections to those characters was Duck the pimp. Was he pissed off enough about me taking Brittney to kill Leitha and kidnap Brittney back? That's what I needed to find out.

I drove north on Blanding Boulevard, traffic heavy but moving at a steady pace. The brakes on Joe's pickup were a hair short of tip-top. I thought about how fragile the human spinal cord is for a minute and then pulled into the T-Mobile store where I'd gotten the phone yesterday. The pain in my arm had eased up some, but my legs felt like I was wading in knee-deep water. I stepped to the counter and told the lady my predicament. She gave me a new phone for eighty plus tax.

I called my home phone to see if I had any messages. There were five: three from Juliet telling me she'd heard about Leitha and how sorry she was about everything and could we please try to work it out; one from Dr. Michael Spivey, asking me to call him as soon as possible; one from an old friend, a retired police officer I call Papa. All Papa's message said was, "Let's go fishing." He uses a bamboo fly rod he made himself and at seventy-three can still cast into an area the size of a hubcap.

I called Dr. Spivey first. A woman answered.

"Mrs. Spivey?" I said.

"May I ask who is calling?" She had an eastern European accent, Russian or maybe Romanian.

I told her my name and reason for calling.

"Doctor Spivey is not available at the moment. May I take a message?"

"Can I talk to Mrs. Spivey?" I said.

"Hold please."

I listened to nothingness for a few seconds. Mrs. Spivey picked up.

"Is this Nicholas Colt?" she said.

"Yes. Your husband left a message for me to call."

"It's about Brittney, of course." From the sound of her voice, I could only imagine the assortment of chemicals coursing through her veins. Xanax, Prozac, possibly a martini or two. "Michael's making rounds at the nursing home right now. I'll give you his pager number."

She told me the number. Her voice was like the Mojave Desert at midnight. Flat and dry, cold and hopelessly distant and dark. I thanked her, hung up, and paged Dr. Spivey. Five minutes later, he called.

"Mister Colt, would it be possible for us to meet somewhere? We're very upset about everything that's happened, of course. Poor Leitha. My God. She told me that she'd hired you to find Brittney."

"That's right."

"I know the police and FBI are involved now, but would you be willing to stay on the case as well? My wife and I love Brittney dearly. Now that Leitha's gone, well, we want to adopt her. Are you available? Leitha said good things about you. I'll pay you, of course."

"When did you want to meet?" I said. I had personal reasons for wanting to find Brittney, but I wasn't above taking a paycheck for my efforts. Especially from someone who could afford a Russian maid.

"Could you come to my house this evening? I'll be home around six. You can have dinner with us and—"

"Can't make it tonight. How about tomorrow?" If Papa wanted to go fishing then, by God, that's what we would do. As determined as I was to find Brittney Ryan, family always came first. Papa and Joe Crawford were all I had.

"Tomorrow's fine. Around eleven in the morning if you could make it."

"I'll be there," I said. He gave me directions.

CHAPTER SIXTEEN

I drove to Green Cove Springs. Papa and I have the kind of relationship where you don't have to call, you just come. He was sitting on the porch reading *The Adventures of Huckleberry Finn.* I've known Papa for twenty years, and he always has his ragged old copy of that book nearby. Like it's his bible or something. He swears it's the only piece of fiction that ever mattered. He looked up and smiled.

"Nicholas. Have a seat, young man."

"Thanks, Papa. Not feeling too young these days."

"It's all relative," he said. "When you're my age, you'll wish you were forty-five again. Enjoy it while you can. You thirsty? You want a beer?"

"I'll get it. You ready for another one?" A sweaty can of Pabst was on the table beside his chair, along with a jar of Planters. Huck Finn was Papa's scripture, Pabst Blue Ribbon and greasy peanuts his communion. He drained the can, crushed it and threw it behind him, answering my question.

I walked inside to the kitchen, opened the refrigerator, and got the beers. He had at least a case lined up on the bottom shelf. I went back out on the porch.

"What happened to your arm?" An edge of white gauze extended beyond my shirt sleeve.

"Gunshot wound," I said.

"You been doing some real work?"

"Don't you ever watch the news?"

Papa opened his beer and took a long pull. "You know I don't watch that shit. Too fucking depressing. I already know something terrible happened somewhere today. Why do I need some punk wearing makeup to tell me the details. Same shit, different day. I could plug in a tape from twenty years ago and it would be the same damn—"

"Don't you care about what's going on in the world?" I said.

"Fuck the world. I know there's a war somewhere. I know someone got raped, robbed, stabbed, kidnapped, or murdered. If it didn't happen on this here porch, I ain't going to dwell on it. It's too loud, and I'm too old. Know what I mean?"

"Sure. Anyway, you want to hear about the case I been working on?"

"I was a beat cop most of my life. A grunt. Strong back, weak mind. I damn near—"

"Don't give me that 'strong back, weak mind' shit," I said. "You could have gone as far as you wanted to in the department."

"Maybe. Just never wanted to play their fucking games. Once I made sergeant, knew I'd get a good pension, that was enough for me. I'm glad I'm out of it."

"Is that why you stayed on ten years past your retirement date? Face it, Papa. You loved being on the job."

He laughed. "You know me too well, Nicholas. Can't hustle a hustler, I guess. So tell me how you got your arm all shot up."

I yawned. My arm hurt, but I knew I'd probably fall asleep right there on the porch if I took another pain pill. "You still want to go fishing?" I said.

"Maybe when the sun goes down. Or maybe we could just sit here on our asses and drink beer all night. You going to tell me about the arm, or you want to play twenty questions or what?"

I told Papa everything that had happened.

"Something sure as hell pissed someone off," Papa said, "for Leitha to be tortured and murdered like that. You don't see that kind of shit every day."

"Thank God."

"And you think that Duck character was involved? You think he was mixed up with the car theft ring?"

"Maybe. He's definitely a criminal, and I imagine payback was on his mind the minute I left his apartment."

"Meaning you think he got Brittney back."

"That's what I'm thinking. If he does have her, he's going to be expecting me this time."

"You'll have to tail him," Papa said. "Wait for the right time. If you go in like Rambo again, you're going to get your ass waxed."

"Precisely," I said.

Papa grinned. He looked at me with narrowed eyes. "I know you better than to tell you to just let the cops handle it. Here's the deal. You're going to need someone inside, someone close to this Duck character, a confidential informant, a snitch."

"Maybe I could pay one of his whores to rat him out."

"That might work. I never had much luck with whores, though. Especially the street bitches. They go one way, then the other. What about that club he works at? What did you say, The Tumble Inn?"

"Yeah, aka The Stumble Out. Think I should try that?"

"Be your best bet."

"Bartender?"

"Best snitches in the world."

"Thing is, they've seen me at the club."

"They haven't seen me," Papa said.

CHAPTER SEVENTEEN

Papa and I drank all the beer in the refrigerator. I overslept and didn't make it to the Spiveys' house in Ponte Vedre until about one fifteen Sunday afternoon. I'd called and left a message on voice mail, hoping my tardiness wouldn't be an issue. The house was stucco, painted khaki with a red tile roof. From the looks of the exterior, I figured the closets were as big as my Airstream. The driveway circled around a fountain, with half a dozen high-end automobiles parked at various angles. I eased Joe's old Ford in between a Jaguar and a Porsche. I put the pistol Joe had loaned me in the glove compartment, which was empty except for an old green metal flashlight and a dozen or so vintage moist towelettes from KFC. Joe's shotgun was behind the seat, along with a small box of tools and my replica Balabushka pool cue. It was an odd assortment of items to carry around in the cab of a pickup truck, but you never know when you might need to make a quick repair, play a game of nine-ball, blast someone to kingdom come, and wipe yourself off in the dark.

The expatriate maid I'd talked to yesterday led me through the house to the back patio. She wore a white cook's uniform and walked along with purpose, her plump fanny seeming to propel the rest of her. She pointed toward Dr. Spivey and then deserted me.

There was a party going on, which explained all the cars in the driveway. Spivey held a tall frosted glass with a celery stalk growing out of it. He wore white shorts, a sky-blue polo shirt, and New Balance court shoes. He was talking to a short guy with curly hair and glasses. I walked over and stood there stupidly for a minute until they shut up long enough for me to introduce myself.

"Sorry I'm late."

"Not a problem," Spivey said. "Excuse us for a minute, John."

John excused us with a polite smile and nod, and then walked toward the food. It was a big spread: corn on the cob, baked beans, several types of salads, fresh fruit, pies. A guy wearing a chef's hat and an apron stood beside two half-barrels topped with grating, stoking the coals. If you ever come to my place for a cookout, you'll get a big steak and a baked potato and a beer from the keg. You'll eat the steak, drink the beer, and throw the potato away. I'm not that great at cooking potatoes.

"You'll be able to stay and eat, won't you?" Spivey said.

"Looks good," I said. "But I really need to get to work."

"Let's walk inside. I want you to meet my wife."

Mrs. Spivey sat in the living room staring out the front window. The room was furnished with a studded leather sofa and love seat, heavy pine tables, travel posters from several Mexican resorts.

"Sweetheart, this is Nicholas Colt," Dr. Spivey said.

She rose, took a couple steps toward us, and extended her hand. Her fingernails were glossy, red, and perfect, but the hand I shook felt like something not quite alive. She had what I call "elsewhere" eyes, the type of gaze I've seen from rape victims and women who were abused as children. I didn't know her story, but I got the distinct vibe it was a whopper. Her forty-something chin was heavily dimpled and reminded me of a humongous canned green pea.

"Mister Colt is going to help us find our Brittney," Dr. Spivey said. "Isn't that right, Mister Colt?"

"You can call me Nicholas," I said.

"Oh, right. I'm Michael and this is Corina."

"What makes you think you can find her?" Corina said, the Xanax coming through again. She was skinny as my Balabushka with approximately half the personality.

"All I can do is try," I said. "No guarantees. She might have left town, but I doubt it. She would have contacted me or the police when she heard about Leitha's murder. I think Brittney's either dead or being held against her will. The two of you haven't heard from anybody, have you?"

Corina grabbed a Kleenex from a box on one of the pine tables. Michael put his arm around her. She wiped her eyes and held the tissue in front of her like a tiny bride's bouquet. Michael said, "You mean, like a ransom note or something?"

"Anything," I said.

"No. Why would anyone get in touch with us? We're not her parents. Not yet, anyway."

"Yeah, but you have money. If someone kidnapped her, she might have told them about you."

"We haven't heard from anybody," Michael said. "We'll be sure to let you know if we do."

"All right."

"Sweetheart, why don't you go on out and join the party," Michael said to Corina. "Nicholas and I have some business to discuss. The Schonbergs are here, and the grill should be just about ready for the steaks."

"I'll go out in a minute," Corina said.

Michael led me down a long hallway, leaving Corina to stare out her window.

Floor-to-ceiling bookshelves lined two walls of Michael's library, and the others were paneled with what looked like mahogany. The aroma of pipe tobacco mingled with the subtle and clean scents of leather conditioner and furniture wax. The room had no windows. Michael sat behind a cherry desk you could have parked a jazz trio on and motioned for me to have a seat in one of the adjacent chairs.

A large gray cat jumped onto the desk. Michael petted him for a minute, then picked him up and set him on the floor.

"His name is Twist," Michael said. "He was a stray we took in. I'm afraid he doesn't do much but eat and sleep."

"Strays are the best," I said. "They always seem to appreciate everything. I have a dog named Bud."

He opened one of the desk drawers and pulled out a large leather-bound checkbook, the kind people use for payrolls.

"I want to make sure every effort is made to find Brittney," he said. "Name your price, Nicholas."

"My normal rate is a hundred an hour," I said. "Plus expenses. I can get started with a five-thousand-dollar retainer. I'll log all my time and present you with any relevant receipts, of course."

"What do you consider chargeable expenses?"

"Everything I need to get the job done," I said. "Gasoline, bar and restaurant tabs, hotel rooms if I have to leave town, informant fees. It usually doesn't add up to a lot, but it could. I don't know if you've thought about this, but a reward would help. People who normally wouldn't talk to a cop or a PI will crawl out of the woodwork if enough money's involved."

"A reward. That's a good idea. How much—"

"Fifty grand. If she's found unharmed. You don't want to go public with it, though, like you see sometimes. I have a select crowd in mind. If it gets out in the local news, you'll have every crackhead in town leading you down every goat path."

"And if you find her by yourself—"

"I'm working for the fee I mentioned earlier. The reward's not for me."

"It seems like I could hire a whole team for the money you're talking about," Michael said.

"Then hire them," I said. "It's your money. Hire whoever the hell you want to. I told you my rate. It's really not negotiable."

I didn't bother to tell Spivey I was dedicated to this case whether he paid me or not. I knew he could afford what I was asking, and the money would help, but I was determined to find Brittney on my own if I had to.

"You probably think I'm rich, don't you, Nicholas? The fact is, my wife is very ill. She's dying. We have very good insurance, but it doesn't cover some of the alternative treatments we've sought abroad. This house is mortgaged to the hilt, and I'm having a hard time just keeping up with my own expenses these days. I want to find Brittney. We love her dearly. But I'm just not in a position to offer a reward of that size." He held up an envelope. "Back taxes in the amount of four hundred forty-three thousand, five hundred fifty-six dollars."

I wondered what the square root of *that* was. "Does your wife have cancer?"

"Yes. It started with a little black mole on her shoulder. Turned out to be a melanoma. There's very little hope now, and we've exhausted nearly all our resources. The barbeque today is a fundraiser. Not for Corina, specifically, but to open a research grant in her name. Some of my colleagues are making sizeable donations, and I'm auctioning some antiques later tonight, all proceeds to go toward the grant. We hope to raise a million dollars by the end of the day."

"I'm truly sorry to hear about your wife," I said.

Michael opened the leather binder, wrote a check for five thousand dollars and passed it across the desk to me. "Here's your retainer," he said. "It's really all I can do right now."

"I understand," I said. "Are you involved in the cancer research yourself?"

"My practice is obstetrics and gynecology. Most of my patients are healthy young women. Have you ever witnessed a birth, Nicholas?"

"My daughter, Harmony."

"It really is a miracle. I still have tears in my eyes, every time, and I've helped deliver over a thousand babies. Corina and I were never able to have children of our own, so we've been interested in adoption for quite some time. I guess it seems strange that we're still interested, with Corina's condition and all, but she wants me to go ahead with Brittney despite the fact that I'll probably end up a widower."

I ripped the check in half, passed it back to him. "This will be my donation," I said. "I'll find her, Michael."

"That's very generous of you," he said.

I shrugged. "Even private eyes have a heart sometimes."

CHAPTER EIGHTEEN

A different freak show stood outside The Tumble Inn when Papa and I drove by Sunday night. Lots of leather vests and chains and heavy black boots and tattoos. A couple dozen shiny motorcycles were parked in the small lot adjacent to the club, and the fat kid named Shep was at the door checking IDs again. Joe's pickup truck would have been about as inconspicuous as a diamond necklace on a squirrel, so we were in Papa's Ford Explorer. I pulled to the curb.

"I'm going to check his apartment. Call me on my cell in a little while."

"You got money?" Papa said.

I handed him two hundred dollars. "Don't spend it all on whiskey now, old man."

"Whiskey hell. I'm going to get myself a woman." He laughed, got out of the car, and walked toward The Tumble Inn. He turned and looked back once but didn't see the thumbs-up I gave him through the Explorer's tinted window.

I traveled north on Roosevelt Boulevard and noticed someone tailing me. It wasn't Roy Massengill this time. Probably another one of Fleming's guys.

I let the tail follow me all the way to Duck's neighborhood. I got lucky this time and found an open space across the street from the apartment building. It only took two tries at parallel parking. I was getting better. The car following me cruised on by. It was a Volkswagen Beetle. I jotted down the tag number. I had a feeling the driver parked nearby, waiting for me to move again. The car was black and shiny and reminded me of Darth Vader.

I rolled down the windows of Papa's Explorer, turned sideways and leaned against the door. I sat there for a long time watching nothing happen at Duck's place.

My arm hurt like hell. I took a Dilaudid tablet, even though it was an hour before another one was due.

I wished I had packed a Thermos. Of all the things to forget to bring on a stakeout. I remembered seeing a Krispy Kreme dough-nut store on Roosevelt, but didn't want to drive off and risk losing my parking place. I decided to walk. I had to have coffee. It was only two blocks to Roosevelt, and if I hurried I could be back to the truck in fifteen minutes. I locked the Explorer and walked a brisk pace toward Krispy Kreme.

My arm felt better by the time I got to the doughnut store. The pain wasn't completely gone, but it was tolerable.

I ordered a large cup of black coffee and two jelly-filled dough-nuts. I exited Krispy Kreme and waited for the traffic light at Roo-sevelt and Cedar to change so I could cross the street. A teenager wearing baggy pants and a Metallica T-shirt sat at the bus stop there, his eyes glued to some sort of portable video player.

"You gotta bump?" the young man said.

"No." I stared at the traffic light. I had Joe's .25 tucked in my pocket, but I didn't feel like shooting anybody tonight.

"Gotta cigarette?"

I set my doughnut bag on the bench and handed the kid a Marl-boro.

I took my doughnut bag and crossed Roosevelt. When I got half a block down Cedar Street, I heard two gunshots from the direc-tion of Duck's apartment.

I moved from the sidewalk into the shadows of moss-draped oaks. It was past midnight, and all the tidy bungalows along Cedar Street were dark and quiet. Crickets sang their lonesome songs in the moonlight. A cat moaned in the distance.

My cell phone trilled and startled the shit out of me. It was Papa.

"Hey," he said. "One of the bartenders says he saw a cute young blonde in Duck's car yesterday. Matches Brittney's description."

"I just heard gunshots," I said.

"Where the hell—"

"I'll call you in a few."

I hung up.

I saw an orange glow above the treetops. I ran to the Explorer and set my coffee and doughnuts on the seat and gazed at Duck's apartment building, which was on fire.

Plumes of black smoke rose and choked the moonlight. No alarms were sounding, but several of the residents were on the lawn in pajamas and housecoats. Duck wasn't one of them. I called 9-1-1 on my cell and trotted toward the inferno while talking to the dispatcher. Help was on the way, she said.

A woman bolted out with an infant in arms and two older kids trailing behind. Duck's Escalade was still in the parking area.

If what the bartender told Papa was true, Brittney was up on the second floor with Duck.

I had to get her out.

"Stop that idiot," I heard someone shout. "Don't go in there. You'll get yourself killed."

I didn't stop. I'd been to Duck's apartment before and knew the way. I figured I could get in and out in under a minute.

I took my shirt off and balled it into a wad. I filled my lungs with one last breath of fresh air, held the makeshift respirator to my face, and walked into the greasy black haze.

Wood crackled hotly overhead. I couldn't see anything. The smoke was too thick. It was like trying to breathe motor oil, and the shirt wasn't helping much. I felt my way to the stairwell and started to climb, my leg muscles already screaming for oxygen. I made it up to the second level. Duck's apartment was right around the corner. I felt the door. It was locked and hot. Everything seemed eerily familiar. I'd been in this nightmare before. I tried to stay in the moment, but I couldn't help thinking about Susan and

Harmony and my band, roasting in that goddamn airplane. I kicked the door, but it was strong and my legs weren't. I rammed it with my shoulder, again and again, and finally felt the frame start to give. I took a couple of steps back to gather some momentum. I was going to make it through this time. I could feel it.

Then someone from behind grabbed my waist and pulled me away.

"You can't go in there," he said. "You'll cause a back draft and blow us all to shit."

"Fuck you. There's a fifteen-year-old—"

He dragged me down the stairs and then outside. I tried to resist, but my oxygen-deprived muscles wouldn't cooperate. I struggled to stay conscious, my peripheral vision rippling with swarms of psychedelic gnats. My lungs felt like they'd been bathed in acid. My face was coated with tears and snot.

The fireman slapped a mask over my mouth and nose. I pulled it off and tried to get up. He held me down, and I felt a needle pierce my thigh. Then everything went black.

CHAPTER NINETEEN

I was treated and released from the hospital.

Papa had taken a cab to where his Explorer was parked. He picked me up, and we drove toward his house in Green Cove Springs.

"Can you roll that window up?" I said. I had the chills. My brain felt like it had gone through the spin cycle in a Maytag.

"Window's not there anymore," Papa said. "Someone shot it out."

"Darth Vader," I said.

"Huh?"

"There was a car following me," I said. "Black Volkswagen. They must have thought I was still in here when they shot the window out."

I stayed the night in Papa's guest room. At five a.m. I switched on the television and watched the news. At six Papa came in carrying two coffee mugs. His hair looked like someone had taken a whisk to it. Scrambled hair.

"You couldn't sleep either?" I said.

"You can't sleep worth a shit when you get old. Have to piss about every two hours." He handed me one of the cups.

"Want to go outside?" I said.

We sat on the porch. I lit a cigarette but my lungs were sore and I couldn't handle it.

"Was the fire on the news yet?" Papa said.

"Yeah. Two people upstairs died. A man and a woman."

"And you're thinking it was Duck and Brittney?"

"I hope not."

"So what now?"

"I don't know. Can I use your computer?"

"Of course. What about that couple who was planning on adopting Brittney? The Spiveys."

"I'm not calling them until I know for sure that it was Brittney who died in the fire. I'll get in touch with Fleming some time today, see if the coroner has anything yet. And, I told Juliet I'd come over and get my stuff. That's the first thing I'm going to do this morning. Right after I run these tags."

Juliet's car was in the driveway. Gas Man's wasn't. I still had my key to her front door, but didn't use it. She answered a few seconds after I rang the bell.

"Please come in," she said. She wore blue denim shorts and a bright yellow shirt with a western-style yoke, and a pair of purple socks with tiny yellow hearts and nickel studs at the top. I remembered her buying them when she coaxed me out shopping one time. Her olive cheeks burned with the kind of flush you associate with a fever.

"Is that my stuff?" I pointed to the plastic bag leaning against one wall of the foyer.

Juliet nodded.

"Is the tape in there?" I said.

She nodded again.

"I guess this is goodbye then."

"It doesn't have to be. Nicholas—"

"Don't even." I held my palms up, fingers spread.

Tears welled in her eyes, and a single one led a trail of mascara down her cheek. "That night with Martin, it didn't mean anything. You're the one I love."

"I almost shot the son of a bitch," I said.

"It wasn't his fault. I told him I was single. He doesn't even know about you, Nicholas. He flirted with me at the hospital one time when he was on my unit seeing a patient, but we never talked much. He asked me to dance the other night at Lyon's Den, and—"

"One thing led to another," I said, finishing her thought. "What did you tell him when he left that morning?"

"That it was a mistake. A drunken mistake. Believe me, Nicholas, that's all it was. And it's not like I was cheating on you. We broke up, remember?"

She took a step my way, hands in her pockets, and buried her face on my chest. She sobbed against me, the warmth of her tears seeping through my shirt. I put my arms around her, felt her fingernails dig gently into my back. A chill rose and terminated on my scalp. Papa once told me that the opposite of love is not hate, but indifference. I hadn't reached the indifference stage with Juliet. Didn't think I ever would. Apathy is an emotion foreign to me. I care about things. I give a damn. It's my nature. At that moment, I hated her.

I lifted her chin and covered her mouth with mine. Our tongues swirled like cyclones, deep and hard. I tore her shirt open, heard the plastic buttons dancing on the ceramic tile floor. I picked her up and carried her to the bedroom and we hurried out of our clothes, kissing and getting very busy with our hands.

But something was very wrong about it all. Before we went any further, I silently stood and walked to the window and gazed out to Juliet's backyard. A hawk flew down and perched on the wooden fence. I couldn't help thinking about her in the same bed with him. It gnawed at me. I didn't know if I could ever trust her again, and without trust a relationship is a shaky and hollow thing. It's like a fat figure skater, ugly and off-balance. It just doesn't work.

I wanted to throw her down and fuck her. I wanted it to hurt. It was wrong.

The hawk flew away.

"Please come and make love with me," Juliet said.

I talked to the window. "I can't," I said. "Not today."

"Will you call me?"

"I don't know."

I put my clothes on and left her there naked and alone.

CHAPTER TWENTY

The black Beetle belonged to a man named Everett Spenser in Orange Park. He was eighty-two years old.

I drove to the address, a ranch-style brick with a one-car attached garage. A government foreclosure notice had been tacked on the front door. The place looked grim and forbidding with tall weeds and neglected shrubs.

I got out and peeked into the garage, which was full of everything but a car. I had my pistol out and at this point was pretty sure I wasn't going to need it when a woman to my left shouted, "Oh my God, he's got a gun." I looked next door and briefly saw one of her legs disappear into the entranceway of her home. I pocketed the .25, walked over there, and knocked, PI license in hand.

"I'm calling the police," she screamed. Her deadbolt snapped to the locked position.

"I can explain, ma'am," I said. "I'm a private investigator. I have a license to carry this weapon. Can I talk to you for a minute?"

Someone from behind, an NFL linebacker maybe, hit me just above the kidneys with a shoulder or sledgehammer or something. I fell to the concrete porch on my sore arm. When I turned over the barrel of a rifle was staring at me.

"Don't move, motherfucker," the man behind the gun said. Assassins never say things like that. They just shoot you. He wore an Elvis hairdo and a nerdy pair of sunglasses with tortoiseshell frames. I might have laughed if my cranium hadn't been in danger of immediate modification.

"I'm a private investigator," I said. "My ID is—around here somewhere."

"Get that pistol out of the holster. Two fingers on the butt. That's right. Now hand it over." I had a feeling he had watched too many cop show reruns.

I gave him my gun. "I'm looking for your neighbor, Everett Spenser," I said.

He bent down and picked up my ID, looked it over. "Just 'cause you're a private detective don't give you the right to go stalking around here with a gun. You scared Mama half to death."

"I'm sorry about that."

"What do you want with Everett?" He clicked on the safety and held the rifle at his side.

"Can I get up now?" I said.

"Yeah. Sorry I had to lay you out like that. We've had some break-ins around here lately."

I got up and brushed myself off. "I just need to talk to Mr. Spenser. Do you know if he owns a black VW Beetle, late model?"

"Never seen one over there," he said. "I think the old man's in a nursing home now. His daughter and her kids were living there with him, then all of a sudden I stopped seeing anyone. I heard he's in that nursing home over on Kingsley, but I ain't sure."

"Do you know his daughter's name?" I said.

"Dawn or Joy, something like that. You know, one of those dish-washing liquid names."

"Palmolive?"

He didn't laugh.

"Thanks for not shooting me," I said. "Can I have my gun back now?"

Walking toward Everett Spenser's room at the nursing home was like walking a corridor in an idiot's nightmare. "Bunny, bunny, bunny," the lady in room 102 chanted. The gentleman in 106 was certain he had not been fed, even though it was well past lunchtime. "I must eat. I must, I must. I will not eat peas," he said over and over.

Spenser's room was quiet except for the hum of a feeding pump mainlining nutrition into his gut. On the way in, one of the nurses told me he'd suffered a stroke a few months back and could only communicate with his eyes.

Just shoot me, I thought.

I asked Everett Spenser if he had ever owned a Volkswagen. Two blinks. That meant no. I decided to track down his daughter and find out for sure, but first I wanted to have a word with Homicide Detective Barry Fleming.

My arm hurt like a bastard. I thought seriously about driving to Hallows Cove Memorial and letting them admit me this time. Instead, I took a Dilaudid tablet and soldiered on.

It was two thirty in the afternoon and I wanted a drink, something high-octane to knock me out for a few hours. I resisted the urge to stop at Kelly's Pool Hall.

I drove to the courthouse in Green Cove and parked at a meter across the street. I knew I would have to pass through a guard station with a metal detector, so I left my gun in the truck. As it turned out, I saw Fleming heading toward his car in the police-only parking lot.

"What do you want, Colt?" Fleming was wearing the same suit he had on the day I shoved him into the hot tub.

"And a good afternoon to you, too, Detective Fleming," I said. "I was just wondering if I might have a few minutes of your time. Just a few questions."

"Make it quick. I have a meeting."

"Who was tailing me in a black VW Beetle last night?"

"Someone was tailing you?"

"Knock it off, Barry. It's no secret you want to burn me."

"I should burn your ass after that little episode at the station the other day. You were out of line. You owe me a cleaning bill for my suit, by the way. But I haven't had anybody following you."

"What about Roy Massengill the other night?"

"Massengill was on his own. Off duty."

"So you don't know anything about a black Bug?"

"Cross my heart and hope to die. I really have to go now." He opened his car door.

"Wait. Anything from the coroner on that fire?"

"What we have on that is confidential at this point. You'll have to wait for the press release like everyone else. Sorry."

"Yes or no, Barry. Was the female Brittney Ryan?"

"You're a persistent son of a bitch. I'll give you that. All right. Yeah, we're pretty sure it was her. We're just waiting on dental records to confirm it. Not a word to anybody, Colt. Understand? And stay out of my way. This is way out of your league now." He climbed in and started his car.

My heart sank. I motioned for Fleming to roll down his window.

"One more thing," I said. I was still curious about what Beeler had said about pocket forty-seven and the plane crash. I asked Fleming if it might be possible to have a word with him.

"Nope," Fleming said.

"It doesn't have anything to do with your case. I—"

"Beeler's dead," he said.

"How did that happen?"

"Gotta go, Colt." He rolled up his window and pulled away.

I walked to the truck and called Papa on my cell.

"Fleming said it was probably her," I said, my voice not quite steady.

"That sucks," Papa said. "What now? I guess the case is over for you, huh?"

"It's not over for me. Someone in a little black car tried to kill me last night. I have to assume they'll try again."

"So what are you going to do?"

"I have to find out who was driving the Beetle. Fleming said it wasn't one of his guys, and the tags were a dead end. Everett Spenser is a goddamn vegetable in a nursing home. He denies ever owning the car. But he might be confused, might have forgotten. I'm going to talk to his daughter. Other than that, I'm not sure. You got any ideas?"

"I guess you could stake out your camper. If someone's after you, they'll probably show up there eventually."

"I'll think about that. You feel like getting drunk and doing a little fishing later?"

"Best idea I've heard all day."

"I'll see you later, Papa."

We hung up.

I punched in the number a nurse had given me for Dawn Block, Everett Spenser's daughter. She answered, and I heard a baby crying in the background.

"My name is Nicholas Colt. I'm a private investigator. I'm looking for the owner of a black Volkswagen Beetle, one of the newer ones." I told her the tag number.

"Daddy never had a car like that," she said. "He didn't believe in buying anything foreign. He was in World War Two, hundred and first Airborne. He still thinks the Germans and Japanese are evil."

"Thanks for your time," I said.

I was still across the street from the courthouse, and I got an idea. I walked inside, made it through the metal detector, took the elevator to the ground floor where the Division of Motor Vehicles was located. I took a number from the dispenser and waited to be called. When my turn finally came, I talked through a hole to a platinum blonde with bright red lipstick on the other side of the windowed booth.

"I lost all the paperwork on my car," I said. "I'd like to get a replacement registration."

I told her the tag number, and she keyed it into her computer.

"You're still at the same address?" she said.

"What does it say there?"

She read the address. "Wait a minute," she said. "The information I have here says you were born in 1924. That can't be right. You're Everett Spenser? May I see your driver's license please?"

"I must have written the tag number down wrong. So sorry. Bad case of dyslexia. I'll go outside and do it right this time. I'll be back."

She gave me an unforgiving look. "You'll have to get a new number and wait in line again."

I had no intention of getting a new number or waiting in line again. I recognized the address when she read it. It was Mark Toohey's.

CHAPTER TWENTY-ONE

The air outside was thick, the way it gets before a storm. My lungs ached, my arm throbbed, and generally I felt like crap.

Toohey answered the door wearing the bathrobe the blonde had been wrapped in the other night, his face swollen with sleep.

"Did I wake you from your nappy nap?" I said.

"What the fuck you want?"

"Anybody ever tell you that you have an attitude problem? Can I come in?"

He opened the door and stepped aside. The air conditioner was cranked, and the place reeked of cologne and marijuana.

"What can I help you with today, Mr. Colt?"

"I'm looking for Brittney Ryan again. Seen her?"

"Nope."

"I assume you know Leitha's dead."

"Yeah, man. I heard about that. What a drag. Swear to God, I ain't heard from Brittney. Maybe she left for California. That's what she was always talking about."

I hit Toohey on the chin with an uppercut. He fell, and I kicked him in the ribs a couple of times to make sure he stayed down.

"Jesus Christ." Toohey cupped his jaw in his hand. He sounded like a bad ventriloquist now.

"You got five seconds to tell me about a black Volkswagen."

"What the f—"

I kicked his ribs again in the same spot and heard a crack this time. Toohey moaned.

"The kneecaps are next," I said.

"Black Volkswagen? You talking about that shit Mandy drives?"

"Who's Mandy?"

"My girlfriend, man. You saw her. My ex. Bitch split on me. Like I really give a fuck."

Something clicked in my brain. "What car lot does she work for?"

"Rent-A-Gem," Toohey said.

Bingo.

I bent over and felt his jaw. "It's not broken," I said. "But you better take care of those ribs. Where can I find Mandy?"

"I told you, she works at Rent-A-Gem."

"I'm pretty sure I'm not going to find her there," I said. "In case you haven't heard, Rent-A-Gem is a crime scene now."

"She rents a house somewhere down in Middleburg. I swear, Colt, I didn't have nothing to do with no stolen cars."

"Did you know she used your address for phony papers on the Beetle?"

"Bitch."

On the way to Middleburg, I stopped at the public library and found Mandy's address on the Internet.

It was a wood-frame house, small, probably two bedroom, and looked pretty much like every other house in the subdivision. A white Ford Econoline van was parked in the driveway.

Thunder crackled in the distance. I parked across the street and waited. I called Papa to let him know what was going on.

"You even sure she's there?" he said.

"I saw a light go on in the front room, so somebody's home. I want to catch her leaving and follow her. I got a feeling she's not going to be very cooperative if I just knock on the door and start asking questions. Plus—shit. She just came out."

"She alone?"

"Yeah. I'll talk to you later."

"Doesn't look like the weather's going to be good for fishing."

"Yeah."

"But we can still get drunk."

"Yeah."

The van went south. I followed it to Middleburg High School. It was late in the afternoon and the students and faculty were long gone for the day.

I pulled in behind her in the parking lot, blocking her exit. The door opened and she took off running across the football field with a suitcase. I tackled her at the fifty-yard line. She tried to gouge my eyes with her fingernails before I straddled her and pinned her arms down.

"Let me go," she said.

"The only place you're going is to jail."

She was panting and struggling beneath me. "You don't understand, man. If I don't deliver this suitcase, I'm dead."

"What's in it?"

"Money."

"For who?"

"I can't tell you."

"I think you should tell me. Otherwise, I'm going to break every bone in your face."

She called my bluff. "Go ahead and hit me, motherfucker. Kill me. I'd rather die than go to prison."

"What if there was a way for you to get out of it?" I said. "Clean. Just walk away."

"What are you talking about?"

"Here's what we're going to do," I said. "You help me, I'll help you. You can take the money in that suitcase and go start over somewhere. Far, far away from Jacksonville. Tell me what you know, and you're free as a bird."

"I could have done that in the first place. That's no deal. Wherever I go, he'll find me and kill me."

"Not if I find him first. It's your only chance, Mandy. Take it or leave it."

Tears welled in her eyes. Her façade crumbled. "Rent-A-Gem was a front. This guy they call Pirate was selling names and social security numbers to Marcus Sharp, and Sharp used the socials for fake bills of sale on stolen cars. All we had to do was get the cars out of state clean, and then Sharp had a buyer up in Atlanta who had them shipped overseas. Sharp was making a mint, and everything looked legit on paper. That black Bug I was driving was supposed to go to Atlanta this week, but when Sharp got killed it kind of blew everything to hell. It was Pirate's idea for me to follow you the other night. I didn't want to use my van, you know, for obvious reasons, so I took the Volkswagen. I can see now that I fucked up royally."

"Where did the money in the suitcase come from?"

"It's one of Sharp's payments to Pirate. A thousand bucks for every name and social. I'm supposed to leave the suitcase under the bleachers."

"Why did Pirate want you to follow me?"

"I don't know. He said he would give me two grand to tail you for a few hours, so I did it for the money. I didn't ask why."

"You know who shot my window out?"

"No."

"How did you and Pirate communicate? If he called you on a cell phone—"

"He sent texts from a blocked number. I've never even heard his voice."

She wasn't much help, but I thought I had it figured out anyway. I thought I knew Pirate's true identity.

"Don't even think about sticking around," I said. "You need to pack your shit and get out of town."

"You're not going to have me arrested?"

"I don't care about you. I want Pirate."

CHAPTER TWENTY-TWO

Brittney must have somehow known about Rent-A-Gem being a front for a car theft ring. It was that knowledge that got her and her sister killed. A man known as Pirate was the killer. Pirate sold names and social security numbers to Marcus Sharp for use on bogus registrations for cars that were shipped overseas. So who was Pirate? It had to have been someone with access to Everett Spenser's records at the nursing home, and it had to have been someone who had contact with Brittney Ryan.

I had a strong hunch that Dr. Michael Spivey was Pirate. He needed money to pay for his wife's medical bills, so he sold patients' personal information to Rent-A-Gem. Patients who were dying, or otherwise unlikely to discover that they had been used. Patients like Everett Spenser. Spivey was a gynecologist, and he probably treated elderly women at the nursing home for one thing or an- other. It would have been easy enough for him to grab the occa- sional stray chart and steal whatever information he wanted. I doubted he ever used numbers from his own patients. Those would have been too easily traced back to him if the authorities ever caught on.

Brittney must have seen something while she was at his house for tennis, the Saturday she ran away from home. That was my guess. She must have stumbled upon something incriminating. Maybe she opened the wrong e-mail on Spivey's computer, or over- heard the wrong phone conversation. It could have been anything. Whatever it was, it had frightened her enough to make her run away from home and take refuge with a pimp.

Now that I had an idea who Pirate was, and where he lived, it was a matter of going there and taking him down. I didn't have any real evidence yet, not enough to take to the police and hope it would stick, so I had to play my cards just right.

But there were a couple of things I wanted to do before dealing Dr. Michael Spivey his final hand.

I stopped and bought a VHS-C adapter on my way home. I'd found the tape in Brittney's secret hiding place, with her condoms and cigarettes, so I knew there had to be something on it, something she didn't want just everyone to see. I hoped it wasn't something she and Mark Toohey had recorded in the bedroom. I didn't feel like going back to Toohey's place and breaking more ribs.

I made it to Hallows Cove around six o'clock. I drove around the lake a couple times to make sure nobody was following me. My Airstream looked like hell with the plastic over the windows, but I saw no signs of visitors.

I switched on the air conditioner and scrounged for something to eat. I found half a loaf of bread and an onion and a full jar of peanut butter so I made a peanut butter and onion sandwich and washed it down with a cold beer.

I slid the videotape into my VCR. I rewound it to the beginning, pushed play on the remote, sat back on the sofa, and watched. I knew it was a long shot, but I was looking for any scrap of evidence that might link Dr. Spivey with the crimes.

Brittney was on a tennis court practicing serves. A man's voice off-camera instructed: "Your toss needs to be a little more to the left for the kick serve." The date at the bottom of the screen was Saturday, the day Brittney had run away. She worked on serves for a while, and then the tape cut to her crosscourt backhands. I fast-forwarded through her forehand and volley practices until the tape went to snowy static. I was about to push *Stop* on the remote when another image appeared. It was a little girl, about two I guessed, lying on a stainless steel examination table. She was naked, and the skin from her chest to her toes was the shade of a ripe tomato. The camera zoomed in on her face. She had an unfortunate dark brown birthmark in the shape of a teardrop near the right side of her mouth. She wasn't crying but she looked terrified. "Me got burned," she said. That was it. Back to fuzz. There were no other people on the footage, just the little girl. I rewound and watched the short scene again, this time noticing the date it was taped—a little over three years ago.

A voice, distant and off camera, said, "We need to get her to the burn unit in Gainesville, stat." I recognized the voice, a deep southern drawl. No mistake about it. It was Dr. Billingsly, who had treated my gunshot wound in the ER. I called Hallows Cove Memorial and got a number where I could reach him.

"I need to know if you remember anything about a little girl who came to the ER about three years ago with severe burns on the lower part of her body," I said.

"She died," Billingsly said. "I remember that case. It was heartbreaking. Baby Doe. The ER was packed that night, and somebody left her on a chair wrapped up in a blanket. When we unwrapped her, half the skin on her legs peeled off. I got a helicopter scheduled to transport her to Gainesville, to the burn unit, but it was too late. She died on the way."

"How do you think she got burned?"

"It looked like she was scalded. Bath water too hot, my guess. We see it more often than you'd think. Sometimes it's an accident, sometimes not."

"So you suspected abuse?"

"Right. The forensics nurse on duty that night made a video, but nothing ever came of it. We had no way of identifying the girl, and the parents never came forward."

"That doesn't make sense," I said. "If someone has a two-year-old kid, and the kid just suddenly disappears, people notice."

"Seems they would. There was a police investigation, but you know how that goes. Shit gets put on the back burner, goes cold after a while."

"Thanks for your time," I said, and hung up. Five minutes later, I was on my way to Michael Spivey's house.

The VHS-C tape had been in Brittney's possession. I'd found it in the lining of her letterman jacket the first day I went to Leitha's house. She had used it to record her tennis lesson, but on playback she must have seen the footage of the scalded little girl. I was pretty sure she had watched it at Spivey's house, because Leitha didn't have the equipment to play the tape. I started getting the idea that this whole thing—Brittney running away and then disappearing a second time from my house, Leitha being tortured and killed, the fire at Duck's apartment, and the attempt on my life that same night—had to do with Brittney seeing what was on that tape.

It started raining like a son of a bitch. I slowed to thirty on the interstate, but the tires on Joe's old truck kept hydroplaning and the tractor trailers kept throwing walls of water on me from the fast lane. I finally had to pull to the shoulder and turn my flashers on.

It was almost eight o'clock and black as a skillet. Rain drummed hard on the truck's roof.

I sat there with nothing to do but think. I tried to smoke, but the cab got too hazy even with the windows cracked open a notch.

I swallowed a Dilaudid dry and soon faded into a light sleep poisoned with bizarre dreams.

I ran naked through a jungle, thorny plants all around, purple berries raining from a yellow sky. I stopped, reached into my mouth, and pulled out a tooth the size and shape of a guitar pick. It was brown and rotten and somehow I saw inside my mouth then and my teeth were all jagged and uneven and sharp like broken lightbulbs and my tongue was cracked and swollen and bleeding. I tasted the bitter coppery blood and tried to swallow but couldn't.

I saw my wife, Susan, and our baby in the distance and I ran and ran but they kept getting farther away. I fell to the ground. Everything went black and then Susan hovered over me like an angel and she crushed a handful of purple berries and rubbed the juice on my wounds like an ointment and all the tiny cuts from the thorns healed instantly. She was in my arms now and the ground wasn't thorny anymore but was covered with something like velvet.

I opened my eyes. Branches of chrome blistered a sky the shade of purple Kool-Aid. The rain had nearly stopped. I started the truck and eased back onto the interstate.

Automatic sprinkler heads whirred on Spivey's saturated lawn, and electric lights illuminated the entire perimeter of his house. No penny pinching here, I thought.

Spivey answered the door himself. He looked surprised.

"Mr. Colt. Please, come in."

I went in. When he turned to say something, I pulled out my pistol and pointed it at his face.

I thought about what Roy Massengill had asked me, if I could take a life with no immediate threat to my own. The kill switch, he called it.

But I didn't need to kill Dr. Spivey. The death sentence was alive and well in Florida, and death row was where he was headed. For the murders of Leitha and Brittney Ryan.

"Jesus Christ, Colt. What—"

"Howdy, Pirate. I'm going to have you arrested for first-degree murder, that's what. And some other charges. Like selling patients' personal information to a car theft ring. Like scalding a little girl to death. I haven't figured that one out yet, but I know it was you. That's why you went after Brittney, because she found that video."

"You got it all wrong, Colt."

"Do I? I don't think so. But I'm sure the DA can work it all out."

A deafening boom preceded Michael Spivey's skull disintegrating before my eyes. I turned, and Corina was there holding a .45 automatic, the kind they once used in the military. She had it pointed at my chest.

"Drop your gun," she said.

Her eyes were glazed. She looked through me instead of at me.

I threw down my weapon.

"Take it easy now," I said. "Let's just talk for a minute, Corina."

She laughed. The cackling, inappropriate laughter of the insane. She finished with a wheezy cough, and then her expression turned grave.

"I'm going to rot in hell, right beside my husband." She spoke slowly and deliberately, with her trademark Xanax slur. I had a feeling she'd taken more than her usual dose. "It was unthinkable, what he did, but he did it for me. For me. He gave me a baby—the most beautiful baby. See, we couldn't have children of our own. We tried—God, we went to all the fertility specialists—and then, then, when Michael had the opportunity to perform a third-trimester abortion on an unwed teen, well, why should that baby have gone to waste? Why should she?"

She made gestures with her left hand as she spoke, but my focus was mostly on the trembling gun barrel pointed at my heart. She had the shakes, and it was making me extremely nervous.

"Put the gun down," I said.

She ignored me.

"We had our own little neonatal ICU set up right here at the house, incubator and everything. Our secret baby. It wasn't easy, I can tell you that. It wasn't easy at all, but after a couple of years we had almost everything we needed, almost all the papers for it to look like an overseas adoption when she just wouldn't stop crying one day, just wouldn't stop. I ran some water and put her in the tub. I didn't mean to burn her. I swear to God I didn't mean to. I just wanted her to stop that goddamn bawling. An ambulance was out of the—I would have gone to prison."

She paused and wiped the tears from her eyes. I thought about rushing her and trying to grab the pistol, but her tremors had me spooked. One wrong twitch would put me in tomorrow's obituaries. I stood frozen while she continued.

"I took my sweet secret baby, my Melanie, to the emergency room and left her on a chair. I thought they could save her. I really thought they could. Later on the news I heard she died and—oh my God—my heart was broken—and a couple of days after that we were contacted by a man who called himself Pirate, and he had seen me leaving Melanie there in the ER. He blackmailed us. We paid him every time, until I was diagnosed with cancer and the bills piled up and the money ran out—the money ran out, and then he wanted names and social security numbers of Michael's patients in place of cash. We didn't know what for, but we had no choice but to give him what he wanted. We had no choice, Mr. Colt. Can't you see that?"

"You need help, Corina."

She put the barrel of the .45 in her mouth and pulled the trigger. The back of her head opened up and a spray of blood and brain and bone splattered on the wall behind her. She lay crumpled on the floor next to her dead husband.

CHAPTER TWENTY-THREE

I drove to a pay phone and made an anonymous call to the police. I believed Corina's confession. Now I needed to look for the real Pirate, the one who killed Leitha and Brittney.

After a couple of unproductive calls, I drove to Hallows Cove Memorial and found Dr. Billingsly in the physician's lounge watching CNN and drinking a Mountain Dew.

"Think you could help me with something?" I said.

"I can try. What is it?"

"The night that little girl with the burns came in. I need to know everybody who was in the ER that night. Patients, family members, staff, everybody. Is that something you can help me with?"

"That's going to be tricky. With all the privacy laws, it's tough these days to get hold of medical records. And there were probably hundreds of people in and out of the ER that night. It could literally take months to track them all down, if it's even possible." His pager squealed. He took it out of his pocket and read the message. "Shit. I have to run. Maybe we can talk later."

"Just one thing before you go," I said. "Can you remember the names of the people who were in the examining room that night with you?"

He walked to the sink and washed his hands. "Let's see—there was Kelly Reynolds, one of the ER nurses. The forensics nurse, Jane Woods. There was an off-duty cop working—"

"Wait. What was the cop's name?"

"I don't remember his name. He seemed to be interested that the patient was a burn victim, though. He had suffered some burns himself, in the Army or something. He had some pretty ugly scar tissue on his neck."

I suddenly felt like the biggest fool who'd ever lived. "Was his name Massengill?" I asked.

"Yeah. That was it. Massengill."

I walked outside and sat in the truck for a few minutes, thinking about where to start looking for Massengill. I decided to try Kelly's Pool Hall first. I hoped he was there. If he was there getting drunk, it would give me an immediate edge.

A shiny white Mercedes was in the parking lot at Kelly's, license tag GAS MAN. I walked inside.

Anil was loading a case of Budweiser into the cooler, and his son Philip was lowering a batch of curly fries into hot grease. I found an open stool and sat down. Massengill wasn't there.

"The usual?" Anil said.

"Just a soda water with lime."

Anil brought my soda in a collins glass.

"Seen Roy Massengill around?"

"You know, Mr. Massengill hasn't been in lately. I'm wondering if he is sick."

"Maybe he found Jesus and quit drinking."

Anil silently considered the possibility and then sauntered back to his case of Bud.

Kelly's back room has ten coin-operated pool tables, the kind you can find in any barroom anywhere in the country. Those tables are seven-feet long, three-and-a-half-feet wide, and are fine for your casual recreational player. The real game, though, the only game I'm interested in playing, is played on a Brunswick, nine-feet long. Kelly's had one such table, upstairs in a private room. My friend Joe and I have it for two hours every Thursday night. I climbed the stairs and saw Dr. Martin Jones practicing bank shots. He was alone.

"You're pretty good," I said.

"Thanks. It's been a while. I was intramural nine-ball champ in college."

"You like to play for money?"

"Actually, I need to get going. You can have the table."

"Come on. Play me a game of nine-ball for ten dollars a game."

He looked at his watch. "All right. But I'll have to leave after a couple of games."

"Fine."

When I play with Joe, or in tournaments, I use a replica Balabushka, a very expensive cue with an Irish linen wrap and a bird's-eye maple forearm. It was a birthday gift from Papa a few years ago, my one and only prized possession. I had it with me, in a leather satchel behind the seat in Joe's pickup, but I didn't figure I'd need it for Dr. Jones.

"Lag for the break?" he said.

"I play on this table all the time. It'll be more fair if we just flip a coin?"

We flipped, and he won.

I took the wooden triangle from a hook on the wall and racked the balls. Jones lined up at a diagonal and broke hard. It was a nice break, sending the six ball to the far left corner pocket where it dropped in. He made two more shots and then played a safety, leaving me what he figured was an impossible position. I walked around the table, cue in hand, layering on the chalk.

This was no friendly game of pool for me. I didn't want to win the game, I wanted to beat him. I wanted him to walk away with his head hung low. I hit the cue ball hard, with top English, sent it three rails into the three. The nine ball broke off the rail, and slowly rolled toward the left side pocket. It hung on the lip for a second, dropped in.

"That's one," I said.

He raised his eyebrows and gave me a nervous little laugh. It was my break now, and I went at it with no mercy. I ran the table on the next five games while he sat and watched. I could have hustled him, played below level on purpose, kept the money flowing, but I wasn't in it for the money. I wanted a slice of his pride, wanted him to see what the game was like against a great player.

"Too good for me," he said. He handed me a handful of cash, and walked toward the stairs.

"You know a nurse named Juliet Dakila?" I said.

He stopped, turned around, looked me directly in the eyes, and nodded.

"If you ever go near her again, I'll kill you."

I left him standing there. I went downstairs and walked outside. The sky was clear now with no moon but plenty of stars. The air felt clean and I took a deep breath of it before climbing into the truck and driving to Roy Massengill's house. My arm was throbbing like a goddamn disco.

I had a theory. Massengill had seen Corina Spivey leaving the little girl on a chair in the ER. He'd somehow tracked Corina down, learned that she was a physician's wife and that they had plenty of money. Prime candidates for extortion. He contacted them, using the name Pirate, and told them he'd seen Corina abandon the baby. He arranged for cash to be dropped somewhere, and when the cash ran out he extorted personal information from vegetative nursing home patients in its place. He sold that information to Marcus Sharp, to be used on bogus registrations for stolen cars.

The scam was going along fine until Brittney got hold of Doctor Spivey's copy of the video. She'd taken the tape to the tennis court, and had given it to Kent Clark, the tennis pro, to record her lesson. Then, when she went back to the Spiveys' house to watch it, the footage with the scalded baby came on. Michael Spivey must have found out that Brittney had seen that footage. There was no way for me to know exactly what happened, or why everyone reacted as they did, but Spivey must have threatened her, or maybe even tried to abduct her at that time. Brittney escaped, and then left the note on Leitha's car saying that she was running away. She didn't run away because Leitha grounded her. She was running from Spivey. She was that scared.

Massengill must have freaked out when Spivey told him Brittney had the tape. In Roy Massengill's mind, Brittney had become a threat, a potential witness against the Spiveys. If Michael and Corina Spivey had been arrested, they might have disclosed Massengill's extortion scheme, which then would have led to the car theft ring. Brittney's knowledge of the scalded baby could have brought down the whole house of cards, and that's why Massengill needed her dead.

That was my theory, but theories don't hold up well in court. Theories don't sign arrest warrants. I needed evidence, and there simply wasn't any.

From a legal standpoint, it was going to be difficult to make a case against Massengill. With Marcus Sharp and the Spiveys dead, there wasn't a single witness to any of the crimes he'd committed. I was sure all his dealings had been done in cash, so no paper trail. I only had one fact to go on: he was in the ER the night baby Melanie died. Everything else was circumstantial.

But I decided not to let a minor detail like the law stand in my way.

Massengill's car wasn't in the driveway, no lights on in the house. I parked around the block. I took the flashlight from the glove compartment, a long screwdriver from the toolbox, and the pistol Joe had loaned me. Joe's 12-gauge Remington was behind the seat, but I didn't want to be seen walking down the street with it. Neighbors get nervous when they see a guy walking down the street with a big gun.

In the movies all private investigators have suede carrying cases full of burglar's tools and they're all experts at picking locks. I laugh whenever I see that. Like breaking and entering is part of our daily routine.

I crept around back, wedged the screwdriver between the door and the jamb and muscled the deadbolt away from the frame with one quick jerk. Brass parts from the lock scattered, jangling on the concrete stoop. I was counting on Massengill using the front door and not seeing the mess I'd made. I walked inside and switched on the flashlight. The most recent edition of the *Florida Times-Union* was spread out on the kitchen table, so I knew he had been there in the past twenty-four hours. It was only a matter of time until he came back home.

I turned off the flashlight and sat at the table in complete darkness with Joe's pistol in my right hand. I had the element of surprise on my side. Otherwise, Massengill was superior in every way. He was a third-degree black belt in Tae Kwon Do and a much better shooter than me. My only chance was to ambush him and try to force a confession.

I sat there listening to the kitchen faucet drip until I realized I had made a terrible mistake. I ran out the back door and drove like a madman toward Juliet's house.

Massengill's truck was parked behind the row of crape myrtles that separated Juliet's front yard from the roadside drainage ditch.

I saw him running from the garage toward the woods behind the house, but I didn't fire. I watched him disappear into the pine forest.

I ran inside and found Juliet on the living room floor, blood pouring from her nose. I knelt down and took her head in my hands.

"I shot him," she slurred. "I got hold of his gun, and I shot him. Oh, my God. Oh, my God."

"Where's the gun?"

"I don't know."

She was hysterical, wild-eyed, in a state of shock. I picked her up and carried her to the bedroom. I wiped her face with a wet washcloth and threw some ice cubes in a Ziploc bag for her to hold on her nose.

"I'll be right back," I said.

"No! Don't leave me. Please, Nicholas. Oh, my God, please don't leave me."

"I have to find him. I promise, I'll be right back."

I left her there sobbing. Her nose was probably broken, but she didn't appear to be hurt otherwise. On my way out, I dialed 9-1-1 and left the phone hanging. Juliet's address would show on the computer, and they would send someone out. I didn't have time to explain. Massengill was a wounded animal now, even more dangerous than before.

When I got outside I heard his truck start and saw the headlights come on. He fishtailed out of the driveway and headed south.

Joe's pickup and Juliet's car both had flat tires, courtesy of a knife or some other puncture tool. I thought I was going to have to hang back and wait for the cops until I noticed that annoying little dirt bike parked in the neighbor's garage. I didn't see anyone around and I didn't have time to seek permission so I hopped on and fired it up and left the driveway with the throttle pegged.

The bike was a Suzuki 125 with a steel plate where the headlight should have been. It had absolutely no business on the street, especially at night. Being invisible was good, because Massengill couldn't see me in his rearview mirror; being invisible was bad, because nobody else could see me either. If a car pulled from a side street to cross the highway, I would most likely end up skewered on an oak branch or doubled over and fried on a power line.

Massengill's taillights shone half a mile in front of me, and the gap was widening. I couldn't keep up. I thought I was going to lose him until his brake lights flared and he slowed down and stopped in the middle of the Shands Bridge.

I didn't want him to hear me coming, so I cut the engine and abandoned the bike and ran as fast as I could.

Massengill threw something over the railing to the river forty-five feet below. He didn't notice me until I stepped up and clocked his jaw with a right hook. While he went down on one knee, I pulled the .25 and pressed the barrel firmly between his eyes. He coughed and spit out a tooth.

I was panting, my lungs rattling like a diesel.

"You're one low-life motherfucker," I said. "Tell me why you killed those girls." I pressed the gun harder against his forehead. "Tell me!"

In a single sweeping motion, he pushed the gun away and somehow managed to swivel and kick me in the throat. I went down. I still had the .25, and I got a single round off before he was on top of me. It grazed the top of his head, and blood trickled down both sides of his face. He grabbed my right arm and hammered it against the pavement. The gun skittered away.

"You're dead, bitch," he said.

I managed to dodge a punch to my head, and I heard something crack like a walnut when his knuckles met the blacktop. He stood, infuriated with pain. I got up and took one step toward the gun before he had me in a choke hold.

Flashes of bright orange exploded in my head, and my arms went numb for a second. I tried to move toward the pistol, the inches like miles.

A whiskey aura surrounded Massengill, as though he had bathed in a barrel of it. He had been drinking, his side was bleeding from Juliet's shot, my bullet had furrowed through the top of his skull, and he had shattered his hand on the road. He must have been in severe pain, but his physical strength didn't seem diminished. All that Navy SEAL training was paying off for him now, and I was huffing like a blown radiator. Like a forty-five-year-old chain smoker who didn't exercise enough.

Massengill's giant forearm clamped tighter on my throat. I struggled to free myself, but it was no use. I was fading.

"I need that goddamn video," he said. His voice sounded muffled and faraway, as though he were speaking through a cardboard tube.

"Fuck you," I grunted.

"That's what Leitha Ryan said just before I put a cigar out on her clit. Her death could have been a lot less painful if she'd been more cooperative."

I managed to croak out a few words. "You're going straight to hell. You started that fire, too, didn't you? You killed Leitha, and then you killed Brittney."

"You think you're so fucking smart, Colt. You don't know shit."

It was something my stepfather had said one time when I was twelve. *You don't know shit.* I'd ridden off on my bicycle after school one day to see a girl, intending to make it back home in time to mow the grass. I was late, and it was dark, and he greeted me inside with a section of Hot Wheels track. I'd expected a beating, but he was way out of control this time. He lashed me with the orange strip of plastic again and again, on the legs and butt where the welts wouldn't show for school. I couldn't take it anymore. I cracked him in the nose with a left jab and drew blood. He had been sitting at the TV, eating a plate of pork chops, and he grabbed the steak knife on his tray and buried it in my gut. On the way to the hospital he said, "When they ask you how this happened, you don't know shit, you understand? You were running with the knife, and you slipped and fell."

Thirty-three years later a furious surge of electricity flowed through me, and I jabbed a thumb into Massengill's left eye socket. I dug in deep and scooped the delicate orb out like a melon ball. His eye was nothing but a blob of goo resting on his cheek now. He released me and staggered sideways. My own vision was clouded with sweat and blood, and it took me several seconds to locate the pistol. By the time I bent over and picked it up, Massengill had climbed over the bridge railing.

"No," I shouted, but of course he didn't listen. Before I could shoot him, he jumped to the black current forty-five feet below.

I staggered over and leaned against the rail. No sign of him anywhere. I stood there for a few seconds, and then I must have collapsed. I woke up in the emergency room at Hallows Cove Memorial.

CHAPTER TWENTY-FOUR

I booked a flight to the West Coast a couple of weeks later. I rented a car at LAX, drove a hundred miles northwest, and checked into the Super 8 Motel in Lompoc. I hadn't been to California in years, but it was still as beautiful as I remembered.

Brittney Ryan's ashes were in my suitcase. Her dental records were never located, but the charred body found along with Donald "Duck" Knight at the Westside apartment was presumed to be hers. Several eyewitnesses had seen them enter the building together.

I took the copper urn from my suitcase, left the motel, drove a few miles south to Jalama Beach County Park. Brittney deserved to rest at "the most beautiful place on the planet."

The Point Conception lighthouse is surrounded by the Jalama Ranch, a huge span of acreage, and isn't accessible to the public. The dirt road that leads there from the park is secured with a locked gate and an armed security guard.

But I had connections.

I waited at the gate until Carlos Del Rio drove up in his burgundy Jeep Grand Cherokee. We had agreed to meet there at six p.m., and he was right on time. Del Rio instructed the guard to open the locks and let me in. I climbed into the passenger's seat, and Del Rio made a U-turn while shouting something in Spanish to the guard. We headed down the dirt road, a cloud of dust in our wake.

Brittney had been in contact with Del Rio through e-mail. He was a foreman at the ranch, and had offered her a job in landscape maintenance. Brittney's plan was to work there and commute to L.A. for auditions on her days off.

An old friend in forensics had lifted Del Rio's e-mail address from her computer's hard drive.

"It's about five miles to the lighthouse," Del Rio said. "Sorry the road is so bumpy."

"Believe me, I've been on bumpier," I said.

"Can you tell me what happened to Senorita Brittney?"

I lowered my visor to block the sun, low in the western sky now. It took us ten minutes to reach the coast, and during that time I told him Brittney's story.

A single tear rolled down Carlos Del Rio's cheek.

"Stay as long as you want, señor. Call me at this number, and I will come when you are ready."

He drove away, leaving me alone on the desolate bluff, the wind kicking and the surf pounding. I gazed toward the vast Pacific and a priceless view of the sunset that no master artist could duplicate.

The lighthouse, completely automated now for several years, blinked to life as the sea went black.

The Chumash Indians, native to the area, consider this westernmost point of their former territory sacred, a holy place linked to the spiritual world. I learned that from a waitress at a hamburger joint called The Jalama Café.

I screwed off the cap from Brittney's urn, told her goodbye and that I loved her. She had given me a very brief glimpse of what it might be like to be a father.

I scattered her ashes along the rocky shore of Point Conception, sat in the sand and thought about nothing until the lighthouse switched off and it wasn't the same day anymore.

CHAPTER TWENTY-FIVE

Seven months later, I was sitting at a bar in St. Augustine, waiting to get some snapshots of a cheating wife and her lover leaving the motel across the street, when I spotted Massengill's angel tattoo through my telephoto lens. I sprinted out to my Jimmy and followed the bike north.

His body had never been recovered, but a fisherman near Palatka had found his jeans and waterlogged wallet washed up on the riverbank. The pants had a few ragged holes where crabs and other underwater scavengers had chewed through to munch on his decomposing flesh. DNA tests confirmed the bloodstains on the pants were Massengill's.

That was that, I thought, until April, when a Harley-Davidson Electra Glide stopped in front of The Neon Phoenix and then cruised through beautiful downtown St. Augustine with the same aptly named disposable douche bag of a human being gripping the handlebars. Shaved head, eye patch, gold hoops in both ears. He looked like a pirate for real now.

Or the ghost of one.

His appearance had changed drastically, but the angel tattoo and the scars on his neck cinched it for me. The same Roy Massengill I had watched take an impossible dive from the Shands Bridge into the St. John's River was now running red lights with a very expensive motorcycle.

I floored the gas pedal and followed him through Green Cove Springs and Penney Farms. We hit a buck twenty at one point, the temperature gauge on my Jimmy creeping toward the red zone.

With no streetlights, and a canopy of live oaks draped with Spanish moss filtering all but an occasional glimpse of the moon, our headlight beams created a tunnel effect as we sped along State Road 16 toward Middleburg.

The miraculously reanimated Massengill hung a sharp left onto an unmarked two-lane. After a series of disorienting back road turns, we ended up on a bumpy dirt road leading to an electric gate on wheels and a guard shack illuminated with floodlights. It looked like the entrance to a military installation, or maybe a prison. I'd lived in north Florida for many years and never knew this place existed. It gave me the creeps, as though I'd suddenly been transported to some hellish dream where drowned murderers stalked the nightscape with stiff legs and glowing red eyes.

I stopped about a hundred feet from the gate. An armed guard waved the motorcycle through. The guard wore a rent-a-cop uniform. Dark blue pants, light blue shirt, patches on both sleeves and a silver badge twinkling in the halogen glare. Black patent leather shoes. He was not a big man. Five ten, one sixty, I guessed. He had a pistol strapped to his hip and what sailors call a "cunt cap" on his head. He was compact and walked with confidence.

A sign on the fence said CHAIN OF LIGHT RANCH. JESUS LOVES YOU. AUTHORIZED PERSONNEL ONLY. TRESPASSERS WILL BE PROSECUTED.

I thought about stomping the gas pedal and chasing the Harley into the complex, but I doubted if trespassers would be prosecuted. More likely they would be shot.

I turned around and found my way back to the highway. I drove back through the tunnel of live oaks. I opened the window and took a deep breath of Springtime, my heart still pounding. A Colt .45 song came on the radio and I turned it off. I didn't pass any cars for a long time. The roads were deserted.

If Massengill really was the man on the Harley, I knew his location now and the police could easily go in and pick him up. Is that what I wanted? A lengthy trial with defense lawyers working every angle? No, I wanted Massengill dead. He'd once been a friend and a crewmember for my band, and he'd saved my life when Marcus Sharp had a revolver pressed against my skull. I still wanted him dead. When I'd thought he was chum in the St. John's, that felt like justice to me. I didn't want to allow myself to sink to his level, but were the police and a trial and all the crap that went along with it the only rational option? I gave it some thought on the ride home.

When I got to my place on Lake Barkley, I Googled Chain of Light and found their website. The home page featured a picture of an angel with its wings spread, just like the tattoo on Massengill's arm. It was an androgynous figure, with curly hair and high cheekbones and full lips. It wore a flowing robe and sash, and every feather in its wings had been drawn with painstaking detail. It was barefoot. Maybe all the members had the same tattoo. Maybe the man on the motorcycle wasn't Massengill after all. Still, I'd caught a glimpse of his scarred neck. At least I thought I had.

A man named Lucius Strychar had founded Chain of Light in 1979, and he seemed to have a solid television and radio ministry now. Lots of money coming in. In addition to the property I'd seen after following the Harley, the organization held real estate near Orlando and Tampa. I browsed the photo gallery. All the pictures were of men, and all the men were white. Lucius Strychar himself was a chubby guy in his mid-fifties. Clean-shaven double chin and puffy pink cheeks, with blue eyes and thinning salt-and-pepper hair. I imagined he drove a high-end automobile and lived in a luxurious home. All paid for with donations from lonely elderly folks on fixed incomes who welcomed him into their home nightly via the miracle of television. All sheltered from government taxes.

I clicked on several links and soon realized this was not your typical, run-of-the-mill fundamentalist Christian outfit. Reverend Strychar's message was one of paranoia, referring to the Catholic Church as "The Antichrist" and United States government agencies as "The Gestapo." A quick navigation through the website convinced me Chain of Light was an extremist organization with a lot of revenue and a dangerous ideology.

Out of curiosity, I clicked the link for "career opportunities." One of the job listings was for a guitar player in Reverend Strychar's music ministry. *Must have experience. Must be a born-again Christian.* "Must have skin the shade of chalk," I said aloud, although the words weren't actually on the screen.

I glanced at my old guitar case. Twice, Brittney Ryan had asked me why I quit playing. Twice, I had denied her an answer. I wasn't sure there was an answer. Maybe, if I hadn't been a musician, I never would have gotten on that plane and my wife and daughter would still be alive now. It was as if music had betrayed me. I'd gotten fiercely angry at it and divorced it. Something like that. I wished I had at least tried to explain it to Brittney. Now I would never get the chance.

I turned back to the computer. Among the Google hits, I found a man named Bart Harmon who claimed to be a former Chain of Light member. Now he was speaking out against the sect, referring to it as a "brainwashing cult." I read through most of his website, and then sent him an e-mail asking if he would be willing to talk with me sometime.

The next morning I drove into Green Cove and waited outside Barry Fleming's office at the courthouse. I sat on a hard wooden bench for over an hour, listening to heels clicking on the terrazzo flooring, cops bitching about how fucked up the system was, lawyers giving sage advice to their clients in hushed tones. A heavily guarded prisoner shuffled by, chains rattling and sneakers squeaking, on his way to one of the courtrooms. He couldn't have been more than twenty years old, but he wore the expression of an ancient soul completely whipped by a lifetime of rotten circumstances and bad decisions.

Barry finally showed up around ten. To my surprise, he invited me in and offered me a cup of coffee.

"I saw Roy Massengill last night," I said.

"No you didn't."

"I swear to God, Barry, I'm pretty sure it was him."

Fleming dumped some grounds into the filter basket, poured some water into the reservoir, and started the coffeemaker.

"He's dead, Colt. He drowned in the St. John's. Brittney Ryan was incinerated in a Jacksonville apartment building, and Massengill took a dive off the Shands Bridge. They're gone. You need to accept it and move on."

"Massengill's body was never found," I said.

"So tell me something I don't know."

"You ever heard of an outfit called Chain of Light?"

"Sure," he said.

"Well?"

"Well, what? You thinking about joining? It's a bunch of right-wing white-supremacist kooks. Jesus freaks and hatemongers who dress up like soldiers and play with guns in the woods. We've known about them for a long time."

"Did you know Massengill was a member?"

"Once again, Massengill's dead. D-E-A-D. Dead as—"

"Fine. Let's say Massengill really is dead. Don't you still think it's a little bit interesting that a militant religious organization had him as a member? If they let Massengill in, what other kinds of pond scum are they harboring?"

Mr. Coffee started gurgling. Fleming took two Styrofoam cups from a stack and filled them.

"Cream and sugar?"

"No thanks," I said.

"How do you know Massengill was a member?"

"He had a tattoo. An angel, on his right arm. There's a picture just like it on Chain of Light's website."

"Okay. So what if Massengill was a member? Like I said, we've known about Chain of Light for a long time. Actually, they've been out there by Penney Farms for thirty-some years now. They're not doing anything illegal, that we know of, so Massengill being a member or not being a member is irrelevant. I have a meeting, Colt. Is there anything else you wanted to talk with me about?"

I wanted to talk to him about Tony Beeler, the man I'd interrogated in a police car after Roy Massengill shot Marcus Sharp.

"You never did tell me how that Beeler guy died," I said.

"Why are you so interested in him?"

"I just am."

"He asphyxiated himself in his jail cell. Used an entire spool of dental floss, if you can imagine that."

"Was there an autopsy?" I said.

"I don't know. Yeah. He committed suicide while he was incarcerated, so there had to have been. It's protocol. Anyway, I'm really running late, so—"

"Thanks for the coffee."

We exited his suite. Fleming went left and I went right. Fleming didn't want to admit the possibility that Roy Massengill was still alive. I couldn't say I blamed him. The case was closed, as far as the police were concerned. But I knew what I had seen, and I wasn't ready to give up.

I got on an elevator and pushed B for basement. An old friend of mine worked down in the Medical Examiner's Office.

CHAPTER TWENTY-SIX

I stepped off the elevator and walked past the courthouse cafeteria. Bacon and sausage and sweet rolls and fried eggs buttered the air. I thought about the food and the stiffs being prepared in such close proximity. I hoped there weren't occasional mix-ups.

I walked down a long corridor. Rubber tiles that had probably once been white were now a dingy shade of yellow from age and wax buildup. The same pale green paint that used to be the standard for hospital interiors covered the walls. The color always reminded me of sickness and death.

The greasy smell of a southern breakfast gradually faded, replaced by the acrid odors of antiseptic and formaldehyde. I wondered who had it worse down here, the cooks or the doctors. All-day nausea or all-day headache. Some choice.

I reached a set of steel doors and pressed the FOR HELP PRESS HERE button. A buzzer buzzed on the other side, and a voice came over the intercom.

"May I help you?"

"My name's Nicholas Colt. Is Chloe Robinson working today?"

"One minute please."

Approximately one minute later, I heard a click and the doors opened automatically. Chloe stood on the other side of the threshold with her hands in her lab coat pockets.

"Hey there, stranger," she said. She had put on a few pounds since last time I saw her, but she still looked good. Long red hair, green eyes, fair skin.

"Hi Chloe. I need a favor. Can I come in?"

"I only have a few minutes. We're doing a John Doe at ten forty-five, possible homicide."

I entered the anteroom and followed her through a narrow hallway to her office.

Chloe and I had been romantically involved for a while before I met Juliet. Everything was going along fine, and then one day I just stopped calling her. I really didn't know why. I think The Righteous Brothers might have said it best. I'd lost that lovin' feeling. When that happens there's nothing you can do but move on. I should have at least called her, though. I felt bad about that.

"How have you been?" I said.

"Okay. You?"

"Good. I was wondering if you could access a file from about seven months ago."

She sat at her computer desk. "Name?"

"Tony Beeler. He was a prisoner here at the jail. Apparent suicide."

"Anthony Beeler. I remember that case," Chloe said. She typed in some information, and a picture of Beeler's head came up on the screen. "What are you looking for?"

"Any hint of foul play," I said. I had my doubts that Beeler's death was a suicide. He had known something about the plane crash, and he had been at least peripherally involved with Massengill in the car theft ring. It just seemed a little too convenient for him to kill himself in the county lockup.

It took Chloe a few minutes to search through the file. Finally, a close-up of Beeler's left hand appeared.

"There was this, but it happened at least forty-eight hours before he died."

"What is it?"

"Slight trauma to the tissue under his left thumb and pinky, consistent with injuries commonly caused by wood splinters. The thumb nail had been penetrated approximately—"

"Maybe he unloaded some two-by-fours before he was arrested," I said.

"Sure," Chloe said. She looked at her watch. "I have to gown up. You can click through the slides if you want."

"Thanks. I think I will."

She stood. "You still seeing that nurse?"

"Juliet. Yeah."

"You still have my number?"

"I think I probably have it somewhere."

"Burn it," she said. "I don't ever want to see you or hear from you ever again. I hate you, and I'm going to keep hating you until you're dead. Got it? Good."

She slammed the door on her way out.

I'm going to write a book some day: *Men Are from Mars, Women Are from Hell.* Nice as pie one minute, fiery tornadoes of rage the next. I'll never figure them out. I stopped trying a long time ago. Then again, I probably deserved her scorn. I shouldn't have ditched her like I did.

I sat in her chair at the computer desk. I didn't find anything interesting until I clicked on the photograph of Beeler's upper right arm and shoulder. He had a number of tattoos, most of them probably India ink stabbed on in a jail cell.

But he had one that was obviously the work of a master. It was the Chain of Light angel, the same tattoo that was on Roy Massengill's arm.

Instead of using the elevator, I took the stairs to the sixth floor. I wanted to give myself a little fitness test. I failed. I almost barfed on Fleming's office door. My lungs felt as though they had been injected with Silly Putty. Black blotches pulsated six inches in front of my eyes.

I waited until my heart rate slowed and then knocked on Fleming's door. No answer. I guessed he was still in the meeting. I tried the knob. The door wasn't locked. I walked in and sat down and wondered if I was having a stroke. I looked at the coffeepot, decided on a cup of water instead. Maybe it was time to think about some lifestyle changes.

I looked at a magazine for a few minutes, an old copy of *Florida Design*. I got a sense of déjà vu on page 129, and it took me a minute to realize I had actually once owned the house featured there.

Fleming walked in a few minutes later. "What are you doing here?" he said.

"Beeler was a member too."

"What?"

"I saw his autopsy pictures. He had the angel tattoo. He was a member of Chain of Light."

"You're starting to get on my nerves, Colt. What does any of this have to do with you?"

"Pocket forty-seven."

"What?"

"It's gangland slang for sabotage. I interrogated Beeler for a few minutes when he was first apprehended. Beeler told me I should have died in the crash with the others, and then he said, 'pocket forty-seven.' Beeler knew something about the plane crash that killed my wife and daughter, and I have a hunch that knowledge got him killed."

Fleming's expression fluctuated between doubtful and irritated as he filled his coffee mug. "Prisoners say all kinds of crazy stuff. They try to manipulate the situation by playing your emotions. Sometimes they even succeed. Beeler was just spouting bullshit in the back of a police car. It doesn't mean a damn thing."

"You weren't there," I said. "I can tell when I'm being played, and it wasn't like that."

"I think maybe you need a vacation, Colt. Get out of town for a month or two. I suggest you and your girlfriend take off to a place you've never been and let time and liquor and the ocean cleanse this crap out of your head."

"You remember the day you landed in the hot tub?" I said. "Right now I feel like throwing your ass out that window."

He said something, but I was already out the door and walking toward the elevator.

CHAPTER TWENTY-SEVEN

Juliet and I had started patching things up soon after my trip to California. It had been touch-and-go for a while, but we were back in full swing now. I'd been staying at her house more and more, and we were seriously discussing getting married.

I drove to her house at seven that evening. She cooked pancit with shrimp and we sat at the dining room table and ate it and drank some wine. I told her about seeing Massengill on the motorcycle, about Tony Beeler and the tattoos and Chain of Light.

"Let me get this straight," she said. "You think Massengill is still alive?"

"The guy on the Harley was a dead ringer. I'm just saying it's possible."

"Maybe your mind was playing tricks."

"Maybe. But I don't think so."

Juliet sighed. "You knew Roy Massengill for, what, twenty years or so? Don't you think you would have known if he was involved in a hate group like Chain of Light?"

"It's not like we were bosom buddies, Jules. He was a roadie, an employee of the band. Then he joined the Navy, and after that went to the police academy. We drank together sometimes and all, but I never pried very deeply into his personal life or his ideological beliefs. He had the angel tattoo, though, so he was definitely involved with Chain of Light. No doubt about that."

"But maybe he wasn't the guy on the motorcycle. Maybe it was someone else. You told all this stuff to Fleming?"

"More or less."

"And?"

"He thinks we should take a vacation."

"Not be a bad idea."

I helped her clear the table, and then we sat on the couch and watched a movie. M. Night Shyamalan's *The Happening*. My mind kept wandering and I didn't enjoy the film much. I was thinking about my own apocalyptic thriller, and mine was more thrilling than M. Night's.

"I'm going in there," I said, as the closing credits rolled.

"What?"

"To the Chain of Light ranch."

"You, a born-again Christian?"

"I'm serious," I said.

"So what are you going to do?"

"I'm going in there. I don't know. I'm going to pretend to join up, train to be a missionary or a revolutionary or whatever it is they do in there. I'm almost a hundred percent certain that the guy I followed to the gate was Massengill. I'm going to go in there and find him and burn his ass."

"If Massengill really is there, aren't you worried he will recognize you?"

"I'm going to shave."

"Your beard?"

"And my head. Even you won't recognize me." I had been wearing a full beard and shoulder-length hair since my southern rock days. Shaving it all off would be the perfect disguise. I'd been thinking it might be time for a change anyway.

"And while you're doing all that, I suppose our plans get put on hold, huh?"

"It's something I have to do, Jules. Your blessing would mean a lot to me."

She stared at the ceiling for about a million years. "I love you," she said. "Whatever you decide, I'm behind you one hundred percent. If you do this, maybe we can finally put the past behind us and move on with our lives."

That's what I needed to hear.

I lived the next two weeks as a recluse, practicing guitar and building calluses on my left hand. It had been a long time since I'd played. I had to go through a painful blister stage for a few days. My fingers were twenty years older and twenty years stiffer, and for a while I wondered if I would be able to pull it off. People who say it's just like riding a bike are wrong. Your brain remembers, but your muscles forget.

I came out of my self-imposed isolation one day to do some shopping. It was a Wednesday, half-price day at the Salvation Army Thrift Store. The place was packed. Little old ladies wearing tremendous applications of little old lady perfume, cruising the bric-a-brac aisles and filling their buggies with sad-faced clowns and silver-plated crucifixes; kids running around coughing and sneezing and playing with plastic dinosaurs that probably harbored more germs than an isolation ward; fat guys with glasses loading up on paperback novels with cigarettes and guns and half-naked dames on the covers; women with one in diapers and one on the way, trying to stretch their meager budgets till payday.

And me. A skinny middle-aged private eye, searching for the perfect Lost Soul costume, as if the one I already wore wasn't quite good enough.

The place was depressing, and I got out of there as soon as I could. I bought pants and a fishing vest and a pair of boots, all sturdy and road-worthy and ugly as hell. The grand total was eight dollars and thirty-four cents. I didn't actually try anything on, thinking I better launder my purchases before wearing them. All I needed was a nice case of the crabs. Anyway, I figured the outfit would look more authentic if everything was a tad too big. As if I'd dropped some weight on my journey toward enlightenment.

My second stop was Shaky Jake's Gun and Pawn. I wasn't in the market for a gun, but I couldn't help glancing at the display case as

I headed toward the musical instruments. I needed the kind of guitar a hobo would carry around. I found a Kay, a poor man's version of the classic Gibson archtop, hanging on the wall next to a tenor saxophone. The wood was dull and dark and had some grease stains on it, but the neck was true and the tone consistent and mellow. The price tag said forty bucks, probably twice what it cost brand new in the '54 Sear's catalogue. It came with a hardshell case plastered with stickers from a variety of music festivals. Perfect.

Fred must have had the day off. Jake was manning the register himself.

"It's me," I said. "Nicholas Colt."

"Holy guacamole. What happened to your hair, son?"

"I got bored and shaved it off."

"Shit. I thought maybe you was getting radiation treatments or something."

"Nothing like that. Anyway, it's chemotherapy that makes your hair fall out, not radiation."

He pressed a knuckle against his lips and nodded thoughtfully. "I see you found yourself a guitar. Nice one."

"We both know it's a piece of shit, Jake. I'll give you thirty for it."

"Shit. That's a fucking antique, man. I been thinking about keeping it myself. But since you're a friend and all, I'll knock off ten percent. Thirty-six even and it's yours."

"I'll give you thirty for it."

"Thirty-four-fifty and I'll throw in some picks and a strap."

"I'll give you thirty for it."

"Damn it, Nicholas, you never was any fun to dicker with. All right, thirty fucking dollars. I ought to have my head examined."

He pulled a silver flask from his back pocket, twisted the cap off, took a slug. He politely tilted the bottle in my direction.

I shook my head. "I need a favor."

"Sure. You waltz in here and practically steal one of my fine musical instruments, and now you want a favor?" He rolled his eyes in a faux expression of disgust.

It's always tricky with alcoholics, but I could tell I'd caught him in a good mood.

"I need a fake ID. Just a driver's license and Social Security card, but it has to be something that'll pass a background inspection."

He took another belt of bourbon. "Ah. That's why you shaved your head. You're going incognito."

"Nah, I did it because chicks dig bald guys. Can you help me or not?"

"That's illegal." But he was already flipping through his old Rolodex. He penciled a telephone number onto a greasy Chinese take-out menu that happened to be lying on the counter. I paid him the full forty bucks for the axe, and then left the store.

CHAPTER TWENTY-EIGHT

Four days later, I drove the Jimmy up to Jacksonville International Airport and parked it in long-term. Juliet knew the truth, but I told everyone else I was going up to Indiana to visit my grandmother. I thumbed a ride back down to Clay County, and then walked the last couple of miles toward the Chain of Light ranch. I was pretending to be a lost transient soul named Matt Recore. I carried a first-rate fake ID in my pocket, a backpack on my shoulder, and a guitar case in my hand. Shaved face and head, Salvation Army duds. I figured my mother in heaven would have had a tough time recognizing me.

Bart Harmon, the dissident I'd found on the Internet, had never called me, but I'd learned some things from his website. I thought I knew a bit of what to expect at Chain of Light. As it turned out, Bart Harmon didn't know the half of it.

When I finally made it to the ranch, I found the drive-in entrance secured with a padlock and the guard shack empty. The big rolling chain-link gate fed into simple split-rail cedar augmented with a strip of guardrail to keep people from driving onto the property. I scooted my backpack and guitar under the bottom rail and then climbed easily over the top. I walked along a winding tree-lined road for half a mile or so. It was a nice walk. Soon I heard something coming around the bend and I stood still while a Hummer squealed to a stop in front of me.

Two armed guards got out. The guy on the passenger's side leaned on the hood and stared at me. He had a pink wad of gum in his mouth, working it furiously. The driver was tall and skinny and had a ski slope for a nose. He reminded me of a stork. He walked to where I was standing and said, "Who are you?"

"My name's Matt Recore," I said.

"You're trespassing, Matt Recore. The sign out front says authorized personnel only. Can you read?"

"There wasn't anyone in the shack."

"So you thought you'd just make yourself at home?"

"I came here to serve Jesus," I said.

"Got some ID?"

I reached for my back pocket.

"Slowly," the guard leaning on the hood chewing the pink bubblegum said. He reminded me of Bazooka Joe. Bazooka Joe and Mr. Stork. It sounded like a movie title.

I pulled out my wallet and handed the counterfeit Texas driver's license to Mr. Stork. He looked it over.

"We're going to escort you back to the gate. You can't stay here."

"I got nowhere else to go."

"The shelter's full. Nothing I can do about that. Get in the car and I'll take you out to the road."

Bazooka Joe pointed at my guitar case. "You play that thing?"

"I do," I said.

"Let's hear."

"We don't have time for this," Stork said.

Bazooka motioned for Stork to follow him. They walked behind the Hummer and conferred privately. In the meantime, I opened the guitar case, strapped on the instrument, and strummed a few chords. In a minute the guards came back around. They watched and listened.

"We might have a place for you here after all," Bazooka said. "Would you be interested in joining Reverend Strychar's music ministry?"

I played dumb. "He has a band?"

"He has a great band. You'll have to audition for the music director. No guarantees. If he can't use you, we'll have to escort you back to the highway. You interested?"

"Sure. I'll give it a shot."

"Get in the truck."

I climbed in the back and we headed out.

Mr. Stork introduced himself and his partner. "I'm Brother Samuel, and this is Brother Thad. I'm going to hang onto your license. We'll need to do a background check if you pass the audition."

"Sure," I said.

"Ever been arrested?"

"No. You'll find a bankruptcy, a foreclosure, couple of car repos. All financial stuff."

"Not a problem," Brother Samuel said. "Almost everybody here has at least one bankruptcy. Including Reverend Strychar, I think."

The guards laughed.

Sam the Stork steered the Hummer toward a metal building and parked in front of it. I got out with my guitar and followed Bazooka Thad inside.

A man standing behind a rack of electronic keyboards raised his hand and closed his fist, signaling for the band to stop. There was a bass player, a horn section with trumpet, sax, and trombone, and a drummer. All of them men.

The keyboard player sourly announced, "This is a closed rehearsal, fellas," into a microphone.

"Hey, Brother Perry," Thad said. "You still looking for a guitar player?"

"Him?"

"Yeah. He wants to try out."

"Come."

I walked to where the band was set up and opened my guitar case. Brother Perry laughed when he saw the cheap acoustic. He was short and fat with a thick mustache that made him look like a walrus. I felt like laughing back, but I didn't. "Hold on," he said. He stalked away and returned holding a gold Les Paul. He handed it to me.

"Thanks," I said. I found a cable and plugged into the guitar amp.

"You ever played religious music before?"

"Music is music," I said. *I haven't played in twenty years, but I can still play circles around your fat brainwashed walrus ass.*

"We'll start with something simple. 'Just a Closer Walk with Thee.' In G."

"Hit it."

Perry the Walrus counted off the tempo. I started out playing chords and melody simultaneously, Chet Atkins style. On the second verse, I tapped an effects pedal and ripped into a solo that would have made Eddie Van Halen proud.

While technically perfect, the band seemed to be just going through the motions. Phoning it in. It was as if all the fire had been taken out of them. They followed Perry with precision and glazed expressions.

I remembered something I'd read on Bart Harmon's website, what he called "chemical castration." He said he'd been given an injection soon after joining Chain of Light, and that a deep calm had washed over him immediately after its administration. The shots were given once a month, he'd said, touted to cast out the demonic spirits of rage and aggression. As an added bonus, they also alleviated members of annoying little human traits such as sex drive and ambition.

Perry raised his hand and closed his fist. The band stopped. "Where'd you learn to play like that?"

"Taught myself," I said.

"As far as I'm concerned, you're in. But Reverend Strychar has the final say."

"I'd be happy to talk with him."

Perry turned to Thad. "Can you arrange that?"

"Not a problem," Thad said.

"If all goes well, I'll see you here tomorrow at four," Perry said to me.

"Thank you," I said. "I won't disappoint you."

I wouldn't really play for your lousy band for all the hooters in

Hooterville, I thought. Brother Perry and the Eunuchs. Coming soon to a cult near you.

I grabbed my guitar, and Thad and I exited the rehearsal hall.

We stood in the doorway as a group of young women passed by. They marched in formation, four abreast, reminding me of a company of boot camp recruits. They wore dungaree pants, chambray shirts, black boots, and blank expressions. I counted ten rows. There were forty of them.

Two guys with automatic weapons walked along with the women, one in front and one in back, like soldiers herding prisoners around a concentration camp. They wore black jeans, black T-shirts, black berets, and black combat boots with red laces. They carried AK-47 assault rifles. They appeared to be focused, sharp, and deadly.

"You all right?" Thad asked.

"I'm okay," I said.

"You were great in there. On the guitar."

"Oh, yeah. Thanks. What's with the girls marching and the guys in the black suits?"

"All in due time, Brother Matthew. All in due time. Come on. We'll get some chow, and then I'll see if I can get you in to see Reverend Strychar."

He called me Brother Matthew. I was starting to feel like a real Chain of Lighter now. We got back in the Hummer, and Sam the Stork drove us to another metal building. The three of us walked into a large dining area with tables arranged like a high school lunchroom. Fifty or so men were sitting and eating.

"This is the men's galley," Thad said. "After supper, I'll take you to talk with Reverend Strychar."

"Where's the women's galley?" I said.

"Like I said, all in due time. We keep the men and women segregated for the most part. It makes everything simpler."

"Okay."

We walked through the service line and received hearty portions of roast beef, mashed potatoes, green beans, and biscuits, doled up by men in white uniforms with the same sterilized expressions worn by the band. We found a seat, bowed for a moment of prayer, and started eating.

"I think you're going to do well here," Thad said.

"Thanks. I hope so, Mister?"

"It's just Brother Thad. We rarely use last names."

"Makes everything simpler," I said.

"Exactly."

Brother Samuel rose abruptly from his seat. "Attention on deck," he shouted.

Brother Thad stood and motioned for me to do the same.

"What's going on?" I said.

"Shh. That's Reverend Strychar."

Reverend Lucius Strychar had lost some weight and gained some hair since posting the pictures on his website. Liposuction and a hair transplant, I guessed. He wore a gray pinstriped suit, white shirt, yellow tie. He held a Bible, the leather binding worn smooth in spots from years of thumping and waving. He surveyed the room.

"Please, gentlemen, be seated," he said.

Everyone sat. All eyes were on Strychar. Using a chair as a step, he climbed on top of an empty table.

"Good evening, friends. I see some familiar faces, as well as some new ones. Welcome all. Let me hear you say amen."

"Amen!" everyone said in unison.

"Ah, that's beautiful. I know you're all enjoying your supper, so I'll be brief. As many of you know, our dear and talented Brother Peter was called to the mission in Peru a couple of months ago. It was a decision he gave much thought and prayer to, and he has made a three-year commitment to spread the gospel of our Lord Jesus Christ there. God bless Brother Peter."

Strychar cupped a hand behind his ear and everyone said, "Amen!"

Strychar continued, "Brother Peter's departure left a vacancy in our music ministry here. He was the guitar player in our wonderful band, and he performed faithfully for the past several years. But, just as Our Savior fed the masses with seven barley loaves and two fishes, today we have witnessed yet another miracle. Today, the Lord has sent us a replacement for Brother Peter. Let me hear you say amen!"

"Amen!"

"I spoke with Brother Perry a few minutes ago and learned that a remarkable talent is among us, a one-in-a-million talent. Brother Matthew, would you please stand and introduce yourself?"

I looked around, slowly pushed myself to a standing position. "Hi everyone. I'm Brother Matthew."

"Welcome, Brother Matthew!" they all said.

"Welcome indeed," said Reverend Strychar. "Normally, I would have met privately with Brother Matthew before making any announcements, but Brother Perry was so enthusiastic and adamant about this man's talents, well, I just had to come and welcome Brother Matthew aboard right away. Gentlemen, meet the new guitar player for the Chain of Light band. Praise the Lord!"

"Praise the Lord!"

"I trust I'll see you all at the prayer meeting in the morning. Enjoy your supper. Brother Thaddeus, please bring Brother Matthew to the house as soon as you're finished eating."

Thad nodded. Strychar stepped down from the table and exited the galley.

I ate my roast beef and potatoes, feeling generally optimistic about how things were going. It would be a long time before I felt that way again.

CHAPTER TWENTY-NINE

After supper, Thad and I got back in the Hummer and he drove me toward Reverend Strychar's house. Brother Samuel didn't come along. He said he had some things he needed to do.

It was getting dark now. The Hummer's headlights shone on a narrow, wooded, winding strip of blacktop. Reflective signs on posts announced JESUS SAVES, JESUS IS THE WAY, JESUS IS COMING SOON. One of the signs said HELL IS REAL in big red letters, and I didn't doubt it for a second.

We approached a massive log home illuminated with flood-lights. Thad parked, and we got out and walked to the front door. The house had a wraparound porch, and I noticed security cam-eras placed strategically in corners of the roof's overhang.

Thad rang the doorbell. A few seconds later, the locks opened automatically, and we walked inside and down a long hallway. Our boots clacked loudly on the pine floors. Something faint and elec-tric wafted through the air, a smell I associated with hot, powerful amplification onstage. Thad stopped at a door and knocked.

"Enter," Reverend Strychar said.

Thad opened the door and motioned for me to go in. Strychar sat at an executive desk smoking a pipe and looking reflective. The room was huge. Mahogany paneling, bookshelves, confederate and Nazi flags, expensive looking paintings.

"Thank you, Brother Thaddeus," Strychar said. "You can wait outside."

"Yes, Father."

The sound of Thad's boots faded as he walked back down the hallway. Strychar got up and shook my hand.

"Once again, welcome to the Chain of Light. I just wanted to meet briefly and give you some things to read."

"Thank you, sir."

"You can call me Father."

"Thank you, Father," I said, smiling.

He eased into his seat and motioned for me to sit in one of the wing chairs across from him. "First of all," he said, "do you have any questions for me?"

"I can't think of any at the moment," I said. *Are you harboring Roy Massengill, who was responsible for the deaths of my client and her little sister? If so, please choose an excruciatingly painful way to die now.*

"Really? No questions?" he said. "See, if I were a man named Matthew Recore, and I made a pilgrimage all the way from Dallas, Texas, in search of truth and enlightenment, or three hots and a cot, or for any reason, and I showed up here and saw the gate in front and the cameras and the guards with guns, I would probably wonder why a Christian organization feels the need for so much security. And, I would probably wonder why there aren't any, how should I say, people of color among the members here. Hmm?"

"Okay," I said. "Those thoughts have crossed my mind."

"It's important that we keep the wrong kind of people outside the perimeter of this property," he said. "That's why we need the security. We've had some trouble in the past. Atheists, agnostics, pro-choice enthusiasts, and some other liberals and undesirables who were not exactly friendly toward our mission. We even had an informant for the FBI one time. You're not an informant, are you Brother Matthew?"

"Me? I'm just a guitar player. I'm an honest Christian. An honest *white* Christian. I came here to serve Jesus and to be among my own kind. If you know what I mean."

"I have to be sure, somehow, before I can allow you into my ministry."

"You have my driver's license. I imagine you've already run some background checks."

"Yes, well, we all know identification can be falsified. The only reason you've gotten this far this fast is because you're such a gifted musician. But I have to be certain that you haven't come here to betray me."

"I'm not sure where you're going with this," I said, trying to sound slightly insulted. "You want me to sign some sort of contract, or what?"

"I'm afraid that's not quite enough. Actually, I've devised a little test." He opened a drawer, pulled out a black bandana, and handed it to me.

"What's this for?" I asked.

"I want you to blindfold yourself."

"Why?"

"It's an exercise in trust and faith," Strychar said. "And obedience. I want you to do it because I told you to. If you refuse, I'll have to have you escorted from the property immediately."

I didn't believe he had any intention of kicking me off the property. I figured he would bury me on it if I didn't play his little game. I was starting to get the distinct feeling that Reverend Strychar was a first-class nut job, and that I had made a grave error in coming here.

I wrapped the black cloth around my eyes and tied it behind my head. It seemed I didn't have much of a choice.

I heard an electronic beep, and then Strychar said, "Bring it."

A few seconds later the door opened and a pair of boots stomped in. Something substantial landed on Strychar's desk with a dull thud and a metallic clank. It sounded like a wooden crate filled with nails. The delivery person walked away without saying anything. His footsteps slowed at the threshold, and he gently pulled the door shut on his way out.

"What's the worst thing that could happen to a guitar player?" Strychar said.

"I guess dying would be the worst thing, for almost anybody."

"Besides that."

"I don't know. Being paralyzed from a stroke or an accident. Not being able to play for one reason or another."

"What about having one of your hands chopped off?"

I made a conscious effort to keep my respirations regular. "Yeah. That would be fairly devastating."

"Allow me to describe the apparatus on my desk," Strychar said. "It's a miniature guillotine, about three feet tall, with an adjustable clamp that can be used for a variety of body parts. One of my craftsmen assembled it for me a while back. He used a modified axe head for the cutting blade. I want you to feel it." He guided my hand to a thick chunk of steel that tapered to an edge. It was in the down position and harmless at the moment. It was cold to the touch. I couldn't see anything, but I knew it was red on the fat end. Every axe head I'd ever seen was red on the fat end. I thought about snatching it loose from its track and burying it in Strychar's throat. I was considering that option when the phone on his desk rang.

"Hello." Strychar listened to what the caller had to say, and then responded with, "Correct. Two hundred pounds of brisket—the best—okay." He hung up and turned his attention back to me. "Now, Brother Matthew, on the base of my little guillotine there are four wooden levers. Three of them are completely inert, but one of them is connected to the pulley mechanism that allows the blade to fall."

The blade was still in the down position. He hadn't raised it yet. He instructed me to touch the four levers to get an idea of their placement and how they operated. They had been sanded and varnished, and felt about as thick as slats on a chair back. They sprang back to position after being depressed, like the keys on a piano. I pushed all four of them, hoping to feel some slight difference in the one that activated the blade. No difference. All four were identical.

Strychar raised the blade. It locked into position with a click. He grabbed my left hand, pulled it forward, and secured my arm into the clamp wrist-up. A bead of sweat trickled down the left side of my face. My heart was pounding, and my gut felt like I'd swallowed a bowl of pennies.

"Why are you doing this?" I said.

"I told you, it's an exercise in faith."

"Seems to me if my left hand gets chopped off then everybody loses. I lose a hand, obviously, and you lose a guitar player. What's the point?"

"If your left hand gets chopped off, then it's the Lord's will. That's the point. All you have to do is choose a lever and press it. Then we can get on with our business. Do it now, please."

I glided my fingertips over the levers. In my mind I had numbered them left-to-right, one through four. I stopped on number three.

"I can't do this," I said.

"Do it."

"I can't."

"Do it," he shouted. "Do it for Jesus. If He wants you to keep your hand, He'll guide you to the right choice. Praise Jesus! Push that lever."

He started hooting and hollering incomprehensibly, what they call "speaking in tongues." The way I saw it, Jesus probably didn't have time to fix the odds on Strychar's demented game of chance. He was probably busy with other projects. I figured I was on my own. It was my choice to push the lever or not push the lever. If I refused, he would probably send in a couple of those boys in black and have my ticket punched. If I went through with it, I still had a 75 percent chance of walking away unscathed.

There was only one rational choice.

I pushed the lever.

Number three.

Immediately I knew I'd chosen wrong. The blade fell fast and hard. The pain shot through my wrist, up my arm and into my shoulder. It terminated in my throat with a gasp. Every muscle in my body contracted, as though I'd been zapped with a million volts of electricity. Tears flooded my eyes, and a coarse roar pushed its way up from deep in my gut. I sucked in a few rapid and shallow breaths and then suddenly realized Reverend Strychar was laughing.

I pulled off the blindfold. There was no blood. My hand was still attached. I wiggled my fingers just to make sure. A sense of relief flooded over me as I struggled to catch my breath. I lifted the blade and examined it. The cutting edge had been grinded flat and dull. It was harmless. You couldn't have cut butter with it. The whole thing was an elaborate hoax.

All the levers were connected to the mechanism that allowed the blade to drop, so the outcome would have been the same regardless of which one I'd chosen.

Har-dee-har-har. Strychar's sense of humor was as twisted as his politics. When he finally stopped laughing, he looked at me appreciatively. "I needed to know your level of trust, Brother Matthew, the way God needed to know if Abraham was willing to sacrifice Isaac. I only want to protect my flock, those who come to me in need, those who are ready to accept Jesus. I have some literature I want you to take, and a questionnaire I'll need filled out by tomorrow morning. Sorry it's so long, but these are things we need to know before your initiation into the Brotherhood."

"You mean that wasn't my initiation?" I said.

He chuckled. "That was certainly part of it."

He handed me a spiral-bound book titled *Welcome to the Chain of Light* and a thirty-page stapled questionnaire.

I could feel the sweat on my body cooling. I took a deep breath. "I'll get to work on it right away," I said.

"Brother Thaddeus will escort you to your quarters. Unfortunately, we're short on space right now, so you'll have to share a room with one of the other musicians."

"I'm just happy to have a place to stay." Deep inside I wanted to snap his neck with a quick jerk.

"There's a men's prayer meeting in the morning, seven sharp in the temple. I trust you'll join us."

"I'll be there," I said.

"Good. After the meeting, Brother Perry will fill you in on rehearsal and performance schedules for the band. And, we'll get you fitted for some new clothes."

"All right."

"See you in the morning then." He rose and shook my hand again. "Oh, before you leave, I'd like for you to sign my book."

He walked across the room to a painting hanging on the wall, an abstract interpretation of a European city on a river. It might have been Paris. He grabbed the frame and swung it out like a door, the piano hinge securing it to the wall moaning in protest all the way.

"Sounds like you could use some WD-40," I said.

"I keep meaning to take care of that squeak. You know how it is. Always something."

There was a recessed vault behind the picture frame. Strychar's head and shoulders hid the safe from my view as he dialed in the combination. He opened the steel door and pulled out a behemoth of a book, a leather-bound volume the size of a briefcase.

"This is The Holy Record," he said. "It's my journal, starting in 1979 when I founded Chain of Light. Every member who has joined my church has signed his or her name in the book. Let me show you a few you might recognize."

He opened the book to an early page and pointed out a couple of signatures. Big name celebrities. I couldn't believe my eyes. He flipped through and showed me more names, people who still caught headlines from time to time, people I never dreamt would be part of such a sect.

The signatures, along with dense handwritten paragraphs chronicling thirty-some years of Strychar's "spiritual journey," filled the first half of the book. After that, the pages were blank. More than enough room for Strychar to keep journaling for the rest of his life. He wrote today's date and then handed the pen to me.

"Would you be so kind?" he said.

I signed my name. I almost screwed up and wrote *Nicholas Colt*, but I caught myself in time.

"Thank you, Brother Matthew. We'll see you in the morning."

I left his study and walked out to the Hummer, rubbing my wrist and thinking about how I might be able to get five minutes alone with that book. Detective Fleming had said that Chain of Light wasn't doing anything illegal, but I suspected otherwise. Especially since they had allowed fine upstanding citizens like Roy Massengill and Tony Beeler into the club.

I hadn't seen a single motorcycle all day, or anyone wearing an eye patch, but it was a big complex and Massengill could have been anywhere on it. Even if he had left the property, I knew he would be back and that I would run into him eventually. I was counting on it.

Thad drove me to the men's dormitory. It was a four-story brick building with a flat roof. I checked in with Brother David, the resident assistant on duty, and then went to my room on the fourth floor. It was a typical dorm room setup: two twin-size beds bolted to the floor, two small closets, and two desks. There was a tin can on one of the desks with some pencils sticking out of it, and a gold-plated letter opener with a picture of a man on the handle. It was either Jesus or Frank Zappa. I examined it more closely and decided it was definitely Jesus. Zappa had curlier hair.

I practiced on the Kay archtop for a while, thinking about Strychar's guillotine. It was a practical joke, and yet a trial by fire at the same time. It was actually sort of clever. I wondered if all the newbies were required to do that, or if I had been singled out for some reason. I hoped Strychar had dismissed any ideas about me being an informant, and that I could stay as long and gather as much information as I wanted to now.

I put the guitar down, kicked back in bed and started reading *Welcome to the Chain of Light*. A few minutes later, my roommate walked in. It was the saxophone player from the rehearsal hall earlier. He wore jeans, a plaid flannel shirt, and a black knit cap. He looked like some kind of lumberjack.

"What are you doing in my room?" he said.

"They assigned me here. Is there a problem?"

"Yeah, there's a problem. I'm a senior band member, and I'm supposed to have a private room."

He threw his horn case in the corner, plopped on his bed, opened a magazine angrily. Something wasn't right. This guy seemed wired and aggressive, not at all docile like the others.

"I'm sure it's only temporary," I said.

"It better be."

What an asshole. I wanted to tell him to go fuck himself. He wasn't even that great of a sax player.

"I think I'll just go for a little walk," I said.

I got up.

"Have you read that book yet?" He pointed toward my copy of *Welcome to the Chain of Light*.

"Not all of it."

"There's a ten o'clock curfew."

"Oh. So I guess I won't go for a walk then. Is there a common area here in the dorm? You know, like a rec room or something?"

"First floor."

I grabbed my backpack, left the room without saying another word. Sax Man obviously wasn't in the mood for conversation.

I took the stairs down to the first floor and wandered around until I found the recreation area. It was a big room. There was a plasma TV on one wall and a cluster of chairs and a sectional sofa. Ping-Pong table. Pool table. Bookshelves stocked with board games and Bibles and paperbacks with titles like *Fasting Can Change Your Life* and *How to Pay Your Bills Supernaturally*.

I took the cover off the pool table, scattered the balls around and started knocking them in. I was hitting softly, trying not to make a lot of noise, but a few minutes later Brother David walked in and told me the rec room closed at ten. He was about my age with a thick head of brown hair and a wooden cane.

"Is there any way you could change my room assignment?" I said.

"Not likely, full as we are right now. Why? What's wrong with your room?"

"It's not the room, it's the guy in it."

"Ah, Brother Simon. He can be a little moody sometimes, but I'm sure you'll be okay once you get to know him."

If I don't kill him first. "Can you work on finding something else for me?"

"I'll work on it."

I told him goodnight. I walked to the stairwell, climbed two flights, sat on a step until he had enough time to get settled back in his room. Then I quietly went back down the stairs and outside into the night.

I walked toward Reverend Strychar's house. I stayed to the side of the road, in the shadows, close to the woods. I figured getting caught would be a death sentence. I could claim ignorance of the curfew, but then Sax Man would rat me out. He would get his privacy back, and I would get dead. Tagged as a spy. They would probably make my last minutes on the planet nice and painful, to make sure I wasn't just the tip of some investigative iceberg.

I wanted to get my hands on The Holy Record. With the right evidence, I could go to the cops and have the whole place shut down. Thinking about it gave he a hard-on. Not only would Massengill finally get what he deserved, Strychar and his neo-Nazi cronies would go down as well.

The trees to my left cut a silhouette against the night sky, black on black. Small nocturnal woodland creatures scampered through the pine needles intermittently, and the occasional eighteen-wheeler burned a trail down SR 21 to the west. Otherwise, the Chain of Light ranch was as quiet as Christmas morning on the dark side of the moon.

That is, until I heard the screams.

CHAPTER THIRTY

I veered into the woods and hiked blindly toward the commotion. I had a penlight in my backpack, but didn't want to use it for fear of being spotted. I only hoped I didn't breeze through a black widow's web or stumble into a nest of rattlesnakes.

The screams were unmistakably human, unmistakably female, and eerily familiar. Then, just as suddenly as they had started, they stopped. All was quiet again.

I kept walking in the same direction, and eventually reached the edge of a clearing. I saw a white van parked in front of a one-story lodge. The women's dorm, I thought. It was a rustic-looking shack of a place, with cedar lap siding and a metal roof. It was about a hundred feet from where I stood. I crouched down, took out my binoculars.

I imagined the porch fixtures ordinarily provided adequate illumination for the building's exterior, but they were off. The van's headlights were off, too, but the parking lights shone redly on one of those creepy fuckers wearing black clothes and a black beret. He closed the back of the van, walked to the driver's side, and opened the door. Just before he climbed in, I lost my balance and nearly toppled sideways. I caught myself with my left hand, but a twig snapped and made enough noise to get his attention.

I lay flat on my belly and took shallow breaths. A flashlight beam scanned the woods. I heard a pair of boots stomping my way and then a voice from behind them.

"Come on, Mike. It was probably just a fox or something. Let's go."

Mike didn't say anything, but he must have concurred with his buddy's assessment. He switched off the flashlight and walked back to the van.

The truck roared to life and sped away in a cloud of dust, springs squeaking and headlights drilling cones of brightness into the gloom. I thought about approaching the building and maybe trying to talk to one of the women inside. I was curious about the screams. Were the Black Berets some kind of rescuers, or some kind of terrorists? The latter was my guess, but blackness and silence engulfed the shack now, and I had far exceeded any boundaries where I might have been able to talk my way out of trouble. I retreated into the woods and found my way back to the road toward Strychar's house.

It was close to midnight when I got there. Unlike the women's dormitory, Strychar's house was lit up like a football stadium. As far as I knew, he lived there alone. I didn't see any guards now, and I hadn't seen any earlier when I'd come with Brother Thad. He had security cameras everywhere, though, and I figured an alarm system had been wired into every door and window. It was a formidable fortress, but not impenetrable. Rule #8 in Nicholas Colt's *Philosophy of Life*: There might be impenetrable people, but there's no such thing as an impenetrable building.

All I needed was a few minutes alone with The Holy Record. I should have found a way earlier, when Strychar had the book out. Now I not only had to break into the house, but I had the safe to contend with as well. The only real hope I had was that Strychar had written the combination down somewhere. People write things down. Computer passwords, PIN numbers for debit cards, burglar alarm codes, you name it. They write things down because they're afraid they'll forget. It makes them feel better to write things down, until they realize they've forgotten where they put the piece of paper they wrote the things down on, or some clever thief breaks in and handily finds all their secret numbers tacked to the side of the refrigerator with a magnet. Then they don't feel so good anymore. Then they feel like crap. I always advise people to memorize the password to their e-mail account, keep it strictly secret, and then e-mail their other confidential info to themselves. People don't listen, though. People write things down, and that's what I was counting on with Strychar.

I stood in the dark at the edge of the woods, in the shadows, thinking about a way to invade Strychar's residence without setting the alarm off. There really wasn't a way, unless I went down the chimney like Santa Claus. I didn't think that would work out, so I decided to wait until morning when Strychar and everyone else would be at the temple for the prayer meeting. The alarm would go off, but maybe I would have enough time to find the combination and open the safe before the Black Berets came running.

So that was my plan, to wait it out until morning. I sat on the ground and settled back against the trunk of a pine tree. I yawned. It was cold and lonely out there, and I kept thinking about Brittney Ryan and how I had ultimately failed her. I never should have driven off and left her alone in my camper that morning.

I rubbed my eyes. The air was still and heavy and I could smell my own sweat. I had a miniature radio and a tiny set of headphones in my backpack, so I listened to NPR for a while to pass the time. An economic expert discussed the president's new tax plan. Big deal. Render unto Caesar what is Caesar's. I just wanted to get the information I needed and get out of Chain of Light alive. If I could manage that, everything else would be gravy. Go ahead and tax my ass off. See if I care.

They started playing some slow jazz. I turned the radio off and rubbed my eyes again. I needed some coffee. I needed it to be administered intravenously.

I thought I might be able to shut my eyes for a few minutes, but, of course, that was a mistake.

I woke up two hours later with an AK-47 pointed at my face.

"Get up," the Black Beret behind the assault rifle said. "Hands behind your head." His buddy, Black Beret Number Two, stood a few feet behind him and also held an AK-47.

I got up and assumed the position. Number One slapped a cuff on my left wrist, pulled it behind my back and then did likewise with my right one.

"Easy," Number Two said. "That's Reverend Strychar's new star guitar player."

"I know who it is. He'll be lucky to have hands at all when I get done with him."

"I need to speak with Reverend Strychar," I said.

They ignored me. Number One shoved me forward, and we walked single file toward the house with me in the middle. When we got to the door, Number One pulled out a cell phone and punched in some numbers. The deadbolt clicked open and we walked inside. I didn't see a keypad for an alarm. I assumed the cell phone had disabled it remotely with the same code that popped the door lock.

"I need to speak with Reverend Strychar," I said again.

"Shut up," said Number One.

I wasn't in much of a position to argue.

They led me through a maze of hallways, and we ended up in a conference room with a long table surrounded by a dozen or so chairs.

"Sit down," Number One said.

I sat. I tried to remain calm, but I could feel my blood pressure in my eyeballs.

Number One propped his rifle against the wall and sat in the chair across from me. "What were you doing in the woods?"

"I need to speak with Reverend Strychar."

Number Two stood by the door with his AK-47 trained on me.

Number One pounded his fist on the table. "We can do this the easy way, or we can do it the hard way. I'm going to ask you one more time. What were you doing in the woods?"

"You have *vays* of making me talk?" I said. It wasn't the time to be a smartass, but I couldn't resist.

"As a matter of fact, we do," Number One said. "Again. What were you doing in the woods?"

"I need to speak with Reverend Strychar."

Number One got up. "If he moves, shoot him," he said to Number Two on his way out the door.

I didn't move, and Number Two didn't shoot me. Number One returned a few minutes later carrying a yellow dish towel, a small stainless steel bowl, and a couple of big thick books. He lifted one end of the conference table and slid the books under two of the legs, creating what I guessed to be about a thirty-degree slant. He left the room again briefly and came back lugging a plastic mop bucket filled with water.

They forced me to lie down with my back flat on the table. They had me tilted, as though I were going to be shot out of a cannon feet first. I stared at the ceiling. I knew what was coming.

"You're not really going to do this, are you?" Number Two said.

"Is he giving me a choice?"

"We always have a choice. Let's just wait till morning and let Reverend Strychar handle it."

"Why don't you go wake him up, and he can handle it right now?"

Number Two didn't say anything. I got the impression Reverend Strychar didn't care much for being aroused in the middle of the night.

Without further ado, Number One dipped the dish towel into the mop bucket and stuffed it into my mouth, leaving a tail draped over my nose and eyes.

The stainless steel bowl clanged metallically as he snatched it from the tile floor. I heard it plunge and emerge dripping. A slow steady stream then trickled over my face, saturating the towel and making it impossible to get enough oxygen. With my wrists and ankles shackled, I bucked and thrashed and gurgled wetly trying to shout. It was no practical joke this time. This fool was going to drown me, and there wasn't a damn thing I could do about it.

The world started to go purple. Number One yanked the rag out of my mouth before I lost consciousness. He waited until I was finished coughing and gagging and sucking in precious air, and then said, "What were you doing in the woods?"

"I need to speak with Reverend Strychar," I tried to say. It came out more like *ah knee ah sneak ah never sniker.*

"What's your real name? Who do you work for?"

"Ah knee ah sneak ah never sniker, you song ah bench!"

He pushed the rag back into my mouth, deeper in my throat this time. He started pouring water on me again, and then an angry voice that wasn't Number One or Number Two barked, "What is the meaning of this?"

The rag came out. I turned my head to the side and puked. Tears blurred my vision, but I was able to recognize Reverend Strychar standing in the doorway with a big shiny nickel-plated revolver at his side. He wore pajamas with a paisley print and a give-me-a-reason expression.

"We caught him in the woods, right outside the house," Number One said.

"Get him up," Strychar said.

Number One and Number Two helped me back into a chair. My face was dripping with water and tears and snot and vomit. Number Two wrung the dish towel out and wiped me off.

"What were you doing in the woods?" Strychar asked.

I acted indignant as hell: "The sax player in your band made it clear he doesn't want me in his room. And he calls himself a *Christian*? He was hostile toward me, and I can't live and work under those conditions. I was going to wait in the woods till morning and then be on my way. I just wanted to tell you in person I won't be able to play for your band after all."

"Why didn't you just tell us that in the first place?" Black Beret Number One said.

"Quiet!" Strychar said, and then turned to me. "I apologize if Brother Simon was rude to you. I assure you he will be dealt with. I'll arrange for alternate accommodations for you first thing in the morning, after the prayer meeting, if you'll agree to stay. In the meantime, I would be honored for you to be a guest in my house tonight."

"Well—"

"I insist. It's settled then. You'll stay here tonight, and I'll find you a new roommate tomorrow. Do you happen to have a coin on you, Brother Matthew?"

"A coin?"

"Please."

I reached into my pocket and pulled out some change. I handed him a quarter. He flipped it in the air and let it fall to the floor. It bounced and spun and wobbled to a stop on tails.

Strychar turned, raised the revolver, and shot Black Beret Number Two in the heart. The AK-47 skittered away. Number Two didn't grab his chest or say anything. He crumbled like a demolished building. His head hit the tile with a moist crack, the sound an egg dropped from a window makes.

"Brother John, take the shackles off Brother Matthew, and then clean up this mess," Strychar said to Number One.

Number One, aka Brother John, took his key out and unlocked my cuffs with a shaky hand. He looked at me in a pleading sort of way. I didn't say anything. I figured his time would come.

Strychar led me to a bedroom, a nicely furnished suite with a king-size bed and a sunken garden tub. My knees were weak. He gave me soap and towels and a fresh change of clothes. He told me to try to get some rest. He apologized again for Brother Simon, the sax player, and for the "reprehensible behavior" of the Black Berets. He told me goodnight and left the room.

Things certainly hadn't gone as planned, but I was in. I was in the house. Now it was time to start looking for the combination to that safe.

CHAPTER THIRTY-ONE

I took a long, luxurious bath with a fancy bar of soap imported from Spain, and some bath beads from a jar. The soap box had a picture of a senorita on it with long black hair and ruby red lips. Her name was Susanna Francisca. She was beautiful. I was in love with her. I soaked in the hot soapy water for about thirty minutes. It was one of the top five baths of my life. I got out and toweled off and put on the clothes Strychar had left for me. Boxers, jeans, a polo shirt, socks, all brand new. I wondered if he had a department store hidden somewhere in the house. I wasn't tired anymore. It's amazing how a rootin-tootin torture session can get the old juices flowing. I felt brand new. I was fresh and energetic and I smelled like a million bucks.

The revolver's blast in such close quarters had left a steady tone ringing in my ears, a B-flat I thought. It was annoying, but no worse than the hum after a concert back when I played arenas with my band. It reminded me of those guys and my wife and baby and the plane crash.

There was a bowl of fresh fruit on the dresser. I selected a shiny red apple and bit into it. Wicked delicious. I peeked through the blinds, saw Number One and another Black Beret loading Number Two's body into the back of a white van. I didn't know if it was the same van, but it was identical to the one I'd seen at the women's dorm earlier. They loaded Number Two's body in what I perceived to be a nonchalant and disrespectful manner, more like a sack of garbage than a human being. Maybe it was a common occurrence for Strychar to become aggravated and capriciously blow someone away. I felt sorry for Number Two, because he seemed to have qualms about the whole waterboarding ordeal. He'd tried to put a stop to it. I wondered if it was an act, though, a good Nazi-bad Nazi kind of thing. At any rate, Strychar had shot and killed him on the basis of a coin toss, which made Strychar verifiably insane in my book and not to be trusted an inch.

I waited until the van left, and then I waited another half hour. I figured Strychar was back to sleep by then. I got the penlight and a paperclip from my backpack and tiptoed out of the room in stocking feet, hoping to find the combination to the safe.

The house was huge, but I'd been through enough of it to know the basic layout. I found my way to the front door and from there to Strychar's study. It seemed like a good place to start, good as any.

It was four o'clock in the morning. Complete darkness. I padded my way to the executive desk, gently rolled the chair out of the way, got down on my knees.

I held the penlight in my mouth and started ferreting through the drawers. They weren't locked, so I didn't need the paperclip I'd brought. I started with the one on the bottom right. It was a deep drawer with hanging file folders arranged alphabetically, K to Z. Personnel files. I looked in the *M*s, didn't find one for Massengill. My own file was there, in the *R*s for Recore, and I saw that my driver's license had been verified by a clerk in Dallas named Mildred Bates. Strychar was checking me out all right. I figured I must have passed. Otherwise, I would have been dead by now.

I examined the dates on a random selection. None of them was more than twelve months old. Longtime members like Massengill probably had records in a warehouse somewhere. These were just quick references for newbies. More of the same in the bottom left drawer, A to J on that side.

I checked the middle drawers next, first the right and then the left. Nothing of interest in those, just basic office supplies and some other miscellaneous crap. Post-Its, a stapler, a box of staples, a staple remover, an obsolete typewriter cartridge still in its original packaging, a Scotch Tape dispenser, a Florida Lotto ticket from ten years ago, a partially eaten roll of Certs, a box of paperclips, a variety of pens and pencils.

Strychar's junk. Years of it. Everything looked old and neglected. I proceeded to the top right drawer. Strychar's revolver lay there wrapped in an oily rag, along with a box of .357 Magnum cartridges and a cleaning kit. It was a Colt Python. The gun had a trigger lock on it, but the cylinder opened freely. It had that just-fired smell. I saw Strychar had replaced the spent round with a new one already.

There was a stray cartridge rolling around on the bottom of the drawer. I picked it up, examined it, and compared it to one of the shells from the box. It was identical, but slightly lighter in weight. I guessed the powder had been taken out of it. Whoever had done it had done a good job. You couldn't tell by looking. It was an impotent dummy round, probably a prop for another one of Strychar's practical jokes. Maybe some of the newbies were forced to play Russian roulette—unaware of the phony bullet in the same way I was unaware of the dull blade on the guillotine. I decided to play a little practical joke of my own. I replaced one of the real cartridges in the gun's cylinder with the dummy, and left the real one on the bottom of the drawer. The next time Strychar played Russian roulette, he would empty the cylinder and use the stray for the game, only now the stray was a live round. If it happened to line up with the firing pin—whoops. KA-BLOOEY! Lucius Strychar, you've been punked!

Still no sign of anything that might resemble a vault combination. I had two more drawers to go, the top left and the top middle, and then I would start searching elsewhere.

When I opened the top left drawer, it hit me like a ton of numbered Ping-Pong balls.

The lotto ticket.

Why would anyone save a ticket for ten years? If the ticket's a winner, you cash it. If it's a loser, you throw it away. Maybe Strychar had absently tossed it into the drawer. Maybe he had forgotten about it. Or, maybe the numbers were chosen because they held some sort of significance.

I went back to the middle drawer on the right-hand side and retrieved the ticket. 20–21–22–31–34–39. I memorized the numbers, put the ticket back, closed the drawer.

Then I heard a toilet flush.

I switched off the penlight and held my breath. I could hear Strychar's bare feet flapping on the hardwood floor, but fortunately the footsteps faded as he walked back to his bedroom. I had absolutely no excuse to be in his study, so I'm not sure what I would have done if he'd come in there.

It was almost five o'clock now. The prayer meeting started at seven, so Strychar would probably get up for good around six. That gave me an hour to get the safe open, tear the pages I needed out of The Holy Record, and get the hell out of there. It was riskier than ever now that I'd heard Strychar awake and walking around, but I didn't know when I'd be able to get back into the house and have such easy access. It was now or never, and never wasn't an option. Plus, I didn't want to waste the suffering I'd gone through under the hand of John the Twisted Baptist. I felt like I'd earned the privilege to be there.

I waited until I heard Strychar's bedroom door click shut. Then I waited a few more minutes, hoping his bladder was sufficiently empty now and that he'd gone back to sleep.

I quietly crossed the room, put my hand on the painting the vault was behind, and then remembered the terrible squeak the piano hinge had made when Strychar swung it out earlier.

Damn.

You could have heard an eyelash land on a rosebud in Strychar's study. Causing that hinge to squeak would have been like announcing my presence with a megaphone. If only I'd come as prepared as, say, Batman, I'm sure I would have had some household lubricant in my trusty utility belt.

The gun cleaning kit. There had to be some oil in there.

I walked back to the desk and opened the top right drawer. Very slowly, very quietly. The cleaning kit was in a nice wooden case with a hinged lid, and the plastic bottle of oil was right on top. I took the bottle over and squeezed a few drops on the piano hinge. I greased it all the way down, working the lubricant in with my fingertips. I lifted the painting slightly, put some positive pressure on it, and swung it out a couple of inches from the wall. So far, so good. I worked it back and forth a few times, then swung it out until the front of the painting rested flush with the wall on the other side. No squeak. With the vault's door exposed and gleaming under my little light, I started dialing in the numbers from the lotto ticket.

I hadn't messed with a combination lock for thirty-some years, since high school. I figured wall safes worked on the same principle as the good old Master I had back then, the one that kept would-be thieves from jacking my Right Guard, my Chucks, and my sweaty tube socks, so I started by turning the dial three times to the right to reset the tumblers. I kept dialing clockwise, stopped on twenty, went the other way and stopped on twenty-one. I continued alternating directions until I reached the final number, which was thirty-nine.

What a beautiful sound, all those tumblers clicking into place. I grabbed the handle, pushed it downward, eased the door open with a gentle tug.

There it was. The Holy Record. I stared at it for a few seconds, thinking there should be some glowing rays and heavenly music, but nothing happened so I reached into the vault and pulled it out.

CHAPTER THIRTY-TWO

I sat Indian-style on the floor with the penlight in my mouth and
The Holy Record in front of me. It was exactly 5:39. I opened the
book to a random page and started scanning the longhand scrawl as
rapidly as I could. More celebrity signatures—divine visions—dia-
logues with Jesus—a missionary trip to the Fiji Islands—and then
*today another victory—Brother Philip—Datsun pickup truck burst
into flames—*

I didn't get any further. At exactly 5:45, Strychar's alarm clock
squealed like a boiled meerkat.

I quickly closed The Holy Record, stood, jammed it back into
the vault. I secured the vault door and swung the painting into
place. I made sure all the desk drawers were closed, the chair back
in its original position. I left the room exactly as I'd found it. I
slinked into the hallway, tiptoed back to my suite.

I took a few deep breaths. My fingers tingled. My inner troll
was doing a number on my stomach now, trying to work his way
out with a soldering iron. I was getting too old for this shit. At forty-
five I was ready to retire, only I didn't have any money. Maybe I
could get the good Reverend to float me a loan before I had his ass
arrested and permanently thrown in the slammer.

I had the combination to the safe now. I felt good about that.
And, I knew the book contained evidence of terrorist activity. *Datsun pickup truck burst into flames.* I didn't know the details, but
someone named Brother Philip had torched a vehicle and considered it a victory. I would have to get back into Strychar's study at a

better time, ideally when he was not at home, and smuggle the book out of the complex.

I kicked back on the king-size bed with my clothes on and stared at the ceiling for a while. At 6:01 someone knocked on my door. I got up and answered it. It was Brother Thad.

"I'm supposed to give you a ride back to the dorm," he said.

"They found me a new room already?"

"Yeah. Actually, you're in the same room as before. They reassigned Brother Simon."

I wondered if they had reassigned Brother Simon the same way they had reassigned Black Beret Number Two.

"Let me just grab my things," I said.

I put the fishing vest on and stuffed my dirty clothes into my backpack.

Thad drove to the men's dorm and dropped me off at the curb.

"See you in a few," he said. "There's breakfast in the chow hall after the prayer meeting."

"All right."

I walked inside and took the stairs to my room. The floor had been mopped with a pine-based solvent that made me sneeze. I opened a window to let in some fresh air.

Brother Simon, the saxophone player, was not there. His closet was empty, but there were still some things on his desk: the tin pencil caddy, the letter opener, a cheap electronic calculator, and a little white Bible like the ones they give away in hospitals and jailhouses. I wondered if he had forgotten those items or merely abandoned them. I wondered if I would see him later at band rehearsal and how awkward that would be. I wondered if he would sneak up behind me and slit my throat.

His bed had been stripped, revealing an ancient mattress with a colorful array of stains and a steel bed frame that was probably forty years old and would probably last another four hundred. I looked around. I wanted my old room back at Reverend Strychar's house.

I threw my backpack on Simon's naked bed, sat on my own and opened the little white Bible to a page that had been marked with a little red ribbon attached to the book's little gold-embossed spine. Verse forty-one of Matthew chapter thirteen had been highlighted in yellow: *The son of man will send out his angels, and they will weed out of his kingdom everything that causes sin and all who do evil.*

Everything that causes sin and all who do evil. That sounded like everything and everybody under the sun to me. What would be left? Just the son of man and his angels, I guessed, living in one hell of a nice shiny sterile sin-free Utopia of a kingdom until one of the angels decided to stage a coup and then here we go again. I tossed the Bible into the trashcan. I had no use for it. God and I hadn't been on speaking terms for quite some time, since the day a fireball of jet fuel consumed everyone I loved.

The stressful night was starting to catch up with me. I felt drained, achy, and flushed, like I was coming down with the flu or something. I needed several hours of uninterrupted rest. I didn't want to go to the prayer meeting, but Reverend Strychar was expecting me and I didn't want to give him a reason to doubt my loyalty and enthusiasm. I needed to play the part for a little while longer, at least until I could get into the safe again.

I walked down the stairs and out into the morning. The sunshine gave me a headache, but the air felt clean and I took some nice deep breaths of it on my walk to the temple.

I got there a few minutes late. The meeting had already begun. Meeting. It was more like a Holy Roller clusterfuck, with everyone shouting gobbledygook and waving their arms in the air. One man was on the floor, apparently having some kind of seizure. Was he full of Jesus or full of the Devil? Impossible to tell. Maybe he was just full of shit. It was all very disturbing. I'd never seen anything like it.

But I didn't want to look like an outsider, so I closed my eyes and raised my hands and joined in the fun. When in Rome, and all that.

"Sha-na-na," I said. "Ramma-damma-ding-dong. Abracadabra. Allah-kazam. Ah knee ah sneak ah never sniker."

Nobody paid any attention to me. Everyone was in his own little mystical world.

After a while Reverend Strychar walked to the pulpit and started saying real words into a microphone between the strings of gibberish coming from the crowd.

"Hallelujah. Praise the Lord. My brethren, God is here with us in this building today. I feel His presence, and I know you do too. I'm going to pass this bucket around now, and I want each of you to take a slip of paper and hold it in your hand. Don't look at it until I tell you, please."

Everyone in the crowd had quieted down. The man who had been convulsing on the floor now sat in a pew to my left with his hands in his lap.

Strychar handed a galvanized steel pail to one of the men in the front row. He took a slip of paper from it and passed it on. By the time the bucket made its way back to me, it was nearly empty. I took a slip and made a fist around it.

"Did everyone receive a chit?" Strychar asked. "Raise your hand if you did not get a slip of paper."

Nobody raised a hand.

"Wonderful. Now, I want you to unfold that piece of paper and look at it. Some of your chits will be blank. If that's the case, you are dismissed from the meeting now. All others are to stay here with me. I have a very special surprise for you."

My paper was blank, so I filed out the door with the rest of the losers. I saw Brother Thad outside.

"What was that all about?" I asked.

"I don't know for sure, but I have my suspicions."

"And?"

"I better not say. Come on. Let's get some breakfast."

I wondered if Strychar's little lottery had anything to do with the two hundred pounds of brisket he'd confirmed over the phone yesterday. I had a hunch that was it, but I couldn't figure out why some members were excluded from the feast.

On the way to the chow hall I heard children's voices in the distance, singing a song I remembered from Sunday school called "I Just Want to be a Sheep."

"There's kids here?" I said.

Thad didn't say anything. We walked into the galley and went through the line. They had eggs to order, bacon, sausage, hash browns, biscuits, and waffles.

I didn't want any of it. The smell of it made me queasy. I took two slices of whole wheat toast and sat down. A couple of minutes later Brother Thad followed with his plate piled high.

"After breakfast I'm taking a few members up to Orange Park for field ministry," Thad said. "I was thinking you might like to join us."

"Field ministry. What's that?" I thought maybe they were going to preach at some cows or something.

"That's where we canvass neighborhoods. We knock on doors, offer our literature, and offer to pray with folks."

I swallowed a bite of toast, chased it with black coffee. "Oh. I'm going to have to take a rain check on that. I'm really pooped after last night. I need a nap before rehearsal later."

"That's understandable. Just be aware everyone who lives on campus is required to log twenty hours of field ministry a week. Even the musicians."

"Okay," I said, but I couldn't see myself selling God door-to-door like a vacuum cleaner. Actually, I figured most folks would get better mileage from a Kirby.

After breakfast, Thad dropped me at the dorm and I went up to my room and slept dreamlessly until three o'clock. I felt better. Someone had left a box outside my door with three more sets of new clothes in it. I took a shower and dressed and walked to the rehearsal hall. I made it right on time.

My former roommate, Brother Simon the sax player, wasn't there. Brother Perry handed me a stack of charts.

"You pretty good at sight-reading?" he asked.

"I think I'll manage."

I walked stage right and picked up the Les Paul. It was in perfect tune already. We played a few songs. Everything was easy. I could have played most of it blindfolded. One of the numbers was the accompaniment for "I Just Want to be a Sheep," the song I'd heard the children singing earlier. We played for nearly two hours straight. My calluses held up nicely, but the Les Paul got heavy after a while and made my back hurt. I wanted a cigarette and a glass of whiskey.

"Let's break for chow," Perry said. He switched off his keyboards and then walked over to me.

"Nice set," I said.

"I think so. Listen, I meant to ask you before, do you write songs?"

"I've written a few."

"We're trying to put an album together, with redemption as the theme. I would welcome a contribution from you, if you're up to it."

"I'll see what I can do."

"Good. You ready to go eat?"

"Yeah. I'm starving."

It was true. I hadn't had anything all day except two slices of wheat toast. We walked to the chow hall. They were serving meatloaf and steamed spinach and I ate triple portions. We rehearsed some more after dinner and wrapped it up around nine thirty.

When I got back to my room at the dorm, I read some more of *Welcome to the Chain of Light*. There was an entire section condemning interracial marriages, calling them "an abomination to the Lord," and not to be tolerated. The more I learned about the organization, the more hate and hostility I saw. The fact that they were bigots came as no surprise, but actually seeing it spelled out in those terms, actually seeing the words—*interracial marriages are an abomination to the Lord*—hit me hard.

I closed the book and flung it across the room. It landed upside-down against the wall. I was mad as hell, but I reminded myself I needed to keep my emotions in check. I walked over and picked up the book and brushed it off. There was a picture of a lighthouse on the cover. I picked up the Kay archtop and started playing around with some chords and lyrics, trying to take the edge off my anger. I wrote a first verse and a chorus:

> *Sailing through the storm, must've lost my way.*
> *My ship was slowly sinking, the mast was ready to break.*
> *Visibility zero, I fell on my knees and cried,*
> *Please somebody save me, I don't want to die.*
>
> *Then I saw the lighthouse, I saw the way.*
> *I saw the lighthouse, bringing me home safe.*
> *Yonder was a guiding light, shining hope and faith.*
> *I saw the lighthouse, I saw the way.*

I needed a couple of more verses and maybe a bridge, but I couldn't focus on it. I kept thinking about what I'd read in *Welcome to the Chain of Light*.

I started connecting some dots that hadn't occurred to me before.

Someone knocked on the door. I got up and answered it. The man on the other side wore a white lab coat and held a metal container the size of a cigar box.

"You're Brother Matthew?" he said.

"That's right."

"I'm Brother Caleb. I work in the clinic."

We shook hands.

"There's a clinic here?" I said. "Wow. You guys think of everything."

"May I come in?"

I stepped aside, allowing him to enter the room. I shut the door. I sat on the edge of my bed and Caleb sat across from me on my previous roommate's bed.

"I was just going through some of the reading material Reverend Strychar gave me," I said. "Interesting stuff. The Vatican is the Antichrist, huh? Who would have guessed?"

"Our Lord Jesus Christ came to Reverend Strychar and spoke to him, just as I'm speaking to you now. The end is near, my friend."

"Kind of depressing. But, you know, who am I to argue with Jesus?"

"It's not sad at all," Caleb said. "His kingdom will be glorious. As His loyal servants, we are obligated to crush the serpent's head and usher our Lord to His throne."

"Amen," I said. "What's in the box?"

Caleb opened the metal container, revealing a syringe and needle, an unmarked vial of liquid, alcohol swabs, and Band-Aids.

"Our ministry takes us abroad at times," he said. "We're all required to receive vaccinations."

He screwed the needle onto the end of the syringe, punctured a port in the vial, drew out the medication. Maybe it really was a vaccination. Or, maybe it was the dreaded chemical castration Bart Harmon had talked about on his website. Maybe it was something else. Whatever it was, I had no intention of letting him put it in my body.

"I'm going to have to pass on that," I said. "I'm terrified of needles."

I glanced out the window. A white van with its lights on was parked at the curb.

"I'm afraid it's mandatory," Caleb said. "Trust me. It'll only take a second. Would you like it in your thigh, or—"

I grabbed the Kay archtop and smashed it over Brother Caleb's head. Caleb and the splintered guitar fell to the floor in a heap.

I looked out the window. Two Black Berets got out of the van and walked toward the dorm's front entrance.

Brother Caleb started moaning and trying to get up. I grabbed the syringe, buried the needle in his leg and pushed the plunger. He went limp on the floor. Vaccination my ass. They'd tried to tranquilize me.

I looked around for a weapon. I grabbed the letter opener,

cuffed it, and slid a couple of the sharpened pencils into one of my fishing vest pockets.

I yanked the door open, looked both ways, and ran for the stairs.

When I opened the door to the stairwell, I heard footsteps coming up. I looked down and saw the boys in black casually climbing the stairs. One of them was Brother John, the guy who had waterboarded me last night.

I was supposed to be unconscious by now, and they were coming to load me into the van.

·I ran back to my room and shut the door. There was no way to lock it. I opened the window, looked down, thought about it, decided four stories was a little too high.

I stood flush with the wall, beside the door. The knob turned and the soldiers stomped in rudely without knocking. Brother John rushed to where Caleb was lying on the floor. From behind, I impaled the other guy's left kidney with the letter opener. I left the blade buried and grabbed his gun. He fell to the floor writhing in pain.

I put a foot near his wound to keep him at bay, and at the same time trained the AK-47 on Brother John. He was carrying a pistol.

"Toss it over here," I said. He looked at me and my machine gun and quickly decided he had no other choice. Both guys had handcuffs on their belts. I made Brother John cuff the other guy to one of the beds, and then I told him to strip.

"You're going to wear my clothes, and I'm going to wear yours," I said.

I put the black uniform on. The boots were a little tight, but otherwise Brother John and I were about the same size. Caleb looked comfortable, still unconscious and peacefully drooling on the carpet. I stuffed a pillowcase into the other Black Beret's mouth to mute his whimpers. A trail of blood wicked along the exposed part of the letter opener, obscuring the image of Christ on the handle.

I dug through the pockets of my new duds and found the keys to the van and the cell phone Brother John had used to enter Reverend Strychar's house last night. I made John lie on the floor face-down while I handcuffed him.

"Come on. We're going for a ride," I said.

I grabbed my backpack, and a spare set of guitar strings from the archtop's case. We walked down the hallway and then the stairs. Outside, a resident on his way back to the dorm walked by and said, "Eighty-eight, brother," to me. Bizarrely, he didn't seem concerned that I was holding a man at gunpoint.

The van had two seats in the front and an empty cargo shell in back. I shoved Brother John to the floor in back and tied his ankles with guitar strings. I started the truck, drove it into the woods where it couldn't be seen from the road. I switched on the dome light, climbed in back and nestled the barrel of the forty-caliber pistol into my prisoner's left eye socket.

"You're going to tell me some things," I said.

"I doubt it. Who are you? You a cop? FBI?"

"I'm a greasy hair in your goddamn porridge, Goldilocks. I'm your worst fucking nightmare. And, believe me, you *are* going to tell me some things."

"Blow me. I don't know shit."

"We'll see. First of all, the guy that walked by a minute ago said, 'Eighty-eight.' What does that mean?"

"It's simple alphabet code. *A* equals one, *H* equals eight. Double H. Heil Hitler. Don't take no rocket scientist to figure that one out."

"I see you guys in the black uniforms from time to time. Who are you? You're some kind of soldiers, right?"

"Fuck you. Strychar'll kill me."

I forced the gun barrel tighter against his eye.

"News flash. I'm going to kill your ass if you *don't* tell me. Be nice and cooperate and I'll drop you near the front gate. Then you can be on your merry way and find another group of neo-Nazis to play with."

I cocked the hammer.

"Shoot me," he said. "We got a code of honor here. I took an oath. Go ahead and shoot me, you son of a bitch. I'll go straight to Heaven and see Jesus tonight."

Damn it. Why did everything have to be such a hassle? I ripped his shirt open, tore a piece of the cloth off, and gagged him with it. A burning cross was tattooed on his chest, along with the angel on his arm. The cross was leaning forty-five degrees to the right, like the one that had been carved into Leitha Ryan's forehead. I didn't know its significance, but looking at it pissed me off. It made what I was about to do seem somewhat less despicable. I unbuckled his pants and pulled them down to his knees. I grabbed his cock with my left hand, and with my right gently inserted the sharpened end of a number-two Mirado Black Warrior an inch or so into his urethra.

The noises he made weren't quite human.

"Here's the deal," I said. "I don't believe in torture, but I'm desperate and you're a racist piece of shit. Now, you can either answer my questions, or I'm going to jam this pencil all the way up your motherfucking dick and then break it in half. You think it hurts now? Just imagine those jagged splintery ends ripping away at that delicate tissue in there. So what's it going to be?"

He made some caveman grunts, sounding like he might be ready to see things my way. Funny how fast all that code-of-honor shit flies out the window when a fat hunk of hickory gets shoved up your pee hole. I pulled the gag out of his mouth.

"What do you want to know?" he said, breathing heavily.

"The guys in black. Tell me about them."

He was almost crying. "Harvest Angels. The H-A. We're the militant arm of the organization. You notice the red laces in our boots? They stand for all the blood that's going to be shed when we take the country back for the white man."

"Bullshit," I said. "How many of you could there be? A couple hundred? A couple thousand?"

"Try a couple of million. Chain of Light is just the tip of the iceberg, brother. The H-A's all over the country. You read the Bible?

Check it out. Matthew thirteen, verse forty-one: 'The son of man will send out his angels, and they will weed out of his kingdom everything that causes sin and all who do evil.' We're going to weed out all the mud races. Niggers, Jews, gooks, beaners—all those evil motherfuckers. The H-A's gonna kick ass and take names."

I twirled the pencil in a little deeper. He clenched his teeth and yawped from the gut.

"There must be an armory here somewhere," I said. "Where do they keep all the weapons and the ammo and shit?"

"You know the chow hall?"

"Yeah."

"Same building. In back." He paused and smiled. "You'll never get to any of that stuff."

"We'll see. I saw some young women marching in dungarees yesterday," I said. "What's the deal with that?"

"Marching in formation? Led by a couple of Harvest Angels?"

"Right."

"They were breeding stock. They keep those girls in a separate barracks."

"Breeding stock. Where do they get the girls?" I said.

"They get them. That's all I know."

"All right. Why did Strychar have that lottery at the prayer meeting this morning?"

His voice took on a wistful quality: "At midnight it'll be April twentieth. Adolf Hitler's birthday. Time for the spring sacrifice. They put up a wooden swastika, tie a virgin to it, douse her in gasoline—it's quite a sight. Invitation only. I got to go last year."

"So where's the big birthday party?"

"A clearing in the woods behind Reverend Strychar's house. Same as last year." He grimaced and swallowed hard. "You going to let me go now?"

"Sure," I said. "Just a couple of more questions. There's a man here somewhere, wears an eye patch and rides a Harley Electra Glide. You know who I'm talking about?"

"Seen him around, don't know his name."

I took the cell phone out of my pocket. "Tell me the code you used to open Strychar's door and disable the alarm."

"Why do you want to get into Reverend Strychar's house?"

"Personal reasons." I shoved the pencil in deeper. It was almost up to the eraser now.

"Jesus! All right, all right. Two-zero-two-one-two-two-three-one-three-four-three-nine."

"Got it," I said. It was the same as the safe combination, the numbers on the lotto ticket. 20–21–22–31–34–39. I had already memorized them last night.

"You going to let me go now?"

I looked into Brother John's eyes and saw pure evil. He was a racist and a torturer. He had a tattoo of a burning cross on his chest. No telling how many lives he had taken in the name of hate.

I pulled the pencil out of his pecker. A few drops of bright red blood dribbled out. He breathed a sigh of relief, and then I clouted him in the forehead with the butt of the forty cal. He was still breathing when I pulled him out of the back of the van by his feet like a sack of manure and dumped him on the forest floor.

CHAPTER THIRTY-THREE

The digital clock on the van's dashboard said 11:38. Only twenty-two minutes before Hitler's big birthday bash and the virgin sacrificing got started.

I figured a fair amount of what Brother John had said was bullshit. Would these low-life racist pricks actually burn someone at the stake? Surely not. Something was cooking somewhere, though. I could smell it. I figured it was the two hundred pounds of brisket Strychar had confirmed over the phone.

I had two objectives in mind: get The Holy Record and get the hell off that ranch. Strychar's house would be empty. He would be at the party with those he invited. Now that I had the code to get into the house, and the combination to the safe, everything should be a piece of cake.

I wanted to find the armory and load up on some firepower. I wanted to blow some shit up. The B movie I seemed to be stuck in should have a blazing molten-hot spectacular ending, I thought, but there was really no point to it. All I needed to do was quietly enter Strychar's house, open the safe, get the book, and drive the van to the Clay County courthouse. I had the AK-47 and the forty-cal pistol from Brother John and his partner, just in case someone got in my way.

I turned the key, put the transmission in Drive, stomped the gas, but something was terribly wrong. I didn't have any control over the steering. I got out and confirmed my suspicion, that the right front tire was flat. I must have picked something up when I drove into the woods. Fuck. I holstered the pistol, grabbed my backpack and the assault rifle, and headed toward Reverend Strychar's house at a trot.

The roads were deserted, but I stayed near the tree line and in the shadows anyway. I didn't want to risk being seen. It was a beautiful, clear April night, temperature in the low sixties. Starry, starry night. No kidding. The weather was practically perfect, and my legs and lungs were practically on fire. They should have hired a more athletic guy to play this part, I thought. I kept waiting for someone to yell *Cut!* and send the stunt man in, but I appeared to be on my own. My feet hurt from the tight boots, exacerbating my misery even further. Sweat poured from my face and trickled down my back in streams.

I ran through the pain and finally found my rhythm. Or, perhaps my numbness. At any rate, I was gliding along like a goddamn gazelle after a while, like a feather in the breeze. Delirium. That's the word I was searching for. I ran through the pain and finally found my delirium.

I saw Reverend Strychar's house and an orange glow coming from the woods behind it. The smell of meat cooking became stronger as I made my way around the perimeter of his lot. It actually smelled great. If nothing else, those Aryan motherfuckers knew how to cook some goddamn good-smelling southern barbecue.

I crouched down and duck-walked to Strychar's front door, my chest heaving and heart pounding. No lights on in the house. I pulled out the cell phone, punched in the numbers, heard the locks click. I waltzed in like I owned the place.

I used my penlight to navigate, but the tiny bulb grew dimmer and dimmer and by the time I got to Strychar's study the battery had died completely. I didn't want to risk cranking on the lights, but I needed to see somehow. I couldn't dial the combination to the safe with the little bit of light that filtered in through the windows.

I unplugged Strychar's desk lamp and moved it to a socket closer to the safe. I took my black Harvest Angel shirt off, shrouded the lamp's shade with it, switched on the light. Perfect. I was able to hold the lamp with one hand and dial the combination with the other.

I felt something akin to euphoria as I worked the dial. It reminded me of when I was seven. I wanted a Hot Wheels racetrack, and had been begging my stepfather for months to buy me one. "Maybe for Christmas," he said, between gulps of whiskey. I ripped a picture of that racetrack from the Sears catalog and taped it to the refrigerator door. No mistake about which one I wanted. In the picture, the cars were neck and neck at the finish line, with a blurry trail of color behind them. That's how fast those damn Hot Wheels went on that damn track. Engines roaring, crowd cheering, rubber burning. I thought about that racetrack every night before going to sleep. I thought about it for months. On Christmas morning, there was a big package under the tree with my name on it. *To Nicky, from Santa.* This was it. I was going to be the envy of every boy in the second grade. The anticipation was overwhelming. I almost peed my pants as I tore the shiny red paper and revealed—

A plain white box. I had seen the racetrack I wanted in the store, and it did not come in a plain white box. It came in a box with a picture of cars neck and neck at the finish line. Blurry trail of color, crowd cheering, rubber burning.

There must have been some mistake. Someone had put my name on the wrong present.

"Go ahead and open it," my stepfather said. He always needed a shave and stunk of booze, even on Christmas. Especially on Christmas.

I opened the package. It was a set of gray pajamas, pocked with pictures of blue Indy cars. Something a little kid would wear to bed, not a big second grader. I started bawling. I couldn't help myself. I knew he would make me wear those PJs until they were threadbare and bursting at the seams, and I knew I would never ever get that Hot Wheels racetrack as long as I lived. When he saw my grief, he called me a spoiled brat, and stomped away to fix himself another highball. I never forgave him, and things were never the same between us. We hated each other until he blew his brains out when I was fifteen.

Now I always tell people with kids to buy them what they really want, even if you have to go into hock to do it. It's something they'll remember for the rest of their lives.

Opening Reverend Lucius Strychar's safe reminded me a lot of Christmas when I was seven. The same sinking sense of disappointment engulfed me when I dialed the last number and opened the vault's door.

The Holy Record was gone. Strychar must have taken it to the party with him.

Now what? I couldn't just go on back to my room at the dorm and pretend nothing had happened. I'd left Caleb there unconscious, and I'd left Brother John's partner there cuffed to the bed and impaled with a letter opener. Not to mention Brother John himself, who was probably waking up in the woods about now with some painful reminders of his own.

I couldn't just hightail it and go on back to being regular old Nicholas Colt living in the Airstream on Lake Barkley. Caleb had come to my room with a tranquilizer shot, and he had been followed by two Harvest Angels. Somebody knew something. My cover had been blown. That was the only explanation, and that meant I was committed to doing something. Immediately.

I wasn't extremely confident about going up against an army of white supremacist goons on what might be their biggest holiday of the year, but my only other option was to leave the compound and seek help from the police. That wasn't much of an option, because as soon as Strychar figured out I was gone he would put everything in super-lockdown mode and make sure any evidence was nowhere to be found. Especially The Holy Record.

Going to the police at that point would have been tantamount to quitting, to giving up, to raising the white flag. I decided I was not going to give up. Either I would leave the Chain of Light ranch with the evidence I needed, or I would leave in a body bag.

I checked the desk drawer for the Python, thinking a little more firepower couldn't hurt, but it was gone too. I crept out of Strychar's study, backtracked through the house and out to the porch. I didn't bother trying to lock the door.

I entered the woods behind Strychar's house, felt my way through the pines and the underbrush and followed my nose until I reached a small hill overlooking a clearing. I stood there for a minute, drenched in sweat, wheezing like an asthmatic iguana, and gazed upon the outrageous scene below.

At the center of attention was a six-foot wooden swastika with a young woman tied to it. Brother John had been telling the truth about that after all. It appeared there was indeed going to be a human sacrifice. I pulled out my binoculars, focused in on the girl. A chill washed through me like a tidal wave. My heart actually stopped beating for a couple of seconds.

At that moment, my agenda, indeed my entire life, changed. It was Brittney Ryan, and she was very much alive.

CHAPTER THIRTY-FOUR

My eyes burned and my throat tightened, and it wasn't from the barbecue smoke. Talk about feeling as though I'd seen a ghost. This was unreal. This was beyond anything I could have imagined. I stood there completely flabbergasted for a minute, trying to soak it in, trying to reason how this could possibly be. Then I gave myself a figurative slap in the face, because if I didn't do something quickly I was going to lose her all over again.

I had expected the meeting to be crawling with black uniforms, but that wasn't the case. The attendees, a hundred or so of them, wore civilian clothes and sat peacefully at candlelit tables. This party was for the drones, the worker bees. That's what the lottery at the prayer meeting had been all about.

I recognized faces from the band and the kitchen help. Not a Harvest Angel in sight. If it hadn't been midnight, and a six-foot swastika with a girl tied to it hadn't been the main attraction, the scene I looked down on might have been any church picnic any-where in the country.

I had worked out some things in my mind earlier, in the dorm room, while reading *Welcome to the Chain of Light*. Reverend Strychar considered interracial marriages an abomination, a sin against nature. His was a ministry of hatred; he and his followers possessed a staunch determination to preserve the purity of the Aryan race, no matter the cost.

My wife, Susan, was from Jamaica, and we were a high-profile couple because of my band Colt .45. We tried our best to maintain our privacy, but the paparazzi followed us everywhere. We were regulars in the tabloids. We were on the cover of *Rolling Stone*, dressed as bride and groom. She was black and I was white and we were man and wife and everyone in the world knew it, and almost everyone in the world was cool with it.

Almost.

We got the occasional stares in public, and the occasional nasty-grams in the mail. We lived in the Deep South, so some of that was to be expected. But, before Tony Beeler blurted the words *pocket-47*, it had never occurred to me that the plane crash had been a planned thing, a result of sabotage. And until now, it had never occurred to me that my sweet Susan and our precious daughter might have fried inside that airplane because of their skin color. It was crazy to think that a religious organization would kill a plane-load of people because of ignorance and prejudice toward a married couple, but the more I thought about it the more it seemed not only possible but probable.

The more I thought about it, the more my blood boiled.

Roy Massengill drove one of our equipment buses. Roy Massengill was a Chain of Light member. He had access to the charter jet, and along with his other talents he was a decent aircraft mechanic. He was the invisible hand that came along and fucked things up. If my suspicions were correct, Roy Massengill, acting under the sanction of Reverend Lucius Strychar, lit what turned out to be the most tragic burning cross in history.

Now, more than ever, I needed to get my hands on The Holy Record. I had seen one other act of terrorism written in the book, the exploding Datsun pickup truck; I figured if Chain of Light was behind the plane crash, that would be recorded there as well.

As I stood and witnessed what promised to be yet another gruesome scene of misguided religious fervor based on ignorance and hatred, a fierce rage boiled up inside of me. I wasn't concerned with justice. I didn't want any of these assholes to go to jail. I wanted to kill them all. I wanted to mercilessly mow them down with the AK-47, and then rush in and rescue Brittney and take her home with me and live happily ever after.

But that's not what happened. Not exactly.

The wooden swastika stood on a platform in the center of the clearing, and Brittney's arms and legs were tied to it with heavy ropes. She was awake and alert and terrified. The swastika was flanked by burning crosses, one about twenty feet to the left of it and one about twenty feet to the right. The crosses appeared to be metal, the flames fed by propane cylinders. Again I was reminded of my wife and baby burning with that airplane. Reverend Strychar stood at a pulpit in front of the platform, with what I assumed was The Holy Record on a stand in front of him.

Reverend Strychar was speaking to his flock: "—and as we proceed in the most solemn of sacrifices, dear brethren, let us remember what our savior said as he hung suffering on the cross—"

"What did he say, Lucius?" I shouted from my position on the hill. I walked toward the pulpit, my rifle pointed at Strychar's chest. "Did he tell you to kill innocent people? Did he tell you to hate folks because of the color of their skin, or because they don't think the same way you do? I'm not a religious man, but I'm pretty sure Jesus Christ taught tolerance and love. Not too much of that 'round here, now is there?"

"Who goes there? How dare you interrupt this holy meeting?"

"Holy? The only thing holey here is going to be your heart if you don't untie that girl in about five seconds."

I advanced, and Strychar finally recognized my face in the firelight.

"You," he said. He looked astonished. He'd already killed me—twice, actually—but there I stood.

In my peripheral vision, I saw someone rise from one of the tables. I kept my eyes on Strychar.

"Brother Matthew. What are you doing?"

I recognized the voice. It was Perry, the music director.

"I'm not Brother Matthew," I said. "My name is Nicholas Colt. I'm a private investigator. He knows who I am. I don't know how he found out, but he knows. If you want to live to see the sunrise, you better sit your ass back down."

"But—"

"Sit the fuck down," I shouted.

He sat. Everyone else kept quiet. I'll never know for sure, but I felt a sense of relief among them, relief that they weren't going to have to watch an innocent young woman burn. Maybe what limited optimism I still possessed emerged, a limited hope that some smidgeon of humanity still existed, even in those cold and listless hearts gathered to witness one of the most heinous crimes imaginable.

"Get your hands up where I can see them," I said to Strychar.

He ducked behind the pulpit, and a ring of fire suddenly surrounded him and the platform where Brittney stood tied to the swastika. The ring was composed of smaller rings, overlapping like links in a chain. The Chain of Light.

I'm sure the fiery ring had originally been set up as a dog and pony show, for drama's sake. Now it acted as a barricade between Strychar and me, and between Brittney and me. I needed to save this young girl's life, but I also needed The Holy Record. As it was, I couldn't get to either of them.

Brittney was positioned behind Strychar, so if I fired my weapon in that direction I risked hitting her. If I tried walking through the flames, I would become a human torch. In short, I was screwed. All Strychar had to do was make one call on his cell phone and a hundred Harvest Angels would swoop down and cut me to ribbons. But Strychar didn't make that call. Strychar panicked. He rose from behind the pulpit, holding his nickel-plated revolver, and fired five shots in my direction. Handguns, even expensive ones like the Colt Python, aren't very accurate. It was hardly a miracle that all five shots missed me. He stuffed the gun into his waistband, grabbed The Holy Record, and heaved it toward the flames, intending to burn it, but he tossed a little too hard and it landed outside the ring.

He then turned one hundred eighty degrees, pulled the Python and pointed it at Brittney. He was only ten feet away from her.

She screamed just before the next shot was fired.

But the next shot fired was not from the gun in Reverend

Strychar's hand. The next shot fired was from a forty-caliber semi-automatic pistol identical to the one I'd taken from Brother John back at the dorm. My head instinctively turned left, toward the muzzle flash, and I caught a glimpse of a man with an eye patch before he grabbed the massive book, The Holy Record, and darted into the woods. I fired a few rounds in his direction, but he kept running.

Massengill.

I wanted to chase him. I wanted him, and I wanted that book. I looked toward the woods, and then I looked toward Brittney. If I chased Massengill, Strychar might finish her off with his last bullet. He might even set her on fire. If I let Massengill go, I might never learn the truth about the plane crash.

Sometimes you have to let go of the past and cling to the love you have now.

I didn't move an inch.

Strychar staggered, faced the crowd, and fell to his knees. A dark stain bloomed from his chest. "Help me," he pleaded.

"Turn the flames off," I shouted.

Grimacing in pain, he reached behind the pulpit and flipped a switch. The ring of fire disappeared.

I ran to Strychar, thinking I might be able to put some pressure on his wound and stop the bleeding. If I could keep him alive, maybe there was still a chance I could learn the truth about the plane crash.

Unfortunately, Reverend Lucius Strychar had other plans.

He still had the revolver. When I got close enough, he pointed it directly at my heart. I pointed the AK-47 directly at his.

Stalemate.

I kept my eye on his trigger finger. When his twitched, mine twitched.

A crushing tide hammered through my neck and jaw. Some sort of alarm wailed in the distance. Strychar only had one more bullet, but that was all he needed. At close range, the .357 mag would tear me in half.

"Drop the weapon," I said.

"You drop it. Nothing can happen to me. I'm a prophet, sent to usher in the return of Christ. Jesus won't allow anyone or anything to hurt me. Surrender now and I might let you live."

"You have one cartridge. I have an entire magazine. Give it up, Strychar. It's over."

"You're right. It is over. For you."

He squeezed that trigger hard and fast and a nanosecond after I heard the *click*, I instinctively and involuntarily opened up and riddled a dozen holes in his chest.

His last bullet never fired. It turned out to be the dummy round I had loaded into the revolver the night before.

CHAPTER THIRTY-FIVE

Strychar lay dead at my feet. I turned and ran to Brittney and loosened her bonds. She fell into my arms crying.

I held her for a few seconds, raked the sweaty hair away from her face.

"We're going to be all right," I said. "But we have to get out of here. Fast."

"The guy with the eye patch!" she screamed. "He killed my sister. Get him!"

"I'm not leaving you, Brittney. I'm never going to leave you again, you understand that?"

The Chain of Light members who had been sitting peacefully at the picnic tables were now stampeding up the hill toward Strychar's house like a herd of cattle. Distant shouts of *Fire!* echoed through the valley, and I remembered I had left Strychar's desk lamp shrouded with my black Harvest Angels shirt. It seemed I had inadvertently created the perfect diversion.

I pulled out Brother John's cell phone and called 9-1-1. I told the dispatcher there was a house fire and gave her the address. When she asked my name, I hung up.

I turned back to Brittney. "Can you walk?"

"I don't know. I'll try."

"I'm not leaving you."

"I can do it. I can walk."

"Have you ever used a handgun?"

"No."

I didn't want to lead her into the woods on a dangerous manhunt, but she wanted Massengill as much as I did. Maybe more. And I couldn't leave her alone.

I took the forty-caliber pistol out of its holster and handed it to her. "It's ready to go. Just aim and pull the trigger."

She looked at the gun, and then at me. "That's it?"

"That's it. Are you sure you want to do this?"

She hesitated a beat, but her tone was emphatic. "Fuck yeah," she said.

We entered the woods, me leading the way with the AK-47. Moonlight trickled through the canopy, dancing on what appeared to be drops of fresh blood on the ground. I crouched down, pinched a droplet, rolled it between my thumb and forefinger, sniffed it. It was blood, all right. I must have at least grazed Massengill when I fired earlier. The trail led west, toward the highway.

We stalked deeper into the woods. The drops of blood on the ground got farther apart, and then stopped altogether. Massengill's wound must have clotted. Now there was no way to track him.

"Now what?" Brittney said.

"State Road Twenty-One's over there. Come on."

"We're giving up?"

"No. He was headed toward the highway, so—"

"Look!"

On the ground, a few feet to our left, lay The Holy Record. Dots of fresh blood on its leather binding shimmered in the diffuse moonlight. I tackled Brittney at the waist and we fell together to the forest floor. My right ear collided hard with a pinecone.

"Stay down," I said.

I remained on top of Brittney, covering her body the best I could, expecting gunfire to erupt any second. It had to be a trap. The book had to have been left there as bait. No way Massengill would have just abandoned it.

I waited, expecting the worst, but nothing happened. Smoke alarms from Strychar's house warbled faintly from half a mile away. No fire truck sirens yet.

"Why are we on the ground?" Brittney whispered.

"Be quiet. I'm trying to save your life."

Something warm and viscous dripped on the back of my neck. A voice from above—way above, in the treetops somewhere—said, "Pocket forty-seven. That's how you figured all this out, isn't it? When Tony Beeler said 'Pocket forty-seven'? That's how you *think* you figured all this out, anyway. Let me tell you something, Nicholas Colt. You've done more damage tonight than you can possibly imagine."

I whispered into Brittney's ear. "I'm going to roll off of you, to the right. At the same time, I want you to roll left. Understand?"

"I'm scared."

"It's all right. Just trust me, okay?"

"Okay."

"I'll count to three. You ready? One—two—*three*."

I rolled right, stopped on my back, opened up with a staccato burst from the AK-47. I fired the entire clip in the direction of Massengill's voice, arcing the barrel in a variety of directions for maximum coverage. I squeezed the trigger like a madman until there was nothing left.

Gunsmoke hovered above me like a ghostly serpent. I was out of ammo now and partially deaf in both ears. I stood, looked upward, saw nothing but a purple haze.

"Brittney, I want you to stay down. Do you hear me?"

No response.

Then a refrigerator fell from the sky and landed right on top of me.

I rolled onto my side into the pad of twigs and pine needles with Massengill straddling my shoulders. He had my head in a scissors lock with his legs, so tight I thought my brain might leak out through my nose.

"How does that feel, Colt? I'm going to crush your fucking skull."

I reached between his legs and grabbed a handful of testicles, squeezing as hard as I could. Massengill roared in pain, and I felt the vice on my head go slack. He immediately slugged me in the forehead with his fist in retaliation. He got to his knees and pulled out the forty-caliber automatic, the same one he'd used to shoot Strychar back at the clearing. He aimed the barrel directly at my face.

The punch had left me dazed. It felt as though my mind and body weren't quite connected, as though I'd been drugged. I couldn't move my legs. I was completely at his mercy, and mercy didn't seem to be one of his strong suits.

He held the gun on me, rock steady, and with his free hand re-moved the eye patch. He pulled a butane cigarette lighter from his pocket, flicked it, and held the orange flame to his face. There was a gruesome cavern where his eyeball had once been, lined with skin grafts that looked like pink modeling clay. It was the result of what I'd done to him on the Shands Bridge several months ago, and that's why he was showing it to me before he blew my brains out.

"This is your handiwork, Colt. Aren't you proud?"

"I did what I had to do."

"And now, I'm going to do what I have to do."

"Why did you save my life?" I asked. "The night you killed Mar-cus Sharp?"

"I was aiming for you, dumb fuck. I missed, but I'm pretty sure I won't this time."

There was a palpable moment of silence, and then Brittney galloped in from stage right with a screeching yawp and stabbed Massengill in the face with a pine branch. For an instant I caught what looked like a ghastly wink as his expression changed from fierce to stunned. The pistol discharged, and two hundred grains of lead whistled supersonically past my left ear. Before Massengill had time to react, Brittney went at him again, jamming her weapon into his only eye this time. He fell back and she stabbed him again, twisting the stick in his socket as though she were scouring a bot-tle with a brush. A thick string of bloody goop followed when she finally pulled it out.

Brittney stepped away as he lay writhing. I thought he was finished, but a few seconds later he sprung to a sitting position like some sort of sightless jack-in-the-box. He fired a round in her direction, missing by several feet. He fired again, closer this time. The bastard must have had radar. Somehow he was honing in on her. She was only a few feet away, so maybe he was catching her scent. Or the sound of her breathing. Or some other voodoo shit he'd learned as a Navy SEAL.

Brittney stood frozen. The slightest sound would be a beacon and a death sentence, and she knew it. I was starting to get some feeling back in my legs, but they still weren't strong enough to stand on. I felt dizzy and nauseated and useless.

"Shoot him," I shouted. I'd given her the pistol before we entered the woods, and I couldn't understand why she hadn't used it. She'd chosen a stick instead, which didn't make any sense.

I hoped the sound of my voice would cause Massengill to train his weapon on me. If he shot at me, it might give Brittney time to run away. But he never wavered. He kept the gun pointed in her direction. He fired again, his third shot even closer than the second. Each time, the muzzle flash gave me a momentary glimpse of the horror on Brittney's face.

The pistol was stuffed down the front of her jeans, the grip sticking out and easily accessible. The only thing I could imagine was that she'd tried to shoot him and the gun hadn't fired. Maybe it had jammed. She'd probably pointed and pulled the trigger like I told her to, and when nothing happened she'd bravely come to my rescue with the only weapon she could find.

Then I thought of another possibility.

"There's a little slide by the handle," I said. "Pull it toward you."

Massengill fired again. He missed, but his barrel was aimed directly at her now. I figured the next shot would take the left side of her head off.

I was wrong.

The next shot was from Brittney, and it blasted a chunk of flesh the size of a rib-eye from Massengill's right shoulder. His arm convulsed spastically, and his gun fell from his hand.

"I'm hit," he said, seemingly amazed by the turn of events.

He was blind and severely wounded and helpless. Brittney stepped forward and, with absolutely no emotion I could discern, pumped an entire clip of forty-caliber rounds into his brain.

She stood there for a few seconds staring at his lifeless body, then threw the gun down and ran to me. She collapsed at my side, gasping for breath.

"You did good," I said. "You saved me."

"I think I'm going to be sick." She got up, staggered away, leaned on a tree, and puked her guts out.

I managed to rise to a sitting position. I was still dizzy, but I felt like I might be able to walk with some help.

Fire engine and police sirens howled in the distance now, growing louder as they approached the ranch. I figured together Brittney and I could make it to the highway. From there, we would need a ride. I called Juliet on Brother John's cell phone. She answered on the second ring.

"Nicholas? Is it really you? You sound drunk."

"I think I have a concussion. I'll tell you all about it in a little while. Can you pick us up at the intersection of twenty-one and sixteen?"

"Us?"

"Brittney Ryan is with me," I said. "Brittney is alive."

CHAPTER THIRTY-SIX

I sat at Juliet's kitchen table with The Holy Record and read the following entry from October 21, 1989:

> A grand mission was accomplished today, the downing of a chartered jet with an interracial celebrity couple and their mongrel child aboard. "Fuel gauge malfunction," I believe the official investigation will show. I have my faithful servants Brother Roy and Brother John to thank for this service to humanity. Pocket-47, as they say. It has been reported that the man actually survived, but that is of no consequence. The lesson remains.

Brother Roy was Roy Massengill, of course. I wondered if Brother John was the same idiot who had nearly drowned me.

And there was that phrase again. Pocket-47. It had come to mean something more than sabotage to me. There was something downright evil about it.

Eight people died on that airplane because of a religious zealot's hatred. I allowed myself to weep openly for one hour, and then decided to put it behind me. Not that I would ever forget Susan and Harmony, but it was time to move forward with my life. They would have wanted it that way.

It worried me some, what Brother John said about the Harvest Angels, that they were two million strong and had cells all over the country. Groups like Al-Qaeda get a lot of news coverage, but it's probably the homegrown terrorists that pose the greatest threat to national security. I had a feeling we'd be hearing about the Harvest Angels again some day.

The Clay County Sheriff's Department shut the Chain of Light Ranch down immediately. From me they got The Holy Record, along with the VHS-C tape. The original videocassette from the ER examining room was found at Massengill's house, as I'd suspected. The State Attorney's Office and the FBI filed boatloads of charges against several members in the upper echelon—charges ranging from false imprisonment of minors to seditious conspiracy against the United States—promising to keep the court system busy for years. The FBI confiscated a considerable cache of weaponry and a ton of terrorist propaganda, and Florida added forty-nine children to its foster home registry.

But one child, who had endured the system for most of her life, was not put back on the list. I made sure of that.

A little over a year after the occurrences at the Chain of Light ranch, Juliet and Brittney and I drove away from the Clay County courthouse with signed, sealed, and delivered adoption papers in hand. Juliet and I had gotten married a few months before, and Brittney was our daughter now.

Brittney had been receiving counseling for the loss of her sister, and for posttraumatic stress disorder. She was back in school, struggling a bit, but that was okay. I was extremely proud of her.

On days she felt like it, we would sit and talk. By and by I learned the horror story that had been her life for eight months. She never went back to Duck the pimp. It was another girl who died in Duck's apartment, a girl named Jennifer. Roy Massengill kidnapped Brittney from my camper the day I chased the old Chevy station wagon, and then brought her to the Chain of Light ranch. They could have killed her right away. Instead, they kept her prisoner and fattened her up, intending to use her as an offering for their Nazi god.

"Did they abuse you?" I asked.

"Not at all. They treated me like a princess. I didn't know about that sacrifice crap until the night they came and got me. I was under the impression they were going to make me have babies, like some of the other girls. I thought they were just waiting until I got a little older."

"What a nightmare," I said. "You know, I took her to Point Conception."

"Who?"

"Jennifer. I took her ashes there. I'll have to try to get in touch with her family somehow."

The first few times I asked Brittney about the videotape I'd found in her bedroom, she acted too upset to talk about it. I didn't push it, but then one day she walked in from school and opened up on her own.

"I needed a tape for my tennis lesson, so I grabbed one from Doctor Spivey's study. I thought it was blank, but when I played my lesson back later I saw something horrible. A little girl who'd gotten burned. Not just any little girl—see, when I first went to live with the Spiveys, I was digging around in a box of junk one day and found a picture of an infant. She was pretty, except she had this weird birthmark on her face. I asked Doctor Spivey who she was, and he said she was his niece and that she'd died of pneumonia soon after that picture was taken. I didn't think anything about it, really, until two years later when I saw her on the tape. I recognized her because of the birthmark. I said, 'Hey, isn't this your niece? I thought she died when she was a baby.' Doctor Spivey freaked out. His whole expression changed, like Jekyll and Hyde or something. He grabbed me by the arm and forced me into one of his spare bedrooms. He slapped me, hard enough to knock me down. He called me a stupid little bitch and said I needed to be more respectful of other people's property. He told me not to leave the bedroom. A little while later, I heard him talking to his wife about their yacht. He said he was going to take me for a sunset cruise. I got really scared. I thought he was going to sail way out and throw me overboard. I had to get out of there. I snuck back into the study and stole the tape, climbed out a window, and hitched a ride home. I knew Doctor Spivey would eventually be coming after me, so I left the note on Leitha's windshield making it look like I was running away. I didn't want her to get hurt—"

She hugged me and cried on my shoulder.

We would never know exactly how it went down, but my guess was that Massengill stole the original tape from the emergency room and sent a copy to Spivey to set up the blackmailing scheme. Brittney then inadvertently taped her tennis lesson over most of the incriminating footage on that copy. When she watched it and saw the scalded two-year-old, Spivey suddenly considered her a threat. He panicked. He was guilty of performing a third-trimester abortion, among other things, and his wife Corina was guilty of manslaughter when the child died.

Brittney had caught Dr. Spivey in a lie. He couldn't risk exposure.

Neither could Massengill. That's why he went to Leitha's house in search of Spivey's copy of the tape. Unfortunately, I had already taken it before he got there. When he couldn't find it, he tried to torture Leitha into giving up Brittney's location.

Leitha died protecting her sister.

Brittney suffered night terrors for a while, but those episodes gradually became less severe and less frequent. Slowly but surely, she was beginning to heal.

I was determined to give her the best life I could. I asked her what she wanted to do to celebrate the big day, the day Juliet and I officially became her parents. Anything she wanted, I told her. I would have taken her to Paris for a month. I would have gone back to Point Conception, if that's what she had wanted.

She wanted to go fishing.

We packed a big lunch and the three of us went to Lake Barkley. The old Airstream was still there, and it made a fine weekend getaway for my family. My family. There was a time when I thought I'd never say those words again.

It was a sunny afternoon in May. We fished for hours and ate fried chicken and rested on blankets and fished some more and ate some more and rested some more. It was the kind of day you wished would last forever. Warm and kind and happy, and quite conducive to somnolence.

In other words, perfect.

As the day faded, I lay in the grass with my guitar while Juliet and Brittney fished from the shore. I gazed past their silhouettes, past the concentric circles of their lures plopping into the still water, past the sailboats anchored in the distance. I gazed beyond the gold and turquoise sky, and prayed no harm would ever come to either of them.